Barry Crump wrote his first b
Man, in 1960. It became a b
numerous other books which followed. His most famous and best-loved New Zealand character is Sam Cash, who features in *Hang on a Minute Mate*, Crump's second book. Between them, these two books have sold over 400,000 copies and continue to sell at an amazing rate some 30 years later.

Crump began his working life as a professional hunter, culling deer and pigs in some of the ruggedest country in New Zealand. After the runaway success of his first book, he pursued many diverse activities, including goldmining, radio talkback, white-baiting, television presenting, crocodile shooting and acting.

As to classifying his occupation, Crump always insisted that he was a Kiwi bushman.

He published 25 books and was awarded the MBE for services to literature in 1994.

Books by Barry Crump

A Good Keen Man (1960)
Hang on a Minute Mate (1961)
One of Us (1962)
There and Back (1963)
Gulf (1964) – now titled *Crocodile Country*
Scrapwaggon (1965)
The Odd Spot of Bother (1967)
No Reference Intended (1968)
Warm Beer and Other Stories (1969)
A Good Keen Girl (1970)
Bastards I Have Met (1970)
Fred (1972)
Shorty (1980)
Puha Road (1982)
The Adventures of Sam Cash (1985)
Wild Pork and Watercress (1986)
Barry Crump's Bedtime Yarns (1988)
Bullock Creek (1989)
The Life and Times of a Good Keen Man (1992)
Gold and Greenstone (1993)
Arty and the Fox (1994)
Forty Yarns and a Song (1995)
Mrs Windyflax and the Pungapeople (1995)
Crumpy's Campfire Companion (1996)
As the Saying Goes (1996)
A Tribute to Crumpy: Barry Crump 1935–1996 is an anthology of tributes, extracts from Crump's books, letters and pictures from his private photo collection.

All titles currently (1997) in print.

BEDTIME YARNS

A collection of short stories and poems compiled and edited by Mandy Herron

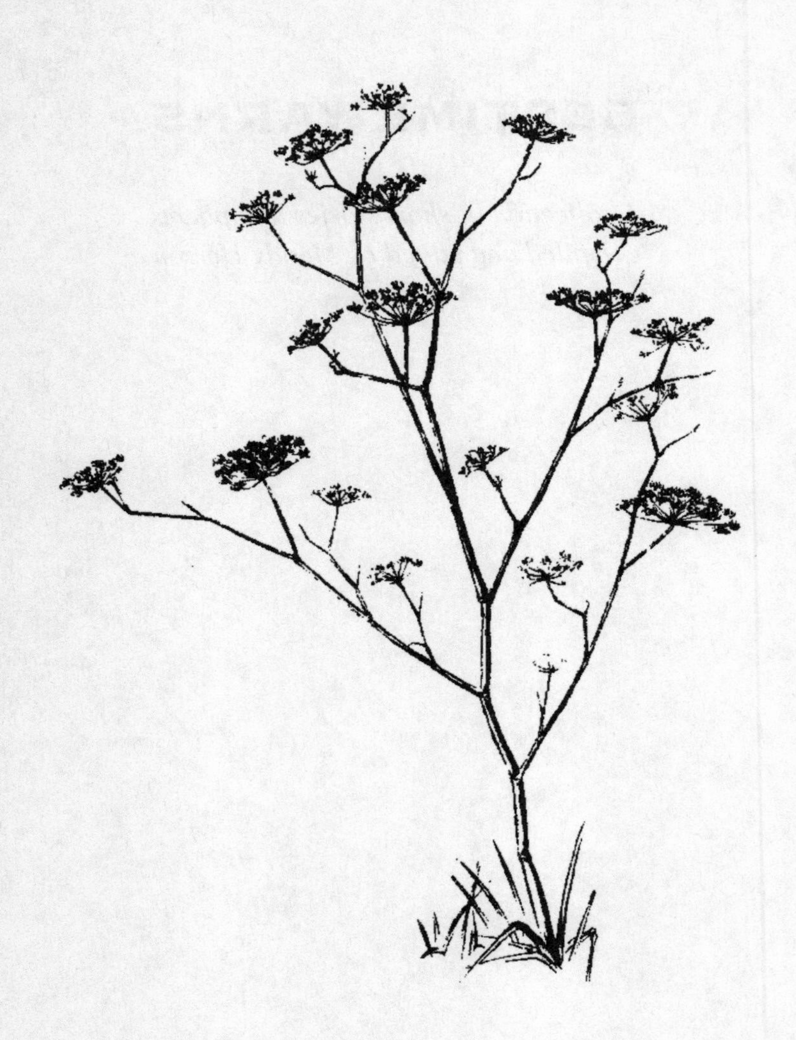

BARRY CRUMP

BEDTIME YARNS

Illustrations in this book by
Linda Poulton, Tony Stones,
Dennis Turner and Kerry Emmerson

Hodder Moa Beckett

First published by Barry Crump Associates Ltd, 1988

This edition published in 1997

ISBN 1-86958-549-6

Published by Hodder Moa Beckett Publishers Limited
[a member of the Hodder Headline Group]
4 Whetu Place, Mairangi Bay, Auckland, New Zealand

Typeset by TTS Jazz, Auckland

Cover photo: NZPL/Evan Collis

Printed by Wright and Carman (NZ) Ltd, New Zealand

Contents

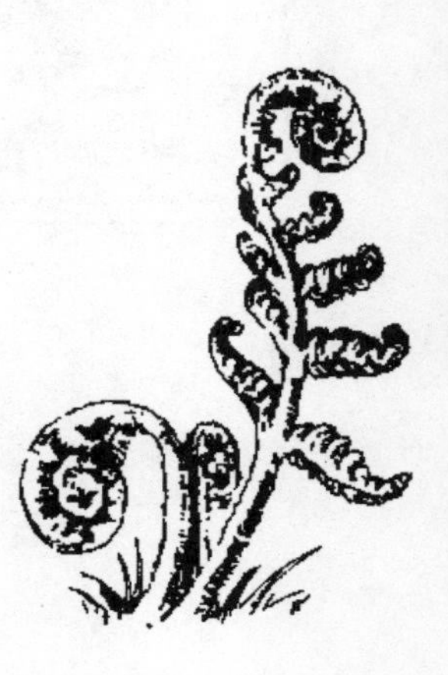

NOTICE

Overheard in the Pub

"Thanks, mate. Y'know, I don't mind accepting your shout. It could easy be me who's shouting you. . . . Yep, if it hadn't been for a shower of rain I'd be one of the wealthiest men in the Territory today.

"A shower of rain was unusual enough, out there beyond Alice Springs, but what that rain done to me shouldn't have happened to a dog. Cost me a fortune, just like that, it did. — Y'see, it was like this. Last year I decided to take a couple of weeks off and treat meself to a little holiday away from all the dust and heat and flies. So I sets off for the coast, Surfer's Paradise, to have meself a good time. — Yeah, thanks, I will have another beer. Ta.

"Well, after a couple of days I got a bit jack of all the noise and racket goin' on round the place, so I took meself for a walk along the beach, away from all the crowds. And I was just wanderin' along thinkin' about goin' home when a dirty big wave came and washed a fish up on the beach right at me feet. Sand mullet it was — about this long. Now here's a go, I says to meself. And I picks up this here sand mullet and carts it back to the pub I was stayin' in to show everyone how I'd caught a fish without even a fishin' line. No one seemed to be very impressed about it.

"The fish was still kinda floppin' around a bit so for somethin' to do I got a four-gallon kerosene tin and filled it with sea water and put me sand mullet in. It started floppin' around in there and pretty soon it was swimmin' about as though it had never been out of the water. After a couple of days I had the thing eating out of me hand. And some of the stuff that thing ate, you just wouldn't believe. Leaves and grass, steak, mutton chops, bread and jam, scrambled eggs, porridge, cigarette butts, chocolate — anything you liked to throw in, that sand mullet of mine'd up and eat it without turnin' a hair.

"Then I got the idea of takin' me fish back to the station, out beyond the Alice there, to show the folks. Some of 'em had never seen the sea in their lives, let alone a real live fish. So I hops on the train with me swag and me kerosene tin with me sand mullet in it.

"Feedin' the thing was no trouble, I just bought it a couple of sandwiches or a pie or somethin' when we stopped for refreshments. But as we got further out into the hot country the water in me kerosene tin started evaporatin'. I didn't have any spare sea water with me so I just had to top her up with fresh water. The sand mullet didn't seem to take any notice of this, and by the time we got out to Alice Springs he was swimmin' around in fresh water as though he'd been born to it.

"When I got me fish out to the station there was a hell of a stir-up. Everyone wanted to pick it up and see what it felt like. I tried to warn them it was supposed to stay under the water or it'd die but they wouldn't take any notice. After a bit me poor old sand mullet got pretty used to bein' picked up and passed around to be looked at, because people from all over were comin' to have a look.

"Then there was a dirty big drought and we couldn't spare the water to keep fillin' up the sand mullet's kerosene tin. So we made it half full, and then a quarter full — and in the end he got so used to it that I just used to throw a wet sack over him and he laid there good as gold. In the finish he was floppin' around the yard with the fowls, pickin' up all the scraps and fowl tucker he could get his hands on. The old rooster got pretty jealous of him in the finish and they had a ding-dong donnybrook out in the yard one day. The sand mullet was doin' pretty good for himself, too. I had to stop the fight in case he knocked off our only breedin' rooster.

"Well, word got around about me sand mullet and a bloke from Melbourne flew up in his private plane and took one look and made me an offer of five thousand dollars for it, but I could see by this time I was sittin' on a goldmine, so I turned 'im down flat. Then I started gettin' phone calls from big outfits all over the world — Thanks, yes, a big one barman — wantin' me sand mullet. I accepted an offer of thirty thousand dollars from a film company in America in the finish. I was supposed to fly over to deliver me sand mullet and collect the dough. The night before I was due to set off, the drought broke. The heaviest rain in the Territory for thirty years. I was quite pleased in a way because I could put me fish back into his kero tin to transport him, now we had the water. So I got everything ready and arranged for a plane to pick us up in the morning and fly us over to Brisbane, where we could take off for the States.

"And you know, mate — you mightn't believe this, but it's as true as I'm standing here — when I went out in the morning to get me poor old sand mullet, he'd fallen into a puddle of water and drowned himself."

Horseplay

My first impression of Laura Trumble was that she would have liked to be able to crawl away somewhere and hide till the rest of her life blew over. She would stand with her hands clutched apprehensively in front of her as though she'd just come from the scene of an accident that she wasn't quite sure whether or not she was responsible for. Interviews with her were like dreams, it was hard to be sure whether they'd actually taken place. Whenever you spoke to her she'd nod her head up and down, depending on how quickly you spoke, as though your words were bouncing from floor to ceiling. And when she spoke to you it was as though she was in a library; as though she was afraid of frightening you away, so you had to lean and listen to catch what she was saying. And her eyes opened and closed in time with her mouth, and you were so fascinated by this that you forgot to listen to what she was saying anyway.

The only time anybody seemed to really notice what Laura said was when she came out with something outrageous that threw everyone out of gear. It wouldn't have been so bad if she could have covered up, but she'd lost faith in lies years before and never trusted them. There was something precarious about her, a kind of anxiety, as though she'd just passed you a poem she wrote to her first boyfriend when she was thirteen. Or as though she'd just felt some elastic give way on her.

Another thing about Laura Trumble was that she seemed to

me to be always trying not to look like an emu. But it never worked. In her best clothes she looked like a dressed-up emu. In her working clothes she looked like a working emu. If she grew her hair long she looked like an emu with long hair, and if she cut it short she looked like an emu with a haircut. Sometimes she even experimented with a home perm, but it only made her look like a moulting emu. For months I had the absurd conviction that if she was to get angry with me she'd reach out her long neck and peck me in the face, so that my left eye would twitch embarrassingly whenever I was talking or listening to her.

I understood that she'd been married until six or seven years before. It seemed that her husband left his car at a garage one day and asked them to check his brakes. The man from the garage ran over him in his own car when he was crossing the street half an hour later and he died of his injuries. Laura moved to Talltree Point and had lived ever since on her thirty-five acres in an old brown house that looked as though it had actually grown up through the fern and long grass that clung thickly around its walls and windows. She usually wore long trousers, gumboots, and a big straw hat, and although she spent most of her time outdoors, she was the only one in Talltree Point who never got sunburnt, even in the summer. It was as though the sun had been ordered to leave her alone.

This, then, was Laura Trumble, the best man with animals that anyone who had ever met her had ever met.

She could take careless cats and have them thoroughly house-trained in two days. In one visit to the cowshed she could stop a new-calved heifer holding its milk. In two days she could teach a dog to sit, come-here and fetch. She could have a magpie saying "Hello" and "Aakawarrk" in less than a week. Even the trout in the little creek that ran through her place would come to be fed scraps when she swished her hand in the water and called them. She was the only one who could get Wally Catch's big bull into the crush when they had to put a ring in its nose to stop it smashing fences. When everyone else had given up trying, she could stop horses from bucking, biting, kicking and bolting. She was the only one who could catch Sam Steven's racehorse the time it ate tutu along the creek and got poisoned and went mad. She was the only one who could do anything with Bill Sutton's Jersey bull the time it went mad from fighting Rod Norton's Shorthorn through the fence and all the fat in its head melted. She spoke to animals in hypnotic whispers, soothed and smoothed and sorted out whatever was troubling them. Ripped pig-dogs that couldn't be stitched up; half-wild bullocks, bloated from breaking into clovery paddocks; sheep-worried dogs and dog-worried sheep; cows in bogs and pigs in trouble. Laura Trumble fixed them all. She had needles and bandages and plaster and splints, knives and liniment, warm sheds, soft hay, advice and comfort. Anything that had to do with animals she could do better than anyone else. Even the veterinary man from over at Swinton used to come to collect Laura when he had a tricky job on. It was often said that if Laura Trumble was anybody but Laura Trumble she'd be a famous animal handler for a big circus, or a zoo or something. As it was she was just Laura Trumble.

It was a hot afternoon the July before last and a few of us were yarning around in the shade of Bruce Walter's garage when a bloke in a big flash Chrysler pulled up beside the petrol-pump and told Bruce to fill 'er up. It took not quite thirteen gallons and we all had to take it in turns to work the pump handle. Then the bloke asked where he could find Mrs Laura Trumble. We pointed out Laura's place and he drove off down there. A couple of hours later he whirled back past the garage without stopping and it was over a week before we found out what he'd come for, Laura not being much of a one to pass on information.

It turned out that the stranger was Carl Middleton, the big racehorse owner. It seems he'd spent thousands of dollars importing a thoroughbred brood mare from England, and more thousands breeding a foal from her. The foal was now a rising four-year-old stallion and nobody could get near it, let alone do anything with it. The experts had finally pronounced that the horse was mad. It wasn't even safe to put it in with valuable brood mares. It was going to have to be destroyed. Then Carl Middleton had heard about our Laura Trumble from the veterinary man at Swinton's brother-in-law, and he'd come to see her as a last resort.

The horse arrived in a big horse-box on the back of a truck. You could hear it kicking at the sides of the box as they went past the garage. Carl Middleton drove along in front in his flash car. They pulled up at Laura's place and she and two men walked around her house-paddock inspecting the fences. Then they backed the truck into the paddock and one of the men climbed up to open the door of the swaying horse-box.

Everyone else got back through the gate and out of the way. The door fell open, making a ramp from the truck down to the ground. And the stallion, a beautiful big bay, about sixteen hands, backed kicking out of the horse-box and half fell off the side of the ramp. Then it leapt, plunged and galloped out into the paddock. It was amazing that he hadn't broken a leg or something.

The stallion was mad all right. He stood there, quivering and snorting, for a few moments and then whirled and galloped, bucking and flinging himself in all directions at once, the full length of the paddock. Just when it looked as though he was going to tear right through the macrocarpa hedge behind the fence at the bottom of the paddock, he propped, skidded a good fifteen yards and wheeled along the fence, bucking and rearing and snorting as though the Devil himself was on his back. At the far corner he stopped and stood with his head drooping and the wind whistling in his nostrils. Then suddenly he squealed and reared and galloped again along the bottom fence to the corner, where he turned to gallop back again, all the time keeping up his crazy bucking and lashing-out.

Laura took Carl Middleton and his men into the house and a couple of hours later they came out and drove away. The stallion was resting a little between his mad fits of running and jumping around, but any activity around the place was enough to set him up in business again.

All that night the mad stallion galloped up and down the fence at the bottom of Laura Trumble's house-paddock. By morning he'd churned a great muddy track along the fence that we could easily see from the garage. We began to wonder when he was going to collapse from sheer exhaustion. He was settling down for longer periods now, and even cropping a few crops of grass now and then, but whenever anyone came within sight of him he'd set up his running-plunging act again and keep it up for long after they were gone.

Now all of us around Talltree Point began to notice how proud of Laura Trumble we were. I suppose we'd been taking her a fair bit for granted. Anyway there was a lot of indignation about this bloke Middleton landing her with this impossible animal. There was some talk of asking the police over at Swinton to order the horse taken away again for Laura's safety. The outcome of it was that we all sat back and waited to see what Laura was going to do with the mad stallion.

And she did nothing. Absolutely nothing. She didn't even keep out of his way, but strutted like a busy emu through and around the paddock whenever she felt like it, completely ignoring the frantic contortions the stallion flew into whenever she appeared. She didn't even look at him, even when he came plunging and snorting along the fence towards her. She just strolled along towards the gate with her bucket of milk, and when the stallion got to within a few yards of her he stopped, snorted and wheeled back along the fence. Not only did Laura do nothing about the mad horse, but she went on doing nothing. Week after week.

And the horse couldn't take it. He got to going through his act right in front of her as she passed through the paddock, but she refused to even look. He ran after her but she ignored his presence as though he didn't exist. He took to coming closer to the house and eventually stood for hours with his head over the yard gate, waiting for her to come out so he could try and impress her. But she went on doing nothing about it. He started running ahead of her across the paddock and then even following her, getting closer and closer to her, but he was wasting his time.

Just as the mad horse got to getting closer to Laura, some of us got to getting closer to the horse. Just about every day one or two of us'd go down to Laura's gate and lean there, looking and saying what we thought might be done with it. The horse ignored us altogether after a while, and Laura went on ignoring the horse.

When Carl Middleton and one of his men came to see how Laura was getting on with their stallion he turned on one of his best performances for them. They talked to Laura at the gate for a while and then drove back past the garage, looking grim.

And with Laura going on ignoring the horse he actually started to fret and look pathetic over the fence while she fed all her other animals in the next paddock and patted them and talked to them. He gave himself the job of escorting Laura safely across his paddock, walking along beside her, bursting for attention — and not getting it. He pretended to get a fright sometimes and bolt down the paddock, but it wasn't very convincing. Nobody ever actually mentioned the horse to Laura and she never talked about him, so we were pretty hard-pushed for conversation sometimes.

Six weeks after his last visit, Carl Middleton, with three other men this time, arrived at Laura's place. The mad horse went mad and they went inside and stayed there for about an hour and a half. Then they left.

Then one day Laura left the gate open and the horse followed her across to the hay-barn and over to where the cows were being fed. He ate a bit of hay and followed her back into his own paddock. The day after that I called in to ask Laura to marry me, and there was the stallion, in the yard of the house, eating the long grass. I froze in my tracks and then he saw me. He raised his head, looked at me for a moment, and then went on eating, swishing his tail at the flies.

That day I came straight out and asked Laura when she was going to start breaking in the horse and would she like me to help. But she just said that he was coming along nicely. It was over a month before I found out that Carl Middleton had given Laura the horse for what he owed her for grazing and time she'd wasted. He'd given up any hope of ever getting the thing quietened down. He'd even made it legal so he wouldn't be responsible for any damage the horse did.

And that's how Laura came to be the owner of one of the best-bred horses in the country, although you wouldn't think so to look at him. He's covered with mud and his mane's all tangled and full of burs. And the calves chewed his tail all to wisps. As a matter of fact he's a bit of a nuisance these days. Keeps getting in the way all the time.

We've got Joe Dobbie's draught mare in foal to him, and Wally Catch's grey hack (but we're not certain yet). We would actually make a fair bit of money with him serving brood mares, but the wife wouldn't hear of it.

I haven't much say in the matter really. After all it was her who went to all the trouble of getting him.

WARM BEER

The short cut across the hills turned out to be a lousy idea. Old Sniffer climbed across the third gully and up to the crest of the fourth ridge. The road he was looking for wasn't in that gully either. Only a straggly sheeptrack wound its way aimlessly across the opposite hillside as though it had been drawn there by a child with a pencil.

He stood looking around the overgrown countryside, sweating beerily in the last of the still sunshine. A sheep bleated somewhere but he couldn't see any sheep, or anything at all except the desertedness of everything.

Already he was beginning to recognise the symptoms of an unfairly premature hangover. It was less than an hour since he'd left the pub. He wiped his face on the sleeve of his shirt and started down the hillside towards the bottom of the gully, where shadows were beginning to lie around, like something spilt and spreading.

It was almost gloomy down in the gully and he was feeling the faint reminder of his old knee. He looked up the slope he had to climb and then at the old road that lay half-submerged in the ferns along the floor of the dry gully. It wasn't the road he was looking for, but maybe it joined it farther down. He began to push his way, limping a little now because of his knee, along the muddy, patchy, overgrown road.

Soon he could hear water trickling in the tiny stream under the fern and scrub just below the road. He began to look for a way down to it, rolling a dried-up gob of saliva uselessly around in his parched mouth. Then the road, if it could be called that, opened out into what had once been a sizeable clearing. He saw the burnt-out remains of what had been a fairly big house, and a few posts and rails rotting in a scattered heap. Stockyards of some kind. Another old house, more like a shack, this one, only a dried skeleton of warped boards and framework. It must have been years since anyone was here.

Old Sniffer looked around, a little bewildered at finding this remote place within such a short time of leaving a pub full of people. He sat on a lump of turf, which turned out to be an old anvil overgrown with weeds and grass, and wondered what the hell to do. It was getting really dark now, and he was obviously miles from anywhere. He was going to have to spend the night in this godforsaken place and probably be crippled up with another dose of rheumatism for a couple of weeks until he drank it out of his bones again. It was then, in the shadowy, creeping dark of the tumbling hidden valley, that he saw, flung carelessly out on a little rise at the foot of a descending ridge, the scattered broken headstones of a long-ago graveyard.

A dirty angel with spread wings swooped eternally into a great clump of fern, and stumpy streaky headstones of all shapes and sizes reared, reached, peered, leaned and lumbered around among the falling fences of the half-acre or so of this astonishing place.

Sniffer pushed his way curiously in the gloom through the undergrowth up the rise, till he stood at the edge of the graveyard. His eyes had grown slightly accustomed to the dark and he pushed his way towards a falling headstone and was bending down to peer at the inscription on it when a voice beside him said helpfully:

"Wattie Beamish. Died eighteen eighty-four from an overdose of nagging. Not a bad bloke when you got to know him. He's on afternoon-shift heart-attacks this week."

Sniffer turned to gaze in astonishment at his informer. A fair-dinkum ghost. Absolutely normal-looking in every respect, except that he was slouching with all his weight leaning against a shimmery frond of fern. He looked as though he'd just stepped off a bus on his way home from work, or something. Sniffer was a bit knocked back by all this, and, perhaps excusably, just stood there gaping. The ghost went on:

"It's not often we get visitors here these days. Forty years ago we almost had to give this place up altogether, there were so many people about. — Sit down." And he set an example by drifting over and perching lightly on the raised edge of Wattie Beamish's grave. Sniffer obediently sat beside him, as far away as he could politely get.

"Er, what are you doing here?" asked Sniffer, for the sake of something to say.

"I'm on guide duty,' said the ghost. "Most of us have to put in a few years guiding at first."

"What about the women?" asked Sniffer. He was trying, for some reason, to keep the conversation on this harmless level.

"Oh we don't have much to do with them," explained the ghost. "We ghosts aren't interested in sex, and without it women aren't much use to us. They're kept in a different place altogther. I believe some of 'em are quite useful in some ways. They've got some kind of training scheme going now, you know. — Would you care for a beer?"

"Well, yes, I wouldn't mind one," said Sniffer thirstily. "Have you got any?" he added suspiciously.

"Sure," said the ghost, producing a bottle of beer from some invisible where. "Not a bad drop the Northern Brewery turns out these days." He flipped the top off the bottle with an enormous opener and passed it to Sniffer. "Got this from a car accident a few minutes ago. Bloke won't be needing it where he's going. Nothing'll make a man crook quicker than warm beer."

"Thanks," said Sniffer. And he carefully took the bottle and drank several hefty gulps of genuine Northern Bitter.

"A bit frothy," observed the ghost, taking the bottle from Sniffer. "It's been shaken up a bit."

"Perhaps you could tell me where the main road is from here," said Sniffer. "I've lost my direction coming over those hills there."

"Roads?" said the ghost as though he wasn't quite sure what they were. "Oh yes. Never use 'em myself. They always seem to go the long way round. I have seen one or two somewhere round here, but I couldn't tell you where one is off-hand, though."

"Doesn't really matter," said Sniffer, taking the bottle again, which he noticed was still nearly full. "I just wanted to get to my hut over on the main road. Tried to take a short cut but I got a bit lost."

"If you want to borrow Wattie's grave here for a snore-off till he gets off work, I'm sure he won't mind," said the ghost helpfully.

"No, thanks all the same," said Sniffer quickly. "I'm not at all tired. It's just that I wanted to get home sometime tonight. Thanks for the offer, though."

"Don't mention it," said the ghost pleasantly. "We can always dig you up a bunk here if you're stuck. — What have they got you doing for a crust these days?"

"Roadman," said Sniffer, passing back the bottle. "Due to retire next year. What about you?"

"Just guide duty. I'm on road accidents at the moment. Hardly enough business to keep us going lately. We get most of our business in the holiday season, you know. Thanks — good luck! So you're due to retire, eh?"

"Yep, I'll be sixty-five next October."

"Well, I don't suppose it'll be long before we'll be seeing you down at headquarters."

"What do you mean by that?" demanded Sniffer.

"Oh, it's always the same," said the ghost with a wave of his hand. "Once they retire they don't last long. Of course we've got one or two little lurks to help things along. Nothing drastic, you understand; a bit of rheumatism during the winter; shut down on the eyesight here and there — increases the possibility of falling down stairs and things like that, y'know — and then, of course, there's always the old booze. That helps a lot, especially in cases like yours. It's really quite surprising how you can boost your tally if you put your mind to it."

Sniffer put the bottle down on the edge of the grave. "You can cut that out, mate," he said belligerently. "I didn't come here to be knocked off by rheumatism and booze. I'm as fit as any bloke half my age. I've got years left in me yet."

"No need to get shirty," said the ghost. "You've all got to go sometime."

"Well I'm not going till I'm good and ready," said Sniffer hotly. "And that's that."

"We've got pretty good conditions here now, you know. Not like the old days."

"I don't give a damn what you've got," insisted Sniffer. "I'm hanging on here as long as I can, and I've got years to go yet."

"Good prospects for promotion, according to ability and length of service," quoted the ghost. "That means that if you join us now, by nineteen ninety-six. . ."

"I'm not joining you now or any other time."

"Come now. Let's be realistic about this. You've got to come sometime — why not make it now? It's all shift-work these days, you know. Time and a half for Saturday mornings and double time Sundays and public holidays. Interesting variety. Only one day a month on hospital duty. Superannuation. — Think what you'll be passing up. The longer you stay here. . ."

"No," said Sniffer definitely, drinking again from the bottle and passing it back to the ghost.

"But think of three weeks' annual leave on full pay," said the ghost eagerly.

"Not impressed," said Sniffer.

“The union intends going to a forty-hour-week at the next annual general meeting of the Federation of. . .”

“You’re wasting your time,” interrupted Sniffer. “I’m not going, and that’s final.”

“That’s too bad,” said the ghost, drinking resignedly from the bottle and tossing it empty into the fern, “because I’ve come to take you in. I always try to make it as easy as possible, but you’d be surprised how stubborn people can be about a simple little thing like that.”

“Well, you’re not taking me anywhere,” said Sniffer. “It might be simple to you, but I’ve got used to it here. I’m not ready to retire yet, anyway. I’d get the sack if I just walked out on the job like that without telling them. Why, I’d probably lose my old age pension over it. I’d never get another job with the county, that’s for sure. Besides, it’d be hard on an old man to change his habits after a lifetime. He gets set in his ways, you know. It could affect his health. And what about my back pay? They wouldn’t know where to send it. And what about my working gear? They dock your pay if you just leave without handing it in. And I’ve got to find out what happens on my serial on the radio. And there’s a lot of things I haven’t finished. And. . .”

But the ghost insisted.

Journey

The hand that felled and split the tree
And sank the posts in sand and scree
And strung the wire and battened up
Now raps the saucer with the cup.

The arm that sprung the hauler-sprag
And slung the axe and strung the stag
And swung the six-horse ploughing team
Now reaches out to play the queen.

The foot that trod the frozen clay
And kicked the winning goal that day;
The foot that once wore hide and steel
Now puts its slippers on by feel.

The ear that heard the southwind roar
And fling the vessel on the shore,
And heard the names of shipmates read
Now hardly hears what's being said.

The eye that saw the car come through,
The Monarch crowned, the ration-queue,
The plastic pipe, the rocket risen,
Now rests its gaze on television.

The soul that since before its birth,
Now weary of its term on earth,
And quickened by a glimpse of light,
Rejoices, and prepares for flight.

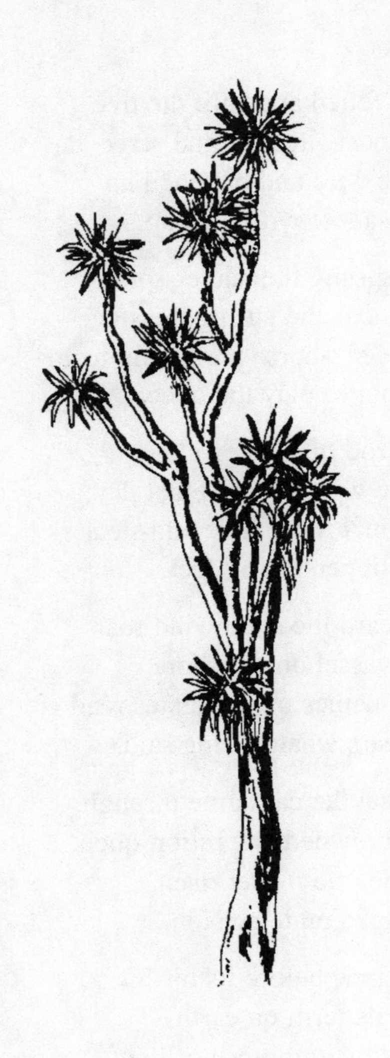

A Clean Swap

Midday and steaming hot. The gentle *kiukiuing* of pigeons in the teatrees. Hushing of air through she-oaks and rifle-fish splashing in the shade under banks. Leaves and debris on the smooth water revolving slowly upstream on a filling tide, and around the bend the coming and going stink of something rotten a crocodile had hidden somewhere.

The twenty-five-foot canoe they'd bought off the blacks down the river for a sack of flour and a packet of Log Cabin tobacco moved sullenly upstream with the current under their lazy paddling. Over the heap of supplies and gear on the platform in the centre of the canoe Ralph could see by the movement of Bill's shoulder muscles that he wasn't putting any weight into the paddle. It didn't matter much. There was no hurry, and Bill would be doing most of the paddling tonight.

One thing about these canoes, they were so big and heavy that once you got them moving they carried along without much effort to the paddlers. Another thing about them was that once you got them moving they took a hell of a lot of stopping or manoeuvring. They missed out on a lot of crocs that way.

If they'd kept off the grog in Normanton that last skin cheque would have bought them an outboard motor. Oh well — next time perhaps.

Bill in the bow stopped pretending to paddle and turned round in his seat.

"Smell that?" he asked.

"Yeah." Ralph paddled slowly on.

"Croc?"

"Could be."

"How much further do we have to go before we can camp?" asked Bill, laying his paddle across the canoe and getting his tobacco out of the hip pocket of his shorts.

"We'll keep going till the tide turns," said Ralph, who was the unofficial head man because of having been at the game for three years. "They don't like you camping too close to the mission and we don't want to louse things up here. We won't get supplies anywhere else."

"What's wrong with camping near the mission?" Bill wanted to know.

Ralph grinned. "The gins," he said. "They sneak away and get hanging around your camp."

He trailed his paddle and steered the canoe away from a petrified stump that showed a few inches under the water.

"You could always hunt them out of it," said Bill.

"You could," agreed Ralph, "but you don't. It's better to having nothing to do with them."

Bill picked up his paddle and turned back to his job. "You'd never catch me having anything to do with those scrawny bitches," he said.

"That's what everyone says," replied Ralph. "But there's still plenty of half-caste kids running around the scrub. You can't blame the mission blokes being a bit down on it."

They lapsed into silence, broken only by the plop-swirling of the paddles, until a couple of bends later Bill pointed to a wet smooth mud-slide on a sloping bank among an isolated stand of mangroves.

"Slide."

"Yeah," said Ralph interestedly. "A big one, too, by the look of it."

They steered the canoe to sweep close in to the bank there.

"Fairly big saltwater croc," announced Ralph. "We might get a crack at him later."

They paddled on and about an hour later the current on the river was still and it was high tide. They found a landing place and nosed the canoe into the shore.

"Unload everything except the shooting gear."

On the leafy bank they made a pile of their supplies and gear and Bill lit a fire. Ralph went away with the rifle to look for meat; he saw a dingo, a king-brown snake, and three wallabies. He shot a wallaby and took the hindquarters and tail back to camp. They ate damper and steaks and put on a wallaby stew with potatoes and onions.

"How much further does this river go?" asked Bill, sipping noisily at a pannikin of weak tea.

"Far as I can remember it breaks up into a lot of small streams not far from here," replied Ralph. "There's a big area of swamp and mud back in there. There'd be crocs in there all right, but it's a hell of a place to get at. Lousy with sandflies and mosquitos. The tide hardly reaches up into it. There's places where you can get nearly-fresh water but you have to hunt round for it. The place changes a fair bit. Hard to say what it's like now. It's two years since me and Baldy Foster shot there. Got a few crocs though, far as I can remember."

"Where will we shoot tonight?" asked Bill, poking at the stew in the camp oven.

"I think we'll go back down on the tide and wait until dark, then shoot our way back up here with the tide again. Should work out pretty right."

"In that case we'd better get going," said Bill. "I'll check the gear."

Harpoon, .303, .22, and ammunition. Knife, spotlight and the battery out of the jeep they'd left at the mission. Gaff, axe, boiling-up gear, quart pots, and mosquito repellent. Box of spares and sacks.

"Everything's here."

"Right. Let's go."

They pushed the canoe out into the river and settled down to a long paddle back down-river.

They had to wait until two hours after dark for the tide to turn before they could set off back up the river. Sitting in the light of their little fire on the bank, Bill said: "Ralph — you know Judy."

"That little gingerheaded piece in the pub at Normanton? Sure, I know her."

"I was wondering — you, er — you took her out a couple of times," he blurted out awkwardly.

"Yeah, that's right. We went over to Croydon once or twice. What about it?"

"Well, it's just that I've been going around with her for a couple of years, and — well, I wondered if you're serious about her or anything."

"Hell, man," said Ralph goodhumouredly. "She's the only

decent sort in the Gulf. Everybody knows that. She's not going to be around much longer anyway. She told me she had a job jacked up in Cairns after Christmas."

"What do you mean by decent sort?" demanded Bill hotly.

"Ar, don't get me wrong, Bill. You know how it is. I didn't know she was going steady with you. At least, she never said anything to me about it. If I'd known you were trotting her . . ."

"It doesn't matter," said Bill sulkily. "If I'd known she was shooting through to Cairns I wouldn't have agreed to come out here with you after you and Toby split up. I only did it to make some money. I don't suppose it matters now."

"Listen," said Ralph kindly. "I don't know how it was with you and Judy, but take my advice and forget her. If she's so keen on you after a couple of years that she'll go out with anyone who asks her, then she's not worth getting yourself worked up over."

Bill said nothing and soon it was time for them to go.

Out in the stream Ralph, in the bow of the canoe, adjusted the light strapped to his forehead and clipped the leads on to the battery behind him. The light speared out through the darkness and raked the banks on either side of the river. The canoe slid silently up the river under the deft paddles, with the light searching for the red eyes of crocodiles.

Half an hour of noiseless progress and then a glimmer of red among some reeds on a bend ahead. Ralph steered the canoe towards a six-foot freshwater croc while Bill paddled steadily on. They got that one easily.

Then they paddled on in the dark silence towards the

glowing eyes of a big croc further up the river. Ralph felt the excitement that always thrilled him when he was on to a big one. He could hear Bill's heavy jerky breathing behind him as he splashed his paddle in clumsy nervousness.

Closer — the eyes vanished. He's gone down. Keep going, he'll come up again — there he is, further on. Keep going. Closer. Deep water here, a harpoon job. Closer. Pole in one hand, steering with the paddle in the other. Here we are! Lay the paddle across the canoe. Careful not to knock on the boat. The ridged snout and the bulging neck just under the water behind the eyes. Got him!

A thrashing, splashing, churning tumult and the croc disappears, but the rope looping out over the bow of the rocking canoe tells that he's fixed on the end of the quill. Lay the pole back in the canoe and grab the knife, just in case.

The rope stops feeding out. There's still a few coils left. Ralph picked up the .303 and closed the bolt on a cartridge. A gentle tug on the rope to get his position and suddenly the rest of the rope runs out and the canoe is jerked half round.

Silence. The river is oil. Crabs crack and plop in the mangroves. Water gurgles into holes in the mud. The canoe turns slackly in the current. He's got to come up for air —

Suddenly red eyes out in the middle of the stream. The comfortable roar of the .303 and the great white belly floats in the light. Quick! Drag him in before he sinks. Loop the rope round his jaws. He's still twitching. Here, let me get at him with the axe. There, that's fixed him. Drag him to the bank and we'll try and get him into the canoe. He's at least twelve feet. Skin'll be worth fifty bucks easy, if it's first grade.

With the croc lying in the canoe between them, Ralph turned off the light and they each rolled a smoke.

"A pretty good start," said Ralph, more nonchalantly than he felt.

"How many more do you think we'll get?"

"Hard to say," replied Ralph. "If we don't get any more tonight we still haven't done too bad. You can sometimes paddle all night around here and not even see one."

They drifted up to another small croc and Ralph shot it with the .22, grabbed it by the snout, chopped it behind the head with the axe and threw it into the canoe. A five-footer.

They lit up another big salty but couldn't get near him, and eventually gave him up and carried on. They got another freshy, about six feet, that didn't give them any trouble, and just before the camp they fluked an eight-foot salty asleep on the bank. Four crocs was a pretty good night's shooting in that area. They threw them into the shallow water by the camp, had a brew of tea by the light of the fire, and turned in at four o'clock.

They woke late in the morning and would have been bad-tempered if they hadn't had such a good night's shooting.

They ate wallaby stew and began skinning. The big crocs took them over an hour to skin, knifing the hide carefully off every inch of the way. It was mid-afternoon by the time they had the four hides scraped, salted, and rolled up in a sack.

"About a hundred bucks' worth," announced Ralph, straightening stiffly from dumping the sack in the shade. "Tonight we'll do from here up the river. It shouldn't be such a drag as last night. Then tomorrow we can shift camp further upstream. Should be able to cover all that water in about a week. Then we'll give the whole river another rakeover down to the mission."

"When are we going back to Normanton?" asked Bill.

"Hell, man," laughed Ralph. "You still thinking about that redhead? We've only been out three weeks. We should have time to do the Roper and the Limmin before the Wet starts. We'll send away what skins we've got from the mission and take the rest back to town when we go for Christmas. We ought to have a few hundred bucks each by then."

"It's all very well for you," said Bill, "but you haven't got a woman to think of."

Ralph looked at him for a moment. "Neither have you, Bill. I told you before."

"Ar, go to hell." Bill turned away and began poking at the fire.

"Look, what's eating you?" asked Ralph reasonably.

"You know bloody well," exploded Bill, turning on him. "You ask Judy to marry you and then turn round and tell me she's no good."

"Where the hell did you get that from?" asked Ralph.

"She told me herself," said Bill belligerently.

"Well in that case why did you come out here with me in the first place?" asked Ralph, frowning.

"She only told me the night before we left," said Bill, "and I thought . . ."

"Look," interrupted Ralph. "I never did and never would ask Judy to marry me. I don't know what line of bull she's been feeding you, but it looks to me as though she's just trying to stir up trouble. Probably trying to get rid of you the easy way; by making you jealous. For God's sake forget her. She's no good to you, me, or anyone else."

"You mean you didn't tell her you'd marry her when you got back from this trip?" asked Bill doubtfully.

"Of course not," laughed Ralph, slapping him on the back. "If I was the marrying kind I'd have taken the plunge years ago. And it wouldn't have been anyone like Judy, I can tell you. Now cheer up and think about all the money we're going to make."

Bill half-grinned ruefully.

"I suppose a man's a bit of a mug at that," he muttered.

They got a fifteen-footer up the river and a couple of freshies on the way back. They shifted camp and shot five more salties in a side-arm of the river. They got a nine-footer out on the bank in broad daylight and an eight-foot freshy on a log near the new camp. They lost a big salty that nearly tipped the canoe over, and harpooned a one-eyed rogue croc in a swamp. They hacked a path for the canoe through miles of overhanging mangrove into a big stretch of open water, where they got a clear hundred and fifty dollars' worth of skins in two nights.

They were nearly out of salt, and Ralph said they wouldn't have time to hunt any more rivers before the Wet, by the time they finished this one.

In spite of all the success they were having, Bill became more and more withdrawn and brooding. He'd often go a whole day without offering a single unsolicited remark. Ralph appeared not to notice, though he knew well enough what the trouble was.

They hacked and dragged the canoe right up into a great spreading area of mud and mangroves at the head of the last creek running into the head of the river, with the intention of shooting their way back to their camp after dark. Even though it was broad daylight the air was so thick with mosquitos that the place droned with them.

"Well," said Ralph, spreading another dose of Kokoda round his neck. "This is as far as we go."

"Yeah," said Bill, slapping at his bare legs.

"Paddle us across to that little island there, Bill. I'll see if I can get a fire going to keep these mossies away. It's still a couple of hours or so till dark. They'll eat us alive by then. A man wouldn't survive a night in this place without a fire."

He stepped ashore and began scouting around for firewood, leaving Bill to hold the canoe against the bank.

"There's a bit of wood in here," he called. "Tie the canoe up, Bill, and come and give us a hand to rake a fire together. It's pretty scattered. And bring the matches with you."

There was no answer.

"Hey, Bill," he called. "Where the hell are you?"

Still no answer. Ralph went to the edge of the mangroves and looked out. Bill was paddling quickly back down the creek.

"Hey, Bill," he yelled. "where are you going? Come back here. Hey Bill — Bill!"

But Bill paddled round the bend out of sight without looking back.

Ralph stumbled and scrambled through the tangled masses

of mangrove roots to the end of the little island. And then he stopped. There was fifty yards of muddy water between him and the main bank of the creek. And then miles of mangroves. Pursuit was impossible and survival in this place was only a matter of time, not counting the likelihood of his being taken by a crocodile on the swim from the island to the creek-bank.

Already, as the repellent wore off, his bare arms and legs were black with mosquitos, and the smaller, more vicious, sandflies. In a grey cloud of insects he waded through the muddy water and began to swim quietly for the far bank.

A great, grey crocodile that had been watching, motionless, from under an uprooted tree since the canoe first arrived, lunged noiselessly into the water.

Four days later, in the early afternoon, Bill reached the mission. He tied the loaded canoe to a stake among several other canoes, climbed the bank and made his way among the huts and staring blacks to the missionary's house on a low hill a little distance away. The missionary greeted him at the gate. Bill had his story ready, but the missionary got in first, which, in a way, was just as well for Bill.

"Your friend said you'd probably be in today or tomorrow," he said.

"Uh — what?"

"Ralph, your mate. He came in the day before yesterday with some of my boys who were out getting beef to salt down for the Wet. He'd been badly bitten by mosquitos, you know. After he left you he lost his way in a mangrove swamp and was hours getting through to open country. It's lucky my boys found him. Terrible mess he was in; mud from head to foot and very weak from mosquito bites and exhaustion."

"Yeah. Er — hard luck," gulped Bill uncomfortably. "Er — where is he now?"

"Oh, he left this morning for Normanton," said the missionary. "I lent him a battery for his jeep. He explained how you were staying on here for the wet season."

"The wet season!" said Bill. "Isn't there any way I can get out of here?"

"Not now," said the missionary. "The last supply truck went back a week ago. There'll be no transport through here until the end of March now. However, we'll be pleased to have you here for the Wet. There's such a lot to be done, we can always use an extra willing man. — Oh yes, and Ralph left a message for you. He said not to worry about his share of the skins. He's making a clean swap for something of yours in Normanton. He said you'd know what he meant."

Tom's Yarn

The early morning sunlight shone through Ponto's big ears and lit them up like a pair of late model tail-lights. Behind him Tom was transferring some tobacco into his pocket from the pocket of Ponto's coat hanging on the door of the shed they'd slept in. Ponto hadn't got much sleep. He'd sat huddled in a corner, shaking like a dog on a river bank, all night. Tom had squatted by the door smoking and thinking and dozing on and off.

They were somewhere north of Murchison. How far neither of them was certain, though they'd agreed it was something between twenty and a hundred and fifty miles.

It was a half-fine morning, with bush all round and the raining-on-leaves sound of a creek somewhere nearby or a big river in the distance. Ponto was sitting in a clump of fern on the bank above the road, brooding.

"That's definitely the last time I'm sleeping on the ground," he complained in a voice as stiff as his knees. "It's no bloody good to a man my age. I'll end up getting rheumatism or something and have to retire. And I'm hungry," he added.

Tom leaned against the wall of the hut watching the way Ponto's ears wiggled as he talked. Not getting an answer to what wasn't really a question anyway, Ponto turned to Tom and said, "Do you know where this road leads to?"

"Well, there's several ways of looking at it," answered Tom, pinching the ends off a thin cigarette and lighting it. "It could lead us to a dead-end, for one thing. It could take us to a flash job and a business of our own. Or it could lead us into a whole swag of trouble. It could lead us to the sea or into those mountains up there. It could lead us into the grave anywhere. Y'see, Ponto old boy, it's not the road itself but the way you travel it. Some blokes bowl straight past some of the best things that are ever likely to happen to them because they don't see them. They're too busy looking towards the end of the journey to get a kick out of the travelling."

Ponto wasn't impressed. "It's all very well to talk about what might happen but I'd sooner have a good feed under my belt than all the talk in the world. A man can get by without talk but he can't go without a feed for long."

"That's just where you're wrong," said Tom. "The way things are today there's more money made with talk than hard work. Take any job you like; who gets the most money, the bloke who does the work or the one that gives the orders?"

He threw Ponto his coat and led the way on to the road.

They strolled along the winding, dipping, bushlined, stony road at a leisurely couple of miles an hour, which Ponto complained was a mad dash to get nowhere on an empty stomach. They were alternately in sunshine and shadow because of the semi-summer clouds that were breathing across the sun on a light west wind.

Tom was telling Ponto a yarn to keep his mind off his stomach.

"Talk about a liar! He was one out of the box, this bloke. One of them blokes who couldn't tell the truth if you paid him to. Must have been knocked around a bit when he was a kid or something. If you happened to mention something about fishing he'd tell you how he used to ride the tiger-sharks around in the sea off the Barrier Reef for a bit of sport. If anyone started talking about horses he'd chip in with a yarn about sneaking up on a brumby stallion in the dark, leaping on its back and riding it into town fully broken in, with a few extra tricks thrown in, by daylight.

"If you said something about cows this bloke'd dig up a yarn about how he kept a mad Jersey bull from doing any more damage by playing it round the paddock like a dirty big trout, using his oilskin for a matador's cape, until the army got there and killed it with anti-tank guns!"

At this point Ponto snorted disgustedly, but couldn't help grinning a little.

"He told me once," continued Tom, "that he used to creep up and hypnotise South American cougars and sell them to the zoos for thirty quid a throw. Once, he reckoned, when he was giving them a hand to load one on to a ship, the cage slipped out of the sling and busted. The cougar got loose and galloped up the main street of Brazil with Shai — that's this bloke's name — flat out after it. He grabbed it just as it was climbing in the window of the Lord Mayor's bedroom and slapped a full-nelson on it and carted it back to the wharf. But he put a bit too much pressure on and broke its neck. Done his thirty quid cold, but he got a medal off the government for bravery. He'd lost the medal in a two-up game a couple of weeks before so he couldn't show it to us.

"Then there was the time this coot reckoned he was logging down south somewhere in the middle of winter. The snow was so deep they used to wander through a block of bush, cutting the heads off the trees so they had all good clean logs to fell when the snow thawed.

"It was so cold the smoke used to freeze as soon as it left the chimney and roll down the roof and pile up in heaps round the hut. They had to spend a couple of hours every day rolling these big hunks of smoke away from the hut and piling them up in a gully behind the camp. When the thaw came they were smoke-bound in the hut for nearly a week. One of the blokes went out to the wood-block for an armful of wood and wandered around in the smoke for two days trying to find his way back to the hut. When the smoke cleared they organised a search party and found him nearly dead from exposure about fifty yards away from the hut. He was as black as the inside of a chimney from all the smoke. They warmed him up and scraped him down, but he never came right."

Tom paused and shook his head. "It must'a been cold all right. Even in the summer they reckoned she was often well below zero. One night there they were snigging a dirty big log out just before dark when she broke off and rolled into a little creek so they left it there till the next day. When they went to drag it out in the morning she was frozen solid. Even the D-9 couldn't shift her so they got another tractor in to do it.

"They pushed and pulled and bladed and ploughed for about three hours but the log stayed frozen into the creek as solid as ever. And when they gave up and knocked off for lunch somebody suddenly noticed that they'd dragged the creek two hundred yards off-course."

Tom glanced at Ponto shuffling along beside him. "How's that for a beaut, Ponto?"

"I'm still bloody hungry," said Ponto ungraciously.

"Then this joker said how the Alaskan Government got to hear how good he was with animals and sent for him to go up there and deal with a pack of timber-wolves that were cleaning up all the eskimo kids on their way home from school. He flew up to the Yukon with a big bag of macaroni and killed off thirty-eight timber-wolves without firing a single shot.

"He hollowed out lumps of meat, filled them with macaroni and dropped them from a helicopter. The wolves ate the meat and the macaroni swelled up inside them till they couldn't move. Then he landed and went round and finished them off with a young bull-terrier bitch he had in the back of the helicopter. He reckoned he could have done a better job using rice but macaroni was easier to get hold of at the time.

"That night he had a few beers with Dangerous Dan McGrew and flew back to Napier. That's where I ran into him. He was heading down to Wellington to see Wally Nash about a job. Very hush-hush, he reckoned it was. All he could say about it was that a big crack was opening up under one of the caissons on the Auckland Harbour Bridge and he was the only one who could save the whole thing from collapsing.

"He stung my mate for a couple of quid because they wouldn't cash his Alaskan cheque at the bottle-store and he'd have to post it up to the Alaskan Embassy in Auckland. He didn't have time to wire his accountant for funds because he'd taken out a contract with the Yale University to supply them with poisonous snakes next year and it only left him three weeks to fix up the bridge and get over to America.

"My mate reckoned that Shai was the best value he'd had for two quid in all his life."

"Serves him right," said Ponto. "If he's dumb enough to believe a bloody joker who reckons smoke freezes he deserves to lose his two quid. He wouldn't get two bob out of me, I can tell you."

"Me mate reckoned it was worth it," said Tom. "Y'see, he was so wrapped up in listening to Shai that he forgot to go and meet his girlfriend. He turned up an hour late, still grinning about Shai. His girl was pretty worked up by this time and what with my mate grinning and scoffing to himself she ups and breaks off the engagement. My mate was tickled pink. He came straight back to the pub and offered Shai another two quid. But Shai said the first two was enough to see him right. Just goes to show. A man never knows which way his luck's going to go from one minute to the next."

"I'm still bloody hungry," was Ponto's only comment.

Dan's Luck

"Strike, Tom. Look at that big fat joker in the lead there!"

"Not so loud," whispered Tom urgently. "And get down. If they spot us we've had it."

Ponto settled back into the hedge and cleared a little opening in the long grass so he could look out.

"They're angling up the hill," said Tom. "They'll probably strike this hedge a bit further along. Keep an eye on them and if they head this way get ready to sneak back over the hill towards the road."

"How long will we have to wait?" asked Ponto.

"It'll be properly dark in about half an hour. We'd better give them about ten or fifteen minutes after that to settle down."

"Are you sure we can manage with only that sheet of corrugated iron?"

"Course we can. You can bake bread on a sheet of iron if you go the right way about it. We'll just cut the meat into strips and lay it on the tin on top of a fire."

"They're going into the hedge," said Ponto excitedly.

"Good," said Tom peering out past Ponto. "Mark the spot where they go in. We don't want to kick up too much of a racket thrashing around looking for them in the dark."

"They're right opposite that forked stump there."

"Good. They must be in good nick. When they bed down this early you can be pretty sure they're well-fed. I'll just keep an eye out on the other side of the hedge to make sure they don’t go right through.”

“Good idea. I’ll watch this side in case they come out again.”

“Ever swiped turkeys before?” asked Tom.

“Yeah, dozens of times. Nearly got caught once or twice too.”

“You’ve got to be careful,” said Tom. “They’re pretty hot on swiping turkeys and stuff these days. I remember once when an old bloke called Dan and I were on a fowl-raid in a shed behind a cocky’s house. We had about four each and just as we were sneaking out Dan goes and knocks a perch down with about thirty fowls on it. You’d think it was New Year’s Eve. Fair go! There was flapping and squawking and dogs barking and lights going on and Dan and I standing in the yard with big handfuls of luminous white chooks. Then someone started yelling out from the house and a big bloke, about six foot four and tare somewhere round two hundred pounds, came out on to the back porch with an old army rifle.”

“You’d have a job talking your way out of that one,” grinned Ponto. “How did you get away?”

“Bloody quickly, I can tell you,” said Tom. “I went one way and Dan stayed where he was. The bloke saw me dash through the yard and took off after me, firing shots in the air. As soon as we were clear Dan ducked back past the house and a woman started screaming her head off. The bloke left off chasing me and went rushing back yelling, “Where? Where?”

“I sneaked back to pick up a couple of chooks I’d dropped

and heard a terrible crash and then shouting and thumping and cursing. I thought Dan must have run fair into this bloke's arms. It wasn't till next day I found out what happened."

Tom began rolling a smoke and peered out of the hedge.

"Getting dark," he said. "We'll be able to get crackin' shortly."

"Well?" said Ponto.

"Well what?"

"What the hell happened?"

"Happened to who?" asked Tom innocently.

"Happened to this bloke Dan with all the yelling and going on?" demanded Ponto impatiently.

"Oh, that! Well the day after, I was going past Dan's place and here he is sitting on the front porch all battered and beaten around with.

"When the bloke heard his wife screaming and went back to see what was going on, he spotted Dan and made a rush at him. Dan jumped a fence and took to his scrapers. He'd just got himself into top gear when a clothes-line caught him fair under the chin. Just about tore the poor sod's head off. He must have done about half a dozen back somersaults. Lost all his chooks. The bloke came charging up shouting, 'I've got 'im! I've got 'im!' Dan dived out of the way just as the bloke pounced on him but he got his clod-hoppers hooked up in the clothes-prop and came another gutser. Dan reckons the bloke was just about frothing at the mouth by this time and roaring like a mad bull. Dan grabbed the clothes-prop and held the bloke off while he got to his feet. Then he threw the prop and lit out for the road. He only got about fifty yards and went fair into a dirty big drain, full of blackberry and up to his guts in water. The bloke heard him fall in and came charging up with the clothes-prop and started slashing and belting and poking among the blackberry with it.

"He didn't find Dan but it was nearly daylight by the time Dan got home. I gave the poor sod one of my chooks so he wouldn't lose too much faith in things."

"He'd a been a bit stiff on it all right," said Ponto. "His luck must have gone crook on him."

"It did that time," agreed Tom. "But Dan was always running into trouble like that and most of the time it was his own fault. He'd never stop to nut things out properly. He got had up once for swiping a Muscovy duck because he didn't even wait till it got properly dark before he started work on the duck-run gate.

"Ten days later he was in court. By that time the charges included the attempted theft of all the ducks — I don't know how he was supposed to carry them — damage to the gate and fence, breaking five panes of a glasshouse and twenty pots with plants in, upsetting a bird bath, turning a herd of cows loose and pinching a little kid's bike. He'd pedalled about a mile before they caught him and Dan reckoned he'd have made it if the back wheel of the bike hadn't buckled on him. He went back for the duck later, just to show he wasn't sore or anything.

"Dan had a big family and he was always on the lookout for a bit of cheap tucker to feed them on," continued Tom. "I remember once Dan and I were sinking a few pots in the local boozer and Dan started wondering what they used to do for meat before bows and arrows were invented. I told him I'd heard somewhere how a crowd of those cave-men blokes used to round up a mob of wild horses or cattle and get them stampeding flat-out towards a bluff. There was always one or two that couldn't pull up in time. They'd fall over and get killed and the cave-blokes could climb down and get them.

"Strike me pink, Ponto, within a week the odd yearling Hereford was falling over a big bluff on a sheep-station near Dan's place; and every time Dan just happened to be passing by. He'd give the skin to the owner and take the meat home for his dogs. And Dan never had a dog to bless himself with. Then he got a contract to fence off the top of the bluff, but he took his time over it."

"He wouldn't get away with it for long," said Ponto. "They'd wake up to that one pretty smartly."

"Yep, Dan gave himself away in the finish," said Tom. "He bowls up to the boss one day and tells him another yearling's gone over the bluff and can he have the meat for dog-tucker. Then the boss says he thinks he'll come out and have a look at where all these cattle have been falling over. Dan tells him not to bother, but the boss says he thinks he'll come all the same. They went out in the boss's Landrover and got there just in time to see two of Dan's boys chase a nice fat little heifer over the top."

"Did they put him up?" asked Ponto.

"No, they didn't put him up," replied Tom. "But Dan did a lot of free fencing for that bloke. Took him about six months to work off the price of the cattle he'd knocked off."

"Well, you can't say he didn't ask for it," said Ponto. "He

was lucky to get away so light."

"On the other hand he was unlucky not to get away scot free," said Tom. "I can't help thinking he could have still been getting a bit of free meat now and again if he'd handled it right. As I said, Dan would never stop to nut things out for himself . . . but it's just about time to make a move. We'll creep slowly up on them. Keep well in under the hedge and don't make any noise or we'll go hungry."

"Would you like me to wait here?" said Ponto nervously. "Two of us might scare them."

"No, you'd better come with me. That way you can keep a better lookout for anyone coming."

Tom led the way on his hands and knees along the hedge. They were about halfway to where the turkeys had settled for the night when Ponto tugged at Tom's foot and hissed: "Hey there's a bloke up there!"

"Where? — Oh yeah, I can see the bastard."

"He's sneaking up on us. Let's get out of here."

"No. Hang on a minute . . . ah, I thought so. He's after the turkeys. We'll just wait here and see what happens."

"Let's get out of it," hissed Ponto. "He's a big joker."

"He's only a kid," corrected Tom. "We'll let him grab a bird and then take it off him. He's going into the hedge now."

There was a bit of rustling and gobbling and flapping from up ahead and the young bloke came out of the hedge and began to walk away. Tom got up and hurried after him. Ponto hung back.

"Hang on there son," said Tom coming up behind the boy. "What do you think you're up to?"

The young bloke got a hell of a fright. The turkey nearly got away from him.

"What do you mean?" he stammered.

"Where do you think you're going with that turkey?"

"Home," said the boy. Tom saw that he was only about fourteen years old.

"I think you'd better give me the turkey," said Tom "and cut along home. If I catch you up here again I'll be down to see your father." He reached for the turkey but the boy clutched it a bit harder and said: "But they're my father's turkeys. I've been sent up to get one for tomorrow — it's Friday."

Tom did a bit of quick thinking. This was a bit awkward.

"Where do you live?" he asked.

"In the house just over the hill there," said the boy pointing.

It was rarely that Tom couldn't think of anything to say. The boy was obviously telling the truth.

Suddenly from along the hedge came tremendous flapping and thrashing, and turkeys flew out of the trees in all directions. Then Ponto backed out holding a struggling turkey by one foot. Sam could just make out his stocky shambling figure as it lumbered off towards the road with all the subtlety of a runaway bulldozer, leaving a trail of noise and feathers half a chain wide behind him.

"What's that?" cried the young bloke.

Tom saw the boy was thoroughly frightened. "That must be the man I saw sneaking up on your father's turkeys," he said sternly. "I'd better get after him. Tell your father I'll be round to see him later. There's got to be a stop put to all this thievery."

And he hurried off after Ponto, catching him down by the road clutching the turkey as though it was going to melt.

"What the hell did you want to go and do that for?" he asked.

"I was bloody hungry," said Ponto.

"Why didn't you wait a bit? I just about had the young bloke talked into thinking we went up there to save his old man's turkeys when you go and flog one and scatter the rest all over the farm. What was all the racket for anyway?"

"The one I wanted got away from me," said Ponto, "so I made a grab at the nearest one I could see and this was it . . . bit skinny but we'll get a feed off him," he added, poking hopefully at the boniest old ewe-turkey Tom had ever seen.

Crossed Wires

Everyone on the line knew that when their 'phones rang medium-long-short-medium-long-short-*dit*, it was Bert Shallcross ringing up Ernie Piper (on short-short-long) and the line was going to be engaged until someone chipped in and asked them to clear it for an urgent toll call.

Bert's wife Betty usually had to ring up anyone else because whether Bert tried to get Sam Dryland on short-long-long or Ray Hope on long-short-short-long or the store on short-long-short or the exchange on one long the result was always exactly the same, and if Ernie wasn't home Bert would often have to crank out his urgent summons half a dozen times before someone answered.

Ernie heard Bert ring as he came in from the shed, and he stepped carefully across the freshly-scrubbed kitchen floor in his gumboots to the phone in the hall.

"That you, Tom?" Bert shouted in his ear. "I think this blasted phone's playing up again. I've been trying to get through to you for I don't know how long."

"That you Bert?" said Ernie.

"Ernie! How the hell did I get on to you? I've been trying to get hold of Tom Cleaser all bloody morning. Been getting wrong numbers all the time, either that or no reply at all."

"Sounded like my ring that time," said Ernie.

"You're short-short-long aren't you? I've been ringing Tom on two longs. There must be something wrong with this bloody telephone again."

"Hang up and I'll try and get through on this phone," said Ernie. "You listen in after I've rung and see if Tom answers. If he does I'll hang up and you can talk to him."

"You want me to hang up?" said Bert.

"Yeah, just till I ring Tom's number."

"Righto then, I'll hang up now."

Ernie rang two longs, and Tom Cleaser's boy answered, "Eight five seven M."

"That you Ivan? Ernie Piper here. Is your Dad in?"

"He's out in the shed. I'll get him for you."

"Yeah, tell him Bert Shallcross wants to get hold of him, will you?"

"Mr Shallcross?"

"Yeah, his phone's crook. I'm ringing for him."

"I'll get Dad," said the boy. "Just a moment."

"You there Bert?" said Ernie.

No answer. Bert hadn't lifted his receiver again.

"That you Bert?" said Tom Cleaser. "What can I do for you?"

"Ernie Piper here, Tom. Bert's been trying to get in touch with you but his phone's playing up. I told him to hang up while I rang through for him but he hasn't come back on the line."

"The line might be crook between Docker's place and the bridge again," said Tom. "I'll give him a try from here. What's Bert's ring?"

"D," said Ernie. "A long and two shorts. Ring us back if you have any trouble and I'll try him again from here."

"Okay, I'll do that. How's the herd?"

"Not bad for this time of year. Sent in just over eighty gallons this morning."

"Good. Well, I'll try and get on to Bert and see what he wants."

"Righto," said Ernie.

"Righto," said Tom.

Ernie hung up and put the porridge on. Bert's ring went three times while he was setting up the table and then Ernie's short-short-long interrupted him stirring the porridge.

"That you Tom?" he said.

"That you Ernie?" said Tom. "Can't get any answer from Bert's number. The line must be crook all right."

"Sounded okay when I was talking to him before."

"Might be between here and Bert's then," said Tom.

"Tell you what — I'll try him from here again. If I get hold of him I'll tell him you tried to contact him anyway. If it's anything I can pass on, I'll ring you back."

"Okay. Let's know how you get on."

"Righto Tom," said Ernie.

"Righto," said Tom. "Sorry to trouble you."

"She's right. Just hope it's nothing urgent, that's all. Bert sounded a bit worried."

"Well, we'll just have to keep trying, that's all."

"Okay, I'll let you know if I have any luck."

"Righto," said Tom. "I'll stay handy just in case."

"Righto," said Ernie.

He rang Bert's number, ate his porridge, and tried again. No reply. So he rang Tom back.

"That you Tom?"

"That you Ernie? How'd you get on?"

"No good. There's no reply from Bert's number at all. It looks like his phone's out of order."

"That's what it'll be all right," said Tom. "The line's as clear as a bell everywhere else. I've just been talking to Arthur Royle out at Broadford and there's nothing wrong with *his* phone."

"I'd better ring the exchange and tell them Bert's phone's out of order. Then I'll drop over to Bert's place and let him know what's going on."

"Good idea," said Tom. "Let's know how you get on. And if you see Bert, tell him I'll be around here all morning, will you?"

"Okay, I'll tell him. Righto."

"Righto," said Tom.

Ernie rang the exchange and reported the breakdown. After he'd carefully cleaned up in the kitchen and wiped the floor where he'd been walking, he got out the tractor and drove down to the creek, crossed into Bert's creek-paddock on the fallen willow and walked up the hill to the house. Betty was down at the cowshed but she didn't see him, and there was no sign of Bert anywhere around the house. Ernie stuck his head inside the kitchen door to yell out if Bert was inside and he was just closing the door again when the phone in the passage rang his own ring. So he went in and answered it.

"That you Ernie?" said Tom.

"That you Tom?"

"Yeah, thought I might just catch you."

"I'm up at Bert's place, as a matter of fact," said Ernie. "I came over to tell him to stay handy. They're sending someone out to have a look at his phone. I heard my ring on Bert's phone so I answered it. I see Betty down at the shed but Bert's not here at the moment."

"That's what I rang about," said Tom. "He turned up here just after we'd hung up last time. Tried to ring you back but there's no reply from *your* phone."

"I've been on my way over here," said Ernie.

"What's Bert doing over there?"

"He gave up trying to get me on the phone. He's here right now. Want to talk to him?"

"Yeah, put him on will you?"

"Righto. Here he is now."

"That you Bert?"

"That you Ernie? Where the hell are you?"

"I'm up at your place," said Ernie.

"My place? I'm over at Tom's. You want to see me about something? I'll be home in about half an hour."

"What happened to you? You were supposed to listen after I rang Tom for you."

" . . . Yeah, well I thought it'd be better to come over and see him in person. You can't rely on that phone of mine."

"Yeah, well I've rung up and told them your phone's out of order. We thought it wasn't ringing but it looks as if it's okay after all."

"You were lucky to get any sense out of it," said Bert. "I was trying for a hell of a time this morning. Gave it up in the finish."

"I'd better get straight on to them and tell them not to come out after all,' said Ernie.

"Just tell 'em we found out what the trouble was and fixed it ourselves," said Bert. "I'll ring them from here if you like. It's closer, and Tom won't mind."

"No, I'd better do it,' said Ernie. "I know the old tart I was talking to before."

"Okay then. I'll tell Tom what's happening. Are you going to wait there till I get back?"

"No, I've got a bit to do before I go into town. By the way, did you get what you wanted from Tom?"

"No, he hasn't got one. I'm going to give Ray Hope a ring as soon as I get back. Tom thinks he might have one. The one I got off you picked up a bit of number-eight wire and stripped a couple of teeth. It's down at the garage, you could pick it up on your way back from town if it's ready."

"Okay. I'll give you a ring when I get back tonight and let you know how it goes."

"Okay. What time?"

"After milking, say about half-past six. You be finished by then?"

"Should be," said Bert. "We'd better make it a bit earlier in case old Linda Forsythe gets talking to that sister of hers in Thames again. We'll never get on the line if she does. How about I ring you as soon as I get in from the shed? I'll try and get 'em finished early."

"No," said Ernie. "It might be better if you let me ring you. Just in case."

"Just in case what?" said Bert.

"Just in case your phone starts playing up on you again," said Ernie.

"Yeah, good idea,' said Bert. "You ring me, I've been having quite a bit of trouble with that phone of mine lately."

"Righto," said Ernie.

"Righto," said Bert.

Ernie hung up and called in at the cowshed on his way down to the creek to thank Betty for all the work she'd done getting his house cleaned up. Then he went home and got himself cleaned up and shaved. Then he got out the old Hudson and set off on the thirty-six-mile drive to town to get married.

Letter to the I.R.D.

Dear Sir,
Your letter says — my conscience burns! —
I've never furnished tax returns.
And, furthermore, you seem to say,
It's getting too late anyway.

And, further-furthermore, you add,
The situation's very bad,
And if I don't, by yesterday,
Produce returns — there's hell to pay!

No problem, sir, we'll put that right;
I'll write it down this very night;
Employers, dates, in each detail —
We'll sort this whole thing out by mail!

You see, I've kept a careful track
Of everything, for income-tack,
And saved it for this very day.
Coincidental, sir? — I'll say!

So with respect for you and me,
I won't put on false modesty,
I'll just stick down the simple fax
Of you and me, and income tax.

I left home, sir, at an early age
And went in search of work and wage
And got a job repairing sacks,
So I could pay some income tax.

I didn't know that from the start
The firm was shaky — fell apart,
And by the time I'd paid the boss,
I stood a quite substantial loss.

I learned to cook and did so well
They made me chef at Brent's Hotel.
The fat caught fire, the pub burnt down
And, broke, I had to leave the town.

At trading I was doing well,
I couldn't get enough to sell.
My profits vanished — every cent —
The victim of embezzlement.

I then moved on to other things,
To seek the revenue they brings,
But one by one my ventures failed
And constant losses were entailed.

For instance in the timber trade
I really thought I had it made,
Until they went and 'sent me through',
To cheat the Inland Revenue!

You know yourself how these things are —
I had some trouble with my car
Then mortgage people haunted me
And drove me into bankruptcy.

And so the years have drifted by;
Regardless of how hard I try
(You might just call it rotten luck)
I haven't made a single buck.

But I didn't need to stay at school
To get damn good at mini-pool
Or learn that life gives nothing free,
It's what you make it, you and me.

Take me, now, who'd have ever guessed
I'd end up too poor to invest
In things like inland revenue —
I think it's rather sad, don't you?

But when it comes to golf, old chap,
I'm on a seven handicap
And, yes, (How sharp of you to guess!)
I play a decent game of chess.

I know what won the Melbourne Cup
And what's the score in Bangladup.
I'll rattle off the All Black Team
And tell you what it should have been.

I know the current price of gold
And just what shares were bought and sold;
I've heard the joke you'll tell tonight —
I guess you'd say I'm pretty bright.

But when it comes to currency
The blasted stuff just dodges me.
I tell you, sir, I've had a lash
At handling everything but cash!

And so, old friend, my point is made,
I give these details unafraid.
And when you come to judge my case
You'll feel the same as me, Your Grace.

But please don't think it's been in vain —
I know I'll soon come right again,
For after all it isn't *who*,
It's *what* you know that gets you through.

And meantime, sir, may I suggest
A way to meet the problem best —
Relying on our mutual trust,
You pay the tax for both of us.

And then when things come right for me
I'll do the same for you, you see?
It's one of nature's basic laws —
You pay my tax — I'll pay yours!

And one day, when I'm all cashed up,
I'll come to town and look you up.
No, really sir — I can't be rude,
I'll *have* to show my gratitude.

And when we're back to square again
And everything's as right as rain,
We'll have the whole thing sorted out
And no, sir, it'll be *my* shout.

And won't we chuckle when we see
How close we've grown, sir, you and me.
The bonds of friendship, forged on facts
Of you, and me, and income tax!

Just one last thing before I go,
You'll understand, Your Grace,
I know. I wouldn't need a large amount,
Let's just say fifty, on account.

The going's been a little tough,
But fifty bucks should be enough.
(A money-order telegram?)
I can't say, sir, how pleased I am!

And any time you need advice,
Just call on me, sir, don't think twice.
I wouldn't put you crook, you'll see —
We'll be good mates, sir, you and me!

I trust you, sir, no need to say
You'll send the fifty right away.
Don't worry, sir, you'll get it back,
See ya, cobber,
Your Friend,
Jack.

WHARF-AND-RAIL

"Things are tough," said the stranger. "There's about a hundred blokes lined up for every job that's going. And there's nothing in my line at all."

"What do you do?" asked Kersey.

"Truck-driver. Been at it all me life. I've driven just about everything from flat-tops to logging artics, but I chucked the big stuff in years ago. I'm strictly a wharf-and-rail man now. You know, general deliveries and stuff. Wharf-and-rail's the caper. You've got to know what you're doing on wharf-and-rail."

"I'll bet," agreed Kersey. "How long since you worked?"

"About five weeks. I was driving for a crowd down south. Wharf-and-rail stuff."

"They put you off, did they?"

"No, as a matter of fact I threw it in."

"Eh?"

"I chucked it in, mate. Had to, more or less."

"How come?"

"Well, there were four of us driving for the same outfit, and one of us was going to get the push, we knew that. But what got my pricker up was when I twigged that someone was trying to put the skids under me."

"Yeah?"

"Yeah. One of the other blokes was dobbing me in to the boss. Shelfing me over all sorts of little odd things that only one of us drivers could have known about. Things like filling in all the dockets at lunchtime instead of after each delivery or pick-up. I tell you, the boss was starting to get it in for me, and I couldn't tell which one of the blokes was putting my pot on. But it had to be one of 'em. We always joked and ribbed each other around the depot, and parked up for lunch and a bit of a yarn together every day. But one of them was a bloody topper, and I couldn't for the life of me work out who it was."

"Did you ever find out?" asked Kersey.

"Too right I did. I wasn't going to let anyone get away with that sort of caper — especially with jobs the way they are. Things are tough, you know."

"They're tough all right,' agreed Kersey. "What did you do?"

"I set a trap for whoever it was. I told one of the blokes on the quiet one morning that I'd lost a crate of cosmetics the day before and signed the delivery docket with a bit of a squiggle, so they wouldn't know where it'd gone astray. He got real insulted when I asked him not to even let on to any of the other blokes. Wanted to know what I took him for and all that sort of thing.

"As a matter of fact it didn't look as though it was him who'd been dobbing me in, but I had to make sure. Then I got one of the other blokes to one side at lunch-time and swore him to the utmost secrecy and told him I'd backed my truck into the front of a flash car trying to get into the cart-dock the day before. It didn't do any damage to the truck, I told 'im, but I'd made a hell of a mess of the grille and one of the headlights on the car. There was no one around at the time so

I took off without reporting it, but now I was a bit worried in case someone had seen it and taken my number."

"How did he take it?" asked Kersey.

"Pretty good. He sympathised with me a bit, and said I'd probably get away with it, and all that sort of thing. And when I told him to keep it under his hat he just sort of grinned and told me to cut it out. Then he tipped me off not to let on to old Pat about it because he had a sneakin' suspicion that Pat was a bit of a you-know-what. Nothing definite to go on, mind you, but he'd be very careful what he said in front of him if he was me all the same.

"Well, this Pat was the other driver, the one that I hadn't spoken to yet. He used to drive the big van — and he was a hell of a good driver, too. Boy, he could really handle the thing. Ugly thing to drive, it was, too, but old Pat could sling it in and out of cart-docks and traffic and lanes and alleyways like nobody's business. The kind of bloke who roars right up to an intersection as if he hasn't seen it and then suddenly slams on the anchors just in time. Chocker-block with confidence and never made a blue. Back the thing straight into places where I'd have to take a couple of cuts with the flat-top. Finish his deliveries away ahead of anyone else and then offer to give you a hand with yours. Couldn't stand the sight of the bastard. All the same, it was hard to see him as a crawler. But it had to be one of them, so I caught him on his own when we were putting the trucks away that night. He had a swept-up sort of a Ford Consul, so I sidled up to him and sort of hinted that the best way to fiddle a bit of buckshee gas was to write in about half a gallon more than you actually put in your truck when you gassed-up every morning. That way it looks as though your truck's hogging the gas a bit, but nothing to cause any suspicions. And at the end of the week you can nick away somewhere quiet and siphon off three or four gallons for your own bomb and no one's any the wiser."

"That's a good one," said Kersey, approvingly. "What'd he do?"

"He just looked at me and said thanks all the same but as far as he was concerned it wasn't worth risking his job for, but if I was getting away with it, good on me. Then offered to give me a lift home in his car and, you know, by the time we got there I was starting to feel a bit of a fool for suspecting him. The only thing to do now was wait and see what happened. And I didn't have very long to wait, either."

"What happened?"

"Well, I'd no sooner bowled into work next morning when they said the boss wanted to see me about something. So I went around to the bit of a place he used for an office and as soon as I saw him I knew straight away that someone had sprung on me.

"'I've had a report that one of our trucks backed into a car the day before yesterday and didn't stop to report it,' he said to me. 'Do you know anything about it?'

"'Not me,' I told him. 'Whoever told you that must have put you crook.'

"Well, at least I knew who the bastard was who'd been trying to put the skids under me. I decided to tip the other blokes off about him. *He* wasn't going to last long, once we all knew we had a topper amongst us. But blow me down, I was loading up some stuff for the wharf just after smoko that morning (hadn't had a chance to talk to any of the blokes yet), when they rang up a message for me to drop in at the depot and see the boss again as soon as possible. And when I got there he had all the carbons of my dockets spread out on the bit of a crate he used for a desk.

"'Are all these dockets of yours in order?' he asked me.

"'Of course they are,' I told him. 'What's wrong with them?'

"'There seems to be some mix-up over a crate of cosmetics,' he said.

"I knew what crate of cosmetics he was talking about, and it had never existed. It only took a couple of minutes to establish that someone had put him crook again and he apologised for holding me up and I went on with the job."

"So two of them were putting your weights up?" said Kersey.

"No mate, the whole three of 'em," corrected the wharf-and-rail bloke. "Y'see, when I got in to the depot that night the boss asked me to bring in my petrol sheets for him to go over with me. He said it was to get a rough idea what my truck's fuel consumption was. But there was no doubt about it — the whole bloody three of them had been trying to put me crook with the boss. They were probably doing the same things amongst each other at the same time. I tell you, things are tough all right."

"They're tough all right,' agreed Kersey. "What some blokes'll do to hang on to a job when they're scared of losing it, eh? What happened?"

"Well, I'd had a proper gutful of it by this time, so I fronted straight up to the boss and told him straight out that it looked to me like some of the other blokes might just be carrying tales to him to try and put me in a bad light because they knew one of us was going to have to be put off.

"I'd have thought that would have at least squared me off with the boss over one or two warnings he'd given me, but it didn't. It put me further up the creek than ever. He turned round and told me that all this business was taking up far too much of his valuable time, and he couldn't afford to keep on drivers who caused trouble among the men. I tried to point out that it wasn't me who'd caused the trouble, but he came back at me by saying he'd give me one last chance. And you know what?"

"No, what?" said Kersey.

"A couple of days after that I found out the boss had told one of the other blokes that I'd been in his office making wild accusations about the other drivers, and he turned straight round and told the other two."

"That's a bit tough, isn't it?" said Kersey indignantly.

"It's tough all right," agreed the wharf-and-rail bloke.

"What did you do then?"

"Well I figured that, even with jobs the way they are, it just wasn't worth it. I knew that I was a goner the moment I made a blue, I could see that. So I made up my mind to get the hell out of it the next payday. That was in just over a week's time, because we were getting paid once a fortnight. I was pretty hostile about the whole thing, I can tell you, but I didn't have any thoughts of revenge or anything like that, until a few days before I was going to leave when I was sitting in my truck filling in a docket for a drum of perfume I'd just loaded, and I was just going to move out when Pat in his big van roared up the street, stopped outside, and shot back into the same building I was in — same kind of cart-dock outfit, only he'd come in a different door further along. He hopped out and went off whistling in the lift to collect something from a warehouse on one of the floors above.

"Now when he'd backed in I'd noticed that the top of his van just fitted under the big steel roll-up doors. They hadn't been pulled right up to the top of the door-way. There was no one else around just then, so I nicked across and pulled out the pin and let the chain out a few links and then put the pin back in again. Then I went back and sat in my truck to wait for a bit of a giggle.

"Pretty soon Pat came back with a lift full of crated outboard motors. He hand-carted them into the van among a whole lot of other stuff he had for rail despatch. He still hadn't seen me parked just along the dock; wouldn't have taken much notice anyway because I was well and truly on the outer by this time. He slammed himself into the van, kicked her in the guts, and roared out of there with his usual burst of speed.

"Well, I'd been expecting a bit of a giggle but I wasn't ready for what *did* happen. The top of the van actually caught on the top of the doorway and the whole van tore away from the rest of the truck with a terrible crash of splintered wood and tearing metal and falling crates and cartons and bales and boxes. And Pat was right out on to the street with the cab and chassis of his van before he could stop. I heard him get out and next thing he ran into the building, pushed the lift button, and then disappeared up some stairs. He was probably going to ring up, or get somebody, or something.

"It must have been the shock of realising what a terrible amount of damage I'd caused — or maybe it was fright, I don't know — but I suddenly got the crazy idea that if only I could put the door back the way it was before I'd let it down things wouldn't be quite so disastrous. So I got out and picked my way among all the wreckage and raised the door about six inches. It was a bit buckled but it went up all right. Then I got back in my truck and by the time I drove out of there the first few people were just arriving to see what the crash had been."

"Hell," said Kersey. "You were taking a fair sort of a risk, weren't you?"

"I don't mind telling you, I was worried all right. I hadn't bargained for that lot. I don't even know what made me do it in the first place."

"Did you get away with it?"

"Yes, I did. But there wasn't much satisfaction in it, even later, when they sent me round to cart away some of the undamaged stuff from Pat's van. The traffic cops were there, and quite a little crowd was watching a bunch of blokes measuring and equating and theorising and arguing and reconstructing; trying to work out how a twelve-foot van could have caught on a twelve-foot-nine doorway. They wouldn't let me touch any of the stuff until it had all been weighed, and I had to stand around and watch and listen.

"Pat was there, being questioned by two blokes who looked like they came from the insurance company. I heard one of them say, 'It's impossible, I tell you!'

"They sealed off the door the way it was and the insurance company paid a man to stand guard all night, and next day they got a van the same as Pat's from somewhere and drove it back and forth, in and out of that cart-dock, with exactly the same load and all sorts of different speeds and angles. But no matter what they tried or how hard they tried it, they still couldn't get the twelve-foot van to catch on the twelve foot-nine door."

"Did they ever find out?" asked Kersey.

"Not as far as I know," said the wharf-and-rail bloke. "I got in just ahead of the boss and told him I was quitting on payday. Pat was going to have to take over my truck when I was gone, so they put him on as my offsider to fill the few days. And all day long he'd shake his head over the disgrace and shock of his first accident in over thirty years of driving. The last thing he said to me before I left was, 'The insurance company is going to pay out but I *still* don't know how it could possibly have happened.' And the last thing I said to him before I left was, 'Don't worry, Pat, I won't tell anyone. But I'd be careful what I said in front of the others, if I were you. I've got an idea they might just be inclined to be a little you-know-what with the boss.'"

"Things are tough, all right," said Kersey.

"They're tough all right," agreed the wharf-and-rail bloke. "And they're going to get a lot worse before they get any better, by the looks of things."

They agreed another couple of times that things were tough all right, and a little while after that Kersey went to sleep. And when the foundry siren over at the railway workshops woke him up next morning, the wharf-and-rail bloke had already gone off to try and get another driving job.

That night, just as they were settling down, Kersey and the wharf-and-rail bloke thought they heard someone coming. They lay quiet and waited, listening.

And after a while a voice at the broken pane of the window said,

"I'm looking for my brother."

"Come round to the door and I'll let you in," said Kersey.

"I was wondering if my brother might be here," said the stranger, as he moved through the door past Kersey and stood in the darkness inside the gymnasium.

Kersey felt his way over to a pile of mats and slapped them to show the stranger where they were.

"Grab a couple of these and find yourself somewhere," he said. "Watch out you don't trip over anyone."

"Haven't you got a light in here?" said the new bloke shuffling his way across the floor.

"We're not supposed to be in here," said Kersey. "We don't come here till after dark and we leave before daylight in the morning."

"Right," said the new bloke, dragging out two mats. "I heard there was a bunch of you blokes around here. Thought one of you might be my brother."

"What's he look like?" said the wharf-and-rail bloke.

"About the same size as me only four years younger, and a

bit taller and heavier build."

"How the hell do we know what you look like?" said the wharf-and-rail bloke.

"No, he hasn't been here," said Kersey. "Where did you last see him?"

"Mangakino, just before the Christmas before last," said the new bloke. "He was coming over this way to paint a woolshed with a Maori bloke, but I've lost track of him altogether."

"He could be any bloody where," said the wharf-and-rail bloke, shrugging down into his mats.

"Yeah," agreed the new bloke. "I might run into him tomorrow," he added optimistically.

The new bloke came back the next night and set his mat up in his place on the floor as though he'd been booked in.

"Did you find out anything about your brother?" asked Kersey.

"No, not a thing," said the new bloke cheerfully.

"What does he do for a crust?" said the wharf-and-rail bloke.

"Same as me," said the new bloke, as though everyone knew.

"And what's that?" said Kersey curiously.

"Just about anything, same as our old man. He was a great worker, the old man. Nothing he wouldn't tackle. And he taught me brother and me the trade from the time we were old enough to walk. We worked from one end of the country to the other, mostly out in the backblocks because the old man didn't like cars and things much. He used to always say that the best way to do a thing was by hand, and he never turned a job down, no matter how tough it was."

"Where is he now?" asked Kersey.

"He retired about twelve years ago now," said the new bloke, thinking back. "My brother and I took over from him and he died of nothing to do about two years after that, and me mother and sister moved into the old shearers' quarters at Maungataniwha to live. Sister married a bloke. Shepherd over there."

"They might be able to put you on to that brother of yours," suggested the wharf-and-rail bloke.

"No, he wouldn't go there. Too much machinery. Everything's being done by machines over that way. That's what caused my brother and I to have to split up."

"Why?"

"Well, the old man didn't really know this, but by the time we took over from him things were starting to get tough in our line of business.

"When the old man died, me and me brother were splitting totara shingles and roofing sheds for cockies with them. But everyone was starting to reckon that the corrugated iron was cheaper and quicker, so we went on to splitting posts and battens. That lasted a while, until they started putting out all them sawn battens and treated pine posts and stuff and we couldn't compete with the prices. After that we took on a couple of fencing contracts, but we couldn't make enough out of it. Everyone else was using tractors and mechanical posthole-diggers; we couldn't handle stuff like that. The Old Man taught us how to do anything with a fishtail peg-and-drag and a team of horses, but by the time we grew up everything was being done with machines. We got born at a bad time, me brother reckons. A few years either way and we'd have been all right."

"But you can learn how to handle a tractor easy enough," pointed out the wharf-and-rail bloke.

"Yeah, but I don't like all this machinery and stuff anyway," said the new bloke. "Makes me nervous. You've only got to pick up a newspaper and see where someone's been killed or hurt by some tractor or something. And at the time there were still plenty of things we could do by hand, without getting involved with mechanical stuff. We did all right trapping rabbits for a while there. And when the rabbit boards took over we went on to possums. Made a good bit out of the skins, until they turned round and devalued them on us.

"It just seemed to happen to us. We'd tackle a thing and just when we'd be starting to make a real go of it, they'd invent something or turn out some machine or other that'd make us superfluous again. Me brother and I had to split up in the finish. Not enough work in one place to keep us both going. He took on a contract to build a couple of swing bridges on a station down south, and after that I heard he wasn't going too bad on water-divining.

"I did a bit of droving on and off for about a year after that, but they gradually got the idea of shifting their stock around in them trucks. It's supposed to be quicker or something. I filled in a bit of time between droving jobs, packing supplies for mustering gangs and shoeing and breaking-in horses and doing the odd bit of roadmakin' with the horse-scoop — things like that.

"But in the finish I had to sell me dogs. There just weren't enough drovin' jobs to be worth keepin' them. But I had a pretty good spin on sowin' grass-seed and superphosphate by hand on some of that steep country around Hawke's Bay. Just used to open up the bags and sow the stuff straight off the packhorses. As a matter of fact I was the only one doin' that kind of work on contract around there. And there was a fair bit of other work goin' to keep me busy between contracts. When they were cuttin' their hay I was in big demand because I could build a better haystack than any of them. It's a dyin' art these days, haystack buildin'.

"And then they brought out them red machines and everyone started getting their hay done up in bales. And on top of that they went and brought in this aerial top-dressin' with them aeroplanes. I reckon they'd be better off puttin' the stuff on by hand, but they still go zoomin' all over the countryside in their aeroplanes, scattering the stock and crashin' into things. It's supposed to be quicker than doin' it by hand, but they must lose a fair bit of time cartin' out their dead aeroplane-drivers and cleanin' up after all the crashes they have. It doesn't make a hell of a lot of difference to me if they want to risk their lives for a couple of bags of super.

"I got a good price for me packhorses and took on a bit of rush-cuttin' and ragwort-pullin'. Things like that. It wasn't bad for a while, but then they got to inventin' all them chemicals to spray the stuff with. And them drain-diggin' machines they've got now cut into our work a lot. There used to be a lot of money to be made keepin' drains open.

"There's still a bit of saw-doctorin' and horse-shoein' and the odd stockwhip or saddle to make. And you can get a job swingin' the old banjo on the road works sometimes, but you have to watch it on that job, believe me. The way they drive them cars these days — especially them red ones! It's bloody dangerous. Just as well the old man's not around to see what's happenin', I can tell you.

"And things are gettin' worse. In some places they're even usin' motorbikes instead of horses for musterin' and riding the lambin'-beat. They don't even cut a boxthorn hedge by hand now, it's all being done with machines. I used to be not too bad on fixing windmills and water-pumps but it's that long since I've seen one I don't know if I could remember. Everyone's going in for these electricity jobs these days. And different types and makes of the same sort of machines being handed out all the time . . . I wonder how me brother's gettin' on," said the new bloke, pausing thoughtfully.

"Have you ever thought of having a go at something different?" said Kersey helpfully.

"Nar, wouldn't dream of it," said the new bloke. "It's not half as bad as it sounds. There's still quite a few things bein' done by hand. And there will be for a good while yet. Don't take any notice of me. As a matter of fact, I've had a bit of bad luck just lately."

"You don't say," said the wharf-and-rail bloke.

"Yes," said the do-it-by-hand bloke seriously. "I just lost a damn good job through sheer rotten luck."

"What was it?"

"Shootin' deer and packin' out the venison. Down on the

West Coast. Two bucks a pound at the road, we were gettin' for it."

"Don't tell me they've mechanised that," said the wharf-and-rail bloke.

"No, no," said the do-it-by-hand bloke. "There wasn't a machine for miles. No, it was far worse than that. It was blowflies."

"Did you say *blowflies*?" said the wharf-and-rail bloke.

"Too right I did," said the do-it-by-hand bloke, flouncing vigorously on his bed of mats. "They done for me good and proper. I tell you, you blokes reckon you've had it tough, but you don't know what tough is until you've run up against them West Coast blowflies. There's hordes of 'em, they come from everywhere. They had me rooted from the start — and they knew it," he added indignantly. "A man's got no show once he runs up against them there West Coast blowflies," he concluded philosophically.

"Much in this meat-huntin' caper?" asked Kersey.

"There would've been if it wasn't for them blowflies," said the new bloke. "They're fair dinkum murder down there, I tell you."

"Blow all your meat or something, did they?"

"You're not kiddin' they blew all me meat! It wasn't so bad when I was gettin' a few deer down near the road. But they got a bit too scarce and scary in all the handy country, so I started huntin' from a hut two and a half hours up the valley.

"The first night up there I shot four deer out on the river flats, just on dark, and I carted the carcases back to the hut on a couple of horses I'd borrowed off a cocky down at the road.

Hung the meat in a tree there. Next morning I got another three deer and by the time I got 'em back to the hut the four I'd got the night before were goners."

"Blowflies?" said the wharf-and-rail bloke.

"Blowflies! You never seen the likes of it. Couldn't believe me eyes at first. I tell you, it looked like four enormous swarms of bees hangin' in the tree there. You could hardly see the carcases — white with blowfly eggs they were. No hope of savin' 'em. I cut 'em down and dragged 'em across and slung 'em in the river. Could hardly see for the clouds of blowflies. About twelve or fourteen dollars' worth of meat down the drain, not countin' all my hard work.

"Fair go, it'd break your heart. And by the time I got back to the hut they'd got stuck into the three carcases I still had on the horses. Dirty great clouds of 'em roarin' around the horses. I belted into 'em with a sack but I had to give it in because it was makin' the horses jumpy."

"What did you do?" asked Kersey.

"I covered the loads as best I could, with sacks and bits of tentage and my good sleepin'-bag cover, and took off down the river to get the meat into a big safe we had down at the road while there was still time."

"Did you make it?" asked the wharf-and-rail bloke.

"Did I make it? — Like hell I did! Never had a dog's show against them bloody blowflies. I tell you, they're diabolical, that's what they are — diabolical. By the time I'd got an hour and a half down the river I knew I wasn't goin' to make it. They blew the meat and they blew the sacks and the tentage and me good sleepin'-bag cover. They blew the horses and

the pack-saddles — the whole outfit was covered with great clusters of blowfly eggs. My three carcases were done for. I cut' em down off the horses and dragged 'em across and slung 'em in the river."

"I didn't know they'd blow leather and things like that," said Kersey.

"They'll blow *anything*, mate, them West Coast blowflies," said the new bloke. "By the time I got back to the hut and hobbled the horses they'd blown the spuds and the onions and even got stuck into me spare pair of socks I had hangin' in front of the fireplace.

"Things being what they are as far as getting jobs goes, I couldn't afford to let them blowflies beat me. There were plenty of deer around up there. I was on to a good thing once I had the flies licked. First off I tried hangin' the meat in the smoke — kept a fire going under it all night and half the next day, but the blowflies seemed to prefer it that way. In the finish I had to cut it down and drag it across and sling it in the river.

"Then I decided to try a lurk someone had put me on to once. Everyone knows that blowflies can't go any higher than about fifteen feet above the ground. The next night I took the horses up the river and got five deer in no time. Packed the carcases back to the hut, swipin' at the blowflies all the way, and slung ropes through the forks of trees and hoisted all the meat right up — about twenty or thirty feet. It was dark by the time I'd done this but I couldn't see any blowflies around up there."

"Did that work?" asked the wharf-and-rail bloke.

"Did it work? — Like hell it did," said the new bloke. "I tell you, if you air-dropped a leg of meat from two thousand feet among them West Coast blowflies, it'd land with maggots on it. By the time I got up next morning it was too late. It's a wonder how the ropes stood up to the extra weight!"

"Hell! what did you do?" asked Kersey.

"I cut 'em down and dragged 'em across and slung 'em in the river," said the new bloke. "All except one carcase that was hangin' in the tree beside the hut. The rope had pulled into the fork of the tree so tight it wouldn't run out when I tried to let it down. Jammed there, it was. And there was no show of me gettin' up there to free it. The tree was too big to think of cuttin' it down. I tried to shoot the rope out of the fork but I had to turn it in. Couldn't spare the ammunition. So the bloody thing had to stay there."

"Spare me days," said the wharf-and-rail bloke. "I bet that lot stunk after a while?"

"Stunk!" said the new bloke. "You're not kidding it stunk. It probably kept some of them blowflies away from me tucker, though. A man's got to be wide awake to get a feed past them West Coast blowflies, y'know. They'll dive-bomb a forkful of bully-beef half a dozen times between the tin and your mouth."

"Hell," said Kersey. "No wonder you had to chuck it in."

"Oh, I didn't chuck it in then," said the new bloke. "I wasn't goin' to let a few million blowflies do me out of me livin'. And besides, I still had a trick or two up me sleeve."

"But how were you going to get your meat down to the

road, even if you could keep the flies off it?" said the wharf and-rail bloke.

"Yeah," said Kersey. "Wouldn't they get at it on the way, like they did the first time?"

"Ah — that's just it," said the new bloke. "Everyone knows that blowflies can't operate in the dark. I could pack the stuff out at night, and no trouble. The horses knew the track and it was easy goin' most of the way. All I had to do was keep 'em off it during the daytime. So I dug a hole."

"A hole?"

"Yeah, a real big one. Took me two days to get it right. Then I laid four fresh carcases in it on rails and put boards across the top and covered the whole thing with sacks and dirt. It was absolutely pitch black in there — I looked."

"That was a crafty move," said Kersey.

"Not crafty enough for them West Coast blowflies," said the new bloke grimly.

"Don't tell us they got in there too," said the wharf-and-rail bloke incredulously.

"They not only got in there, mate, they waited till I was out of the way before they did it. I watched that hole for a good twenty minutes after I put the meat in it, just to make dead sure, and there were no more blowflies around it than any other area the same size around there. And when I got back that evening with another couple of carcases to make up a full load to smuggle out to the road that night, I could hear 'em roarin' away in that hole twenty yards away."

"Was the meat ruined?" asked Kersey.

"Never even bothered to look, mate. I just filled the hole in on top of it."

"Is that when you quit?" asked the wharf-and-rail bloke.

"No," replied the new bloke. "Me professional pride wouldn't let me give in to 'em. I had enough tucker left to last another couple of days, and if I could get just one load of venison down to the road I'd make enough out of it to stock up again and buy gauze and stuff to build a proper flyproof meat-safe up the river. So I played me last card.

"I shot six deer along the river and as soon as I got the carcases cleaned up I dragged 'em across and slung 'em in the river and weighed 'em down with rocks and marked the places where they were. You should have seen them blowflies! Angry as hell, they were. Buzzin' and swoopin' and circlin' around over where the meat was. I reckon some of 'em even had a go at blowin' the river when I wasn't looking. But I had 'em bluffed this time.

"Just to make dead certain, I waited till about an hour after dark that night before I sneaked out and saddled up the horses. There were still a few blowflies bombardin' around in the hut when I left, but that was only because of the light from a candle I'd had goin' in there. Outside there wasn't a blowfly to be seen or heard anywhere — except the odd bunch that roared off like mobs of quail when I picked up a sack or a packsaddle or anything that'd been lying around.

"I got the meat loaded up and took off for the road without seeing or hearing a single blowfly, hardly. Got there about midnight and hung the meat in the safe and camped there.

"And next morning when I went to trim up the venison for the factory bloke it just about broke me heart."

"Blowflies?" asked Kersey and the wharf-and-rail bloke almost at once.

"No, mate. Maggots. Thousands of 'em. Bloody whoppers, right through the lot. Everywhere they were — droppin' off on to the ground."

"What did you do?" asked Kersey.

"What did I do? I cut 'em down and dragged 'em across and slung 'em in the river, that's what I did. Then I took the horses back to the bloke I'd borrowed 'em off and got a lift to town with the venison bloke when he came. Professional pride or not, a man's got to know when he's cut his load. You've got to hand it to them West Coast blowflies, though. They're fair dinkum diabolical, that's what they are. Bloody diabolical!"

"So that's how you came to be here," said Kersey.

"Yeah mate. That's right. I registered for the dole down south but I couldn't stay on there. Had to get out of it."

"How come?" asked Kersey curiously.

"Well, it was like this, mate," said the new bloke. "I was a bit light for a feed so I decided to try the old maggot trick on a restaurant. And you've got no idea the trouble I had trying to get hold of an ordinary maggot. There's no justice. I finally rounded up a weedy lookin' specimen and put it in a matchbox and went into that flash new place on Curnew Street there. Had a slap-up feed of steak, eggs, onions, chips, tomatoes and three lots of bread and butter. And when I'd finished I put me maggot on the side of the plate and yelled out for the waitress."

"She went and got the cook, but he wouldn't wear it. Great

big joker he was, too. Reckoned that if the maggot had been in the tucker it wouldn't be still alive. I could see that he had his mind made up about it so I didn't bother stayin' around to argue with him. They followed me for a while but I lost 'em down around the waterfront.

"I kept out of the way till I got me dole money and then I caught the train to here — and here I am," concluded the blowfly bloke.

A Stroke of Luck

Windy Long had had a stroke of luck and wound up at a party in Ngongotaha.

There was a bloke, mill-worker by the look of him, who'd latched on to them. Everyone thought he was with one of the others. Windy didn't go much on the look of him in the first place, but it wasn't him who'd invited him to the party. Nor had anyone else, as far as they could work out later. He just tagged along and when things were starting to get warmed up, around one o'clock in the morning, this bloke whose name nobody knew decided to get crook. He was sitting in a big old armchair that everybody reckoned later should have been given to one of the women, only no one thought to say anything about it at the time.

He started getting a bit wild in the eye at first. Then he looked around worried and swallowing and shifting his bottle of beer round on the carpet from one side of his chair to the other. Then he got to gurgling and waving and trying to get out of the chair.

Puketu and the boys would have just shunted him outside for a look around and a bit of fresh air and left him to it, but not Mrs Puketu. She fussed around him like an old mother hen, telling him what was wrong with him and what to do about it.

"A nice big feed. That's what you need," she said, helping him on to his feet. "I'll just bet you haven't had a decent meal all day. Now you take this plate and go out to the stove and help yourself to some lovely hot stew. There's a whole big pot of it. Nice mutton stew, with carrots and parsnips and kumara and puha."

The bloke took the plate and spoon as though he was hypnotised and wandered into the kitchen. He lifted the lid of the pot on the woodstove and as soon as the steam from the stew hit him in the face he cut loose. All over the hot stove. Then he sat down against the wall by the stove and passed out, dribbling all over his shirt as though it happened every day. Everybody crowded into the kitchen doorway, looking at this character and the terrible mess he'd made. Then it started to pong.

It pongs a bit when you burn rubber or hair. It pongs when you're stripping the wool of a dead sheep, or the knife slips when you're gutting a poisoned cow. Cattle-trucks pong and so do rotten cabbages. Everybody's got their pet pong that they can't stand, but this was the pongingest pong Windy had ever tried not to smell. It was so bad that he was scared to take his next breath, and then it didn't matter because he couldn't. It went through the house like rotten steam under pressure. Everybody reeled back into the sitting-room. Puketu threw a couple of buckets of water at the stove but it was as much use as trying to put out a fire with diesel oil.

The party was a goner. It occurred to Windy at the time that it'd be a hell of a good way to bust up a party that wasn't going too well, but a bit on the drastic side. It would have stopped a riot.

They took the beer outside and stood around Windy's van, drinking and arguing who ought to go in and drag out the bloke who done it before he got asphyxiated and pegged out all over Mrs Puketu's kitchen floor. That was when they found out he'd never been invited in the first place.

In the finish, Windy ducked in and dragged him out to the porch and threw a coat over him and left him there to sleep it off. Then he shifted the van a little further away from the house and they carried on with the party, which was beginning to pick up a little. Puketu lit a big fire and business was almost back to normal.

Around daylight they were down to the last few bottles and everyone was getting sleepy. Mrs Puketu took Puketu by the ear and led him gently up to the house to do a bit of mop-swinging and the rest of them decided to blow. Puketu called out that their guest of honour had gone from the porch. He must have woken up and slunk off somewhere.

Windy drove some of the other blokes in to Rotorua, gassed up his van and took off for Auckland, where he'd decided to look for work. At the bottom of a long hill he saw a bloke on the other side of the road, thumbing a lift. He was nearly past before he recognised him. It was the feed-of-stew bloke, padding the hoof for Tokoroa or Putaruru, most likely. Poor sod must have been stony. Windy pulled up to give him a lift. They'd been a bit rough on him the night before. He was probably lonely and wanted a bit of company. Can't blame a bloke for that really, Windy thought to himself, it could even have happened to me.

As his hitch-hiker came up to the van Windy reached over to open the door for him.

"Hop in. Where are you going?"

The bloke got in, slammed the door as hard as he could, and snarled: "It's about time one of you bastards stopped. You've been going past for bloody hours."

This knocked Windy back a bit. The only time this bloke had opened his mouth the night before it was to spew on Mrs Puketu's stove, and now he was packing a snotty.

"It's not me who's been going past for hours, mate."

"Ar, you're all the bloody same," said the bloke. And he opened the door and slammed it again.

"Where are you going?" Windy asked him again.

"You got any cigarettes in this thing?" said the bloke, opening the glovebox and poking around among Windy's things in there.

Windy would never see a man stuck for a smoke.

"Yes, there's some rolls on the seat here. Help yourself."

"Haven't you got any tailormades?"

"No."

The bloke opened the door again and slammed it as hard as he could again. "Don't go so fast," he said. "You'll make a man nervous."

"That door's okay," Windy said shortly. "You don't have to slam it all the time."

"Don't trust the bloody things."

"Where do you want to get off?" Windy asked impatiently.

"Did you bring any beer?" the bloke asked, ignoring Windy's question.

"There's a bottle or two in the carton in the back here," said Windy, a bit put off. "You should be able to reach it over the back of the seat."

"Where are you going?" asked the bloke, not reaching for the beer.

"Auckland," said Windy. "What about you?"

"What part? Auckland's a bloody big place."

"Takapuna," said Windy at random.

"Got your own place?"

"No. I stay with friends there."

"That'll do," said the bloke, settling into the seat.

"Now look here, mate," said Windy. "You're not staying with me and that's flat. There's not enough room for you and I'm only a guest there myself. Just tell me where you want to go and I'll drop you off there."

Again the bloke opened the door and slammed it.

"And you can stop slamming that damn door," Windy said hotly. "You'll end up breaking it. Now where do you want to be let off?"

"Do you believe in God?" asked the bloke.

When Windy recovered from his surprise he said: "I never discuss my religious views in public."

The man was obviously as mad as a meat-axe.

"I thought as much. All you religious blokes are the same. Talk big about helping your fellow men, but you'd charge a dying man for a drink of water if you owned a river."

"Now look here, mate . . ." began Windy.

"You needn't bother preaching your sermons to me," said the bloke, waving his hand in Windy's ear. "I've been listening to you blokes for years and I've never run into one of you yet who practised what he preached. A pack of hypocrites, that's what you are. A pack of bloody hypocrites!"

This was getting too much altogether. "If there's any more of that kind of talk you can get out and walk," said Windy.

"Seventh Day Adventists," announced the bloke. "I can pick 'em a mile off."

The bloke was off his rocker all right. Windy decided to kid him along till they got to Hamilton and put him off there. He was a fairly hefty bloke and Windy didn't want any trouble with him.

"You're wrong," he said for a joke. "Salvation Army."

"In that case you won't mind lending me five dollars when we get to Auckland," he said.

"Like hell," said Windy angrily. "You're not getting any five dollars off me. I'll give you a lift as far as Hamilton."

The bloke didn't seem to be able to hear what he didn't want to. He slammed the door again and picked up Windy's tobacco and started rolling thin smokes which he carefully put in his shirt pocket.

"You might as well keep the packet," Windy told him after a while.

"Don't need your charity," said the bloke, shaking the last of the tobacco into the corner of the packet for one more smoke out of it. He put that one in his mouth and lit it, pocketing Windy's matches when he'd used them for the job. Then he threw the empty tobacco packet out the window and reached into the back of the van for a bottle of beer.

"Where's your opener?" he demanded, dragging a bottle out of the carton.

"On the key-ring," said Windy. "Here y'are." He passed him the opener.

"Any glasses?" he wanted to know.

"What do you think?" Windy asked him sarcastically. "Do I look like the kind of bloke who carts glasses around with him? You can drink out of the bottle, same as I do."

He did drink out of the bottle. Every drop of it. And when Windy asked him politely if it would be too much trouble to offer him a drink, he said: "Not on your life. Your driving's bad enough as it is, without boozing on top of it."

"You don't have to put up with it," Windy pointed out. "You can get out and walk any time you like."

"Shut your window," said the bloke. "It's as cold as hell in here. You want a man to catch pneumonia or something and wind up in hospital?"

They arrived at a small town and Windy's passenger said: "I'm hungry. How about you?"

It was the first time he'd taken Windy into consideration and Windy felt ridiculously touched by it.

"Yeah, starving," he said.

"Well, pull up here and I'll get something to eat," said the bloke magnificently.

Windy stopped by a little shop that said they sold pies and things and the bloke got out and went into the shop. He came back eating a pie, with another one in a paper bag. He got in, slammed the door as hard as he could and said; "Right. Let's get going."

Once they were under way again Windy reached out for the other pie, but the bloke grabbed it off the seat and put it in his lap.

"No, you don't," he said indignantly. "If you wanted a pie

you should have got one when we were at that shop back there."

Windy pulled over to the side of the road and stopped.

"Righto, mate," he said. "This is as far as you go. Out you get."

The bloke opened the door and Windy thought for a moment that he was going to leave without any trouble, but he only wanted to slam it again.

"You might wait till I finish me pie," he said throwing the crust from the first pie on the floor and starting on the second.

They sat there in silence while he slowly ate the pie. When he'd finished dropping the crust on the seat and floor, Windy got out and went round to his side and opened the door.

"Come on, mate. Out!" He was determined that this bloke wasn't going to talk him out of it this time.

The man got a smoke out of his shirt pocket and carefully lit it. When it was going properly he stepped out on to the roadside and looked at the sky.

"I hope the next driver is a bit more sociable than you," he said. And he walked off in the direction they'd just come from without looking back or another word. Windy got back into the van and drove quickly away without looking back.

A few miles later he saw another man walking and didn't take much notice of him, but when he got close he saw that he was well-dressed, and he turned and smiled for a lift. Windy had been getting a bit sleepy, and a bit of a yarn was just what he needed to keep him awake. So he stopped.

The man put his bag on the floor and got in, closing the

door so carefully it wouldn't latch properly and Windy had to tell him to slam it.

"Where are you heading for?" he asked.

"The next settlement will do, thank you," said the man.

He was a quiet sort of bloke this one. He didn't say another word for about a mile and Windy was working out how to get a conversation going when the man suddenly said:

"Do you believe in God, sir?"

Windy nearly went off the road.

"Er — why?" he managed to say.

"Well you see, I'm going around making sure that there is a Bible in every home I visit, so that people are always in touch with the Lord. If you haven't a Bible I'll be happy to provide you with one. We don't charge anything but if people feel that they'd like to make a small contribution towards our work we are always happy to accept it. You see, we feel that if everybody has access to God, whether they make use of it or not, it will be a great step towards better understanding. You'd be surprised at the number of people who turn to the Lord in times of trouble and hardship and loneliness. People who never go to church from one year to the next. For them the Bible represents . . ."

And he went on and on and onandonandon . . . Windy was having trouble keeping his eyes on the road, and the sound of the man's voice was only making him sleepier. He thought of stopping for a spell, and he most likely would have if he hadn't had the passenger. He decided to wait till he got him where he was going and then pull into the side of the road for a spell.

He didn't make it. Windy didn't know exactly what happened. One minute he was driving along and the next he was lying in some grass with glass everywhere and people standing around talking urgently.

Two policemen came to see him in hospital and get a statement. Windy couldn't tell them as much as they told him. He'd run off the road on a corner. Going too fast to take it, they said. The van was a write-off.

"Were you insured, sir?"

"No."

"That's unfortunate."

Windy's passenger was in the same hospital, pretty badly knocked around, they said. His door had sprung open and he'd been thrown out.

The police said they'd found an empty beer bottle in the van and some broken full ones. Windy had smelled strongly of liquor when he was dragged from the wreck, and on this evidence there was some talk of bringing charges of drunken driving, or at least negligent driving against him.

"You're lucky not to be being charged with something even more serious than that, sir. Manslaughter."

Somehow Windy couldn't help blaming the bloke who was sick on Mrs Puketu's stove. If it hadn't been for him Windy would at least have had a feed before he set off. Then he'd smoked all Windy's smokes and drunk all the beer and ate all the pies and kept slamming the van door. If it hadn't been for him he might even have had a bit of sleep at Puketu's place the night before. But how could he ever explain a thing like that to the police? He couldn't even *tell* them about him: he'd make a great witness!

No. It was just a typical run of Windy's luck. He'd lost his van and he lost his driver's licence for three years.

So much for his stroke of luck. If Aunt Meredith hadn't left him all that money, he wouldn't have bought the van and ended up at Puketu's place and run into the door-slamming bloke and ended up on the way to Auckland, where he met up with the religious bloke who talked him to sleep, and caused him to run off the road.

No, the stroke of luck wasn't Windy being left all that money. The stroke of luck was when the magistrate lost patience with trying to get some sense out of him and dismissed him on the negligent driving charge the police had brought against him.

Hot Stuff

About eighteen feet by twelve; four-by-two frame and corrugated iron. An axe stuck in a worn away woodblock surrounded by chips and bits of firewood — the nearest thing to a garden it was ever likely to have.

To a city woman the old roadman's hut would have been nothing less than unsightly chaos, but from Squinty Bill's angle it was a good camp, and he was the one who had to live in it. Had lived in it for years. Everything had its place and uses. Even the big stone on the floor by the wall was to hold the door open on hot days, or when he needed more light inside. The sacks on the steps, the porch, the floor and the window all served an obviously useful purpose, and the ones hanging on the fence outside were spares.

The pile of passed-on magazines and newspapers in the cardboard box at the foot of the bed was for lighting fires, and the bed itself sagged in the middle where it was always sat on, just enough so your feet comfortably reached the floor. Nails for hanging things on were banged into the unlined timbers with things hanging on them. A bow-saw, spare hats and old elbowy jackets; a big frying-pan; a rabbit trap; a coil of fuse; a two-year-old Dalgety's calendar, with a picture of a place where Squinty Bill had worked once; a mended bridle; a semi-retired rifle rusted patiently in a corner alongside a curly stick waiting to be carved into a walking stick for his old age. Things like that.

His good clothes hung on a single hanger in the space

between a corner and a tall cupboard, with his going-to-town shoes on the floor beneath. The table was under the window with a row of sauce bottles and salt and pepper tins against the wall at the back. An up-ended box and two chairs with sack seats made one part-time and two permanent seats. Oilskins, gumboots, shovels, slasher and pick on the porch, and the bachelor smells of damp clothing, tobacco, woodsmoke and meths and kero for the Tilley lamp gave the place a dim, wet-weather atmosphere.

Squinty Bill himself was one of those men who seemed to have been in the bush longer than the trees. He had, so to speak, cut his teeth on a whetstone. There were no teeth left now but he was a tough old rag, for all his age. And what he didn't know about huts and camps hadn't cropped up in the last sixty years or so.

Admittedly his hut was in a bit of a mess at the moment. A crate of empty beerbottles in the middle of the floor, with an empty flagon beside it and wet patches where beer had been spilt. Cigarette butts, matches and bottle tops that had missed the fireplace lay scattered around the hearth, and all that was left of the armfuls of firewood we'd brought in before dark was a heap of bark and some dead ashes in the grate. The lamp had gone out and a candle stuck in its own wax on the table was the only light.

There were three of us left, sitting round the table. Old Squinty, still wearing his too-big hat, with a nearly full bottle of whisky in front of him. Big Andy, who always wore a black bush-singlet. Dumb as hell and he knew it. Always on the lookout for someone trying to put it across him because he was easy to put one across. Andy was okay as long as there was no funny business, and he never actually started any trouble. Just watched for it all the time and was far from slow over dealing with it when it came. And me, sitting there blankly watching him trying to roll a cigarette with one big end and tobacco hanging out of it everywhere.

It must have been about three in the morning and we'd been going well till the beer cut out and we started on the whisky. Now we were too bleary and tired to be bothered calling it a day.

The whisky bottle slid loudly across the table towards me. In the silence it sounded like a car crossing a loose cattle-stop.

"Have a beer," ordered Squinty, "and I won't hit you when you're drunk."

At the mention of hitting, Big Andy looked up interestedly, and as Squinty's meaning sank in he returned to his cigarette, which was in a worse mess than ever.

"It's not beer," I said. "It's bloody whisky." I raised the bottle and blew a few bubbles into it, letting a little of the stuff trickle into my mouth. Then I slid the bottle on round to Andy. The sliding of the bottle on the bare boards of the table had the nerve-grating effect of rusty tin on teeth, but it served to bring the next man's attention to the fact that it was his turn to force a drink down or admit he'd cut his load and couldn't take any more.

Andy raised the bottle in one huge paw, drank two noisy gulps, and banged it back on the table with a crack that interrupted me wondering whether old Squinty wore his big hat to bed or not.

"Bloody stuff," said Big Andy to nobody in particular. "Should have got another crate of beer."

"I know what," said Squinty. "Let's try a drop of my sister's honeymead. She sent me a bottle last Christmas and I've hardly touched it. It's real hot stuff."

Big Andy's interest revived at once at the mention of a new kind of drink, and mine at the idea of Squinty having a sister. He somehow didn't seem the kind of bloke who had relatives. A young Squinty was a hard thing to imagine, he'd been old for so long.

He rose stiffly to rummage in the dark corner cupboard and returned with a bottle three-quarters full of something that looked like thick sherry. He put it on the table and got an eight-ounce hotel glass from a shelf.

"Try some?" he asked, waving the glass in my direction.

"Not just now," I said quickly. "Think I'll stick to the whisky," I added, reaching for the bottle in front of Big Andy.

"I'll give it a go," said Andy superfluously.

Squinty uncorked the bottle with a loud *squick* and began to pour the honeymead into the glass.

"Say when," he said to Andy.

Andy still hadn't said anything when the glass was two-thirds full so Squinty stopped pouring.

"This'll do you for a start," he said, passing Andy the glass. "You've got to be careful how you handle this stuff. She'll burn holes in your singlet."

Andy raised the glass, looked at it for a moment, and then drained it in one smooth movement. Then he put the glass on the table and sat back to wait for the taste and results. Squinty and I watched for his reaction to this impressive performance. It wasn't long in coming.

His eyes screwed up, then opened wide and settled back to their normal bleariness. Without saying anything he looked back and forth between me and Squinty as though he couldn't remember who we were. Then he reached a hairy arm past me and turned the label on the honeymead bottle towards the candle: It read:

Raw Linseed Oil
Leather Dressing
Not To Be Taken

Big Andy slowly put the bottle down and began to rise from his seat with a look on his face that left no doubt about what was going to happen to Squinty Bill — and me. Nothing was going to convince him that there hadn't been a conspiracy between us to trick him into drinking linseed oil and he clearly intended "sewing us up", as he was in the habit of describing it, by way of preserving his pride. I sat helplessly watching, knowing that nothing I said was going to prevent a nasty beating-up.

Then Squinty Bill, who'd been looking at the bottle with pursed lips, spoke.

"Wrong bottle, eh?" he said calmly. "Well, I don't give a guest in my camp anything to drink that I won't drink myself." And he grabbed the glass, poured himself a full eight ounces of Raw Linseed Oil and drank it in three gulps.

Big Andy stood half-crouched over his chair with a puzzled frown. Squinty took the whisky bottle, drank from it and passed it across to Andy.

"Better wash the taste out of your mouth," he said. "That oil's a hell of a brew."

Slowly Big Andy subsided back into his chair. Then, as though suddenly coming to a decision, he accepted the bottle Squinty was holding out to him and drank a hefty slug.

"Sure is," he nodded.

The whole hut relaxed as Big Andy did. Even the candle seemed to perk up a little, but Squinty Bill gave no sign he realised what had nearly happened. He got out the genuine bottle of honeymead — ghastly stuff it was — and we sat around the table drinking and waiting for the effects of the linseed oil to hit Squinty and Big Andy. But nothing happened, except that the more they drank the more sober they seemed to get.

We finished the bottle of whisky and by dawn I could scarcely keep my eyes open, while Andy and Squinty chatted over the last of the honeymead. The last thing I remember before going to sleep in my chair with my head on my arms was Squinty saying indignantly: "Y'know Andy, that linseed oil hasn't got any kick in it. Doesn't make a bit of difference to a man."

And Big Andy replying sadly: "No. A man could drink it all night and not turn a hair."

"Shall we try a drop in the honeymead?" suggested Squinty.

"Yeah, good idea," said Andy brightly.

SEPARATE ROOMS

I was travelling south to meet Dan with the car. The first to arrive at the Fentonbridge Hotel was to book us both in and then wait for the other. It looked as though Dan would be there well before me, as I'd been held up and wouldn't arrive at the hotel until late that night.

I was bowling along at a fair speed, trying to make up a bit of time, when I saw the hitch-hiker on the road ahead, thumbing for a lift. I wouldn't have bothered wasting time with hitch-hikers, except that this one was a girl, a young one, and on her own. Good-looking too, and not *too* young. So I stopped and picked her up.

She was passing through the town I was going to and by the time we arrived there, at about half past ten that night, we were getting quite friendly. We'd been to different schools together. She was on a kind of working holiday and was looking for work as she'd almost run out of money.

I drove straight to the hotel and put the car in the parking lot at the back.

"My mate will have booked me in here," I told her. "Why don't you do a ringbolt in my room? It's a hell of a night to spend out and there's no point in paying for hotel accommodation when you can get in for nothing. You can sneak out early in the morning and no one'll be any the wiser."

She had a few halfhearted objections at first. She had a sleeping-bag . . . She didn't usually. . . She might get caught.

The usual guff. She didn't take much persuading. It had been raining up until an hour or so before and it was a freezing cold night.

I left her to wait in the car and went round to the lobby of the hotel and rang a buzzer at the receptionist's counter. A fussy, thin, pimply, dapper little chap came through a door into the office.

"Yes sir?" he lisped.

"Name's Watson," I told him. "Has Mr Curtis booked me in here?"

"Yes, I think so, sir. I'll just check."

He opened the usual big book on the counter. "Let's see now — yes, here it is. You and Mr Curtis are in woom seventeen. It's the fourth on the left at the top of the stairs."

This was a bit awkward.

"Ah — you haven't put us both in the same room, have you?" I asked.

"Oh yes, sir. I remember Mr Curtis especially asked for a double woom."

In spite of him spraying a fair bit of spit around as he talked, I leaned over towards him and said, "Look, I don't want to cast any aspersions on Mr Curtis's character, he's a very nice man, but — well, it's just that I'd rather have a room of my own, that's all. You see. . ." I whispered confidentially in his twitching ear for a few moments.

His response was, I thought, a bit on the drastic side.

"Well!" he said, after a short pause for what appeared to be intense concentration. "That is exactly what I suspected. I knew there was something wong with that man the very moment he walked into this hotel. Disgwaceful, absolutely disgwaceful! Don't you wowwy, Mr Watson, I'll find a sepawate woom for you. Disgusting. That's what it is. Disgusting. If the manager was to discover what kind of — person — was under his woof, I don't know what he'd think."

"I don't think it'd be a very good idea to tell anyone about it," I said quickly. "Let's just keep it to ourselves, eh?"

The receptionist drew himself up to his full five foot six or seven, aimed his Adam's apple right between my eyes and said, "I have no desire to discuss such things with anyone, sir." And after a short pause for effect he began to look through his big book for a room to put me in.

I was eventually installed in "woom nineteen", right next to the one Dan was in. The little receptionist, with several more "disgustings", a "disgwaceful" or two, and an "outwageous", left me with a conspiratorial warning not to make any noise and "awouse that man in the next woom".

I had the uncomfortable feeling that my little white lie was being taken entirely too seriously, but I didn't worry too much about it just then. I had other things on my mind.

I gave the receptionist about half an hour to get clear of the lobby and then went out and smuggled my freezing hitch-hiker up the stairs and into the room — and out again at about half past five next morning. It wasn't worth all the trouble I'd gone to. She made me wait in the shower while she got into bed, and then generously gave me a blanket and pointed out how comfortable the chair looked. When I tried to point out to her the various advantages of double beds, she threatened to scream if I so much as laid a finger on her. I couldn't risk calling her bluff. I'd stuck my neck out far enough as it was.

I got in about an hour's sleep after she left and heard Dan moving around in his room while I was still straightening things up in mine. I rang him up on the telephone.

"Hullo," I heard him say through the wall.

"Hullo, Dan," I said. "Dick here. Where are you?"

"Room seventeen," he replied. "What the hell happened to you yesterday? Where are you?"

"Got in late," I said. "They put me in room nineteen. Hey, that must be somewhere near where you are."

"Next door," said Dan. "Aren't they beauts! I told them to put you in here with me."

"They must have a different receptionist on at night," I said. "He probably didn't know about it."

"The bloke who jacked it up wouldn't know whether he was Arthur or Martha," said Dan. "Did you get everything fixed up before you left Ingleton?"

"Yep."

"Right, I'll see you at breakfast. We'll get away from here as soon as we can. We've lost enough time on this trip as it is. Can't afford any more holdups."

"Okay."

It looked as though I was going to get away with it.

In the dining room Dan was sitting alone at a table. The waitress sat me with him as though she was directing me to a brothel. We talked about the stupid inefficiency of the hotel until our breakfast was brought and flung down on the table as though the waitress was dealing us a hand of poker. While we were eating lambs' fry and bacon Dan suddenly stopped

and looked around the other occupied tables.

"What the hell's everyone staring at us for?" he hissed.

"Staring at us?" I said, as surprised as I could manage. "You must be imagining things. I haven't noticed anyone staring at us," I lied.

Dan looked around again and then went on eating. Then a few minutes later he dropped his knife and fork on the table.

"What the *hell* is wrong with everyone around here?" he snarled. "They *are* staring at us."

"Garn," I said uncomfortably. "You must be a bit on edge this morning."

"There's something queer about this dump," he announced. "I'm not staying here again, that's for sure."

Then the manager of the hotel appeared at our table and addressed himself to Dan.

"We don't encourage your type in the hotel, Mr Curtis," he said stiffly. "I would like you to vacate your room as soon as possible — and I wouldn't bother trying to seek accommodation here again, if I were you."

And he turned and walked out of the room, leaving Dan sitting there stunned and speechless. And me squirming in my chair.

"What the hell's crawling on him?" Dan finally managed to gasp.

"Damned if I know," I said. "Let's get out of here. They're all crazy. It's no good trying to reason with nuts like that."

"Nuts is right," said Dan with a bewildered glance around the silent dining room. "The whole place is crazy. I've a good mind to demand an explanation."

I only just managed to convince him it would be a waste of time. We left the dining room and collected our odds and ends from our rooms. The dapper little receptionist bloke came in answer to the buzzer, looking as though he'd just discovered a nasty smell.

"Yes, sir?" he sniffed.

"Want to pay our bill," I said shortly. I'd like to have had a chat with him about keeping his big mouth shut, but with Dan standing there in the explosive state he was in it was out of the question. The best thing to do was get out of there as quickly as possible.

"Forty-seven dollars, eighty-five", intoned the receptionist, slapping the receipt book on the counter as though it was someone's face.

I paid him and took the receipt. We were just turning away towards the front door when he suddenly held up a pair of black, lacy panties, delicately pinched between finger and thumb. "These were found in your bedclothes by the house-maid," he said to me. "We don't want such things here."

Dan croaked some astonished thing and I grabbed the panties the receptionist was waving in my face and stuffed them in my pocket out of sight.

I shouldn't have admitted knowing anything about those pants, but they'd taken me by surprise. It was too late now. Dan followed me out of the hotel with a look of grim curiosity that was going to demand satisfying.

I was desperately trying to think of a way to square off with Dan when we came in sight of the car. My hitch-hiker was sprawled out on the front seat with her feet on the window.

Waiting for a lift, she reckoned.

Dan took one look and really did his block. He didn't even bother to ask what had really been going on, or give me a chance to explain. No one would have believed me anyway, come to think of it.

That's why I'm back in here. You see, I was only allowed out on probation as long as Dan guaranteed my good behaviour. It just doesn't seem fair somehow.

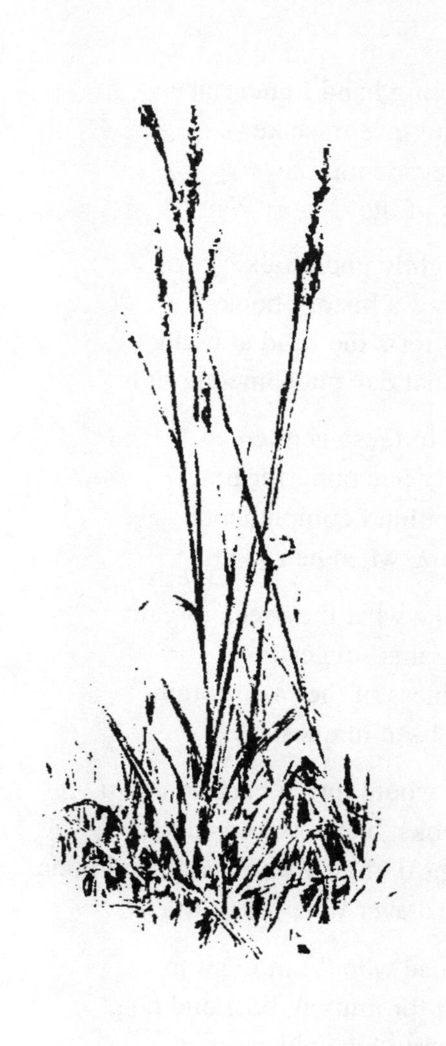

BATTLE

With trembling hand I undertake
To rectify a grave mistake —
Of certain academic flaws
In versions of the 'Maori Wars'.

I haven't lightly undertook
Correction of a history book,
But snugly rests the head at night
What has that day put someone right.

According to these gentlemen
There's only one thing for it;
A maori couldn't comprehend
A good thing when he saw it.

I don't know what they seek to gain
By making this suggestion,
The soundness of the maori brain
Has never been in question.

What fool would turn a bargain down
Like fishooks, blankets and an axe,
When all he'd known were wood and bone
And all he'd ever worn was flax?

What maniac would fail to swap
Some land for mutton, beef and hog,
When hitherto his only chop
Was bird, or rat, or skinny dog?

Who'd fail, unless he'd lost his wits,
To emulate the wily ones
Who sailed the world in mighty ships
And brought him tomahawks and guns?

And having got these wondrous things,
Who wouldn't want to try them out?
And that's what all the quarrelling
And all the fighting was about.

Any mother anywhere
Will understand the claim:
Give little boys the best of toys —
They'll quarrel just the same.

And as the flag of God unfurled,
The different tribes across the world
In deadly clashes such as this,
Attacked each other's prejudice.

In spite of who believes they're right,
Or what men say they're fighting for,
The only kind of war we fight
Is still the same old human war.

So in the broader sense, you see,
The 'Maori Wars' will cease to be,
And future books will only say
That humankind grew up this way.

Country Correspondent

The first person Cosgrove asked when he got off the bus told him how to find Mrs Mobberley.

"Well, you go out past the cemetery and turn left just before you get to Millers'. Mobberleys' is the last place on the right past Bluskers' before you get to where the Driddles used to live before they shifted into their new place next to Cross's."

Cosgrove thanked her and went out to the street to look for a taxi. He found it parked outside Ongapuni's one garage, and then he was sent, twice, from one end of the town and back again by people who didn't like to admit that they didn't know where the taxi-driver was to be found. He eventually traced that gentleman to the public bar of the hotel, where he'd come from in the first place almost an hour before.

Cosgrove had never been able to appreciate the langourous mental and physical attitudes of these country folk, though he always managed to keep his irritation private. But when he was bumbled around by them like this he often became very agitated, and he didn't like being agitated because he could never safely express his agitation for fear of copping a smack in the kisser. It was very frustrating.

And after an hour of the mounting tension involved in something so simple as finding the local taxi-driver, the taxi-driver himself proved uncooperative. Cosgrove asked the publican if he would mind pointing out which was the taxi-driver, and the publican, whose both hands were occupied with something in his pockets, nodded his head wisely in the general direction of two men deep in urgent conversation at the far end of the bar.

As he approached these two men Cosgrove saw that they were both so un-taxi-driverish-looking that he was tempted to suspect the publican of having played some kind of joke on him. And when he was close enough to address them they went on talking as though he was invisible.

"Well, as I said at the time, Bert, there's no tellin' how many's going' t' turn up, and that's a fact."

"Yeah, there's no tellin' how many of em's goin' t' turn up alright. I backed yerrup on that, remember?"

"I think I did 'ear somethin', Bert. But it was me told 'em t' git another twenty tickets extra, above and beyond what they reckoned they was goin' t' need."

"Yeah, well I mentioned it t' Stu Miller when we first went in in the first place and he said f' me t' bring it up after the meeting' but you got in first. Stu'll tell y'. You arst 'im if I come up to 'im when we first went in . . ."

"Excuse me," said Cosgrove politely. "Is one of you gentlemen the taxi-driver?"

For a moment it didn't look as though either of them were going to answer him. They didn't turn their heads to look at him, as he had every right to expect them to; they turned their whole bodies, ever so slowly, until they'd about-faced and were leaning with their drinks in their hands and their backs against the bar, looking at him.

For a long time they stood like that and then Cosgrove saw that one of them was actually going to speak. He saw the

decision on the face, the bracing of the lungs, the intake of breath, the pause, the mouth beginning to open. . .

"Yeah. That's right," he drawled.

It took Cosgrove a moment to remember the question and then relate it to the answer. Then he addressed himself to the talkative one.

"I was wondering if you could run me out to where Mrs Mobberley lives?"

The taxi-driver thought it over for a few seconds.

"Not me, mate," he said. "I'd like to be able to help y', but I can't. Haven't got a car or anythin'."

Another pause, this time from Cosgrove.

"Is your taxi not working at the moment?" he enquired.

"'S'not *my* taxi, mate, it's me mate 'ere's."

Cosgrove felt his temper begin to rise alarmingly and then slowly subside as he deftly reduced the consequences of saying what he felt to its lowest probable common denominator — a belt in the ear from both sides at once. He turned to the other man, who looked even less like a taxi-driver than the other had.

"Could *you* drive me out to Mrs Mobberley's place?" he asked through politely clenched manners.

The second taxi-driver thoughtfully considered the proposition for a few moments. Cosgrove's thumb went through the lining of his pocket with a loud *brip* that caused both taxi-drivers to deepen their looks at him warily. At last the second taxi-driver spoke.

"I s'pose so," he grunted. "Don't see why not." He turned to his mate for approval of the decision.

"Sure, don't see why not," his mate agreed.

"Thank you," said Cosgrove, turning to lead the way out to the footpath.

"I'm goin' right past Missus Mobberley's place this afternoon," went on the real taxi-driver. "I could drop you off on the way if you like," he added generously.

Cosgrove, frozen in his half-turned-away position, felt all his pores open and close like anemones. "I'd really prefer to go now, if you could manage it," he said. "I'm in a rather urgent hurry as a matter of fact. I only have a few hours to get a lot of work done. I have to meet a deadline."

"In a hurry, eh?"

"Yes, I *am* in a hurry."

"Well if you're in a hurry I might be able to help you out." He drank from his glass.

"That's very kind of you," said Cosgrove, prepared to think a little more kindly of the man, now that he had things moving.

"She's right, mate . . ." He paused as though he'd just made a curious discovery. ". . . You're new around here, aren't you?"

"Yes. Look, could we go now please? I am in a hurry. It's urgent."

"In that case I don't see why we shouldn't get away right now," said the taxi-driver actively.

"Well let's get along, shall we?" urged Cosgrove.

The taxi-driver drained his glass and put it on the bar. "Don't fill that one up again, Bert," he instructed. "I've got to dash now. Got to get this bloke over to Missus Mobberley's. He's in a hurry."

"Okay then," replied Bert understandingly. "See y' when y' git back."

"Righto, see you when I get back . . . Will y' be in 'ere?"

"Think so. Either in 'ere or over Bill's place."

"Okay. If y' not in 'ere I'll 'ave a look over at Bill's place."

Cosgrove was following the taxi-driver out the door when Bert spoke from behind them at the bar. The taxi-driver stopped and Cosgrove cannoned into him.

"I'll most likely be in 'ere," Bert said.

"Okay," said the taxi-driver. "I'll look in 'ere first."

"Righto."

"See y'."

And suddenly Cosgrove and his captive taxi-driver were out on the footpath, actually moving towards the taxi, which was parked about 150 yards from the hotel.

"Are you very busy at the moment?" he enquired pleasantly, to dispel the odd feeling that it had all been too easy and something would yet intervene to prevent him from getting to Mrs Mobberley.

"Comes and goes," replied the taxi-driver. "As a matter of fact," he confided, "I don't know too much about the taxi business. I just took over the outfit."

"Is that a fact?" said Cosgrove uneasily.

"Yeah, bought Ronnie Wall out. Matter of fact I been a farmer all me life. The doc made me sell out the farm and take on a lighter caper because of me 'ealth."

"Really?"

"Yeah. Got a crook ticker on me. Coronary Thrombosis."

"I'm very sorry to hear it," said Cosgrove absently,

reaching to open the front passenger's door of the taxi.

"Yeah," agreed the taxi-driver sympathetically. "It's a bit of a blow to a man all right, havin' to take it easy after workin' 'ard all me life."

Cosgrove had got into the taxi and closed the door, so the taxi-driver went round to his side and opened that door and began to climb in.

"Still it's no good complainin'," he went on. "Worries the missus more than me." He slammed the door. "Yeah, when a man's time's up he's a gonner, I reckon. No use worryin' about it."

Cosgrove watched in rising apprehension as the taxi-driver fumbled at his pocket openings. He sat there in silence for a moment and then he said: "I'm gunner have t' get out again. I've forgot to take me keys out of me pocket before I got in. Always doin' that. Funny, isn't it?"

Cosgrove didn't think it was funny enough to be worth the strain of making a polite comment. The taxi-driver got out and plunged his hands into his cluttered pockets several times each. "I'm a beaut at losin' things," he announced with a bashful grin.

This was the final straw. Cosgrove felt his willpower begin to smoulder restlessly inside him. If the taxi-driver announced the loss of his ignition key Cosgrove wasn't going to be responsible for his words or actions. He half closed his eyes and waited fearfully for the terrible pronouncement.

"Ah," said the taxi-driver. "Got 'em. Knew all along they was in me pocket somewhere."

Cosgrove relaxed. Then the taxi-driver bent down to

look into the car.

"Just hold the fort 'ere for a mo, will y' mate?" he said. "Just remembered somethin'. Won't be a tick."

Cosgrove nodded dumbly. The taxi-driver began to cross the street and stopped to look both ways for traffic on the silent thoroughfare, then moved towards the other side. Out of the corner of his eye Cosgrove saw him pause, think, and slowly retrace his steps. He came and opened the door of the cab and looked in again.

"Anything y' want from the shop, mate?" he asked.

"Nup," was all Cosgrove could say to thank him for his thoughtfulness.

"Okay, just thought if there was something y' wanted I could have picked it up f' y', seein' as I'm goin' along there meself."

As Cosgrove couldn't answer he closed the door, looked both empty ways again, crossed the road, and ambled slowly out of sight along the footpath.

When the driver had gone Cosgrove sighed loudly several times in the hot cab and wondered if he wished he were back in the office. He couldn't decide, so he wondered about Mrs Mobberley. From a dozen cross-pollinations of the stock that bred men such as the taxi-driver, Mrs Mobberley would have sprouted, flowered briefly, and then married back into. Cosgrove had known exactly what kind of woman she was as soon as he'd heard about her. He'd met them in dozens of country places, just like this one. Even the same smells and times of year. He'd met them in hundreds of different interviews in thousands of different shapes and dresses and faces and circumstances. In fact Cosgrove had decided that they lacked variety in only two respects: they were all colourless, and all ignorant. What other kind of woman would fit into the environs of the country's stately cowsheds and woolsheds?

And her husband would come in from his labours and hover within earshot, on hand to see that nothing bad for the family got into the papers. ("I knocked off and went up to the house when that reporter bloke came to see the missus the other day, Jim. You can't trust them bastards as far as you can kick 'em. They put words in your mouth, that's what they do. If he'd tried any of his funny stuff with my missus he'd have been out the gate quicker than he came in, I can tell you!")

After all, Cosgrove reflected, you can't blame these men. Mrs Mobberley had only done what is expected of the wives of men of this calibre. No strangers to violence, these sturdy fellows. (One of them once punched Cosgrove in the face and split his lip because the typesetter on another paper had got his name wrong in a list of people convicted and fined for after-hours drinking.) Such a man would have handled Mrs Mobberley's story without any of this newspaper nonsense. He would have simply walked on up, drawn back his powerful right arm, and pulled out his holstered tobacco in one smooth movement. . .

Cosgrove was so engrossed in taking out his frustrations on these absent members of the taxi-driver's kin that he failed to hear him returning. The sudden rattle of the door started Cosgrove's visions into guilty cover.

"Forgot me smokes," said the taxi-driver gravely, settling

into his seat and fumbling patiently on the wrong end of a new packet of cigarettes for the cellophane tag opener. "I'm no good without me smokes."

He got the packet open and broke the ends of two cigarettes with his clumsy fingers before he succeeded in extracting one. Then he patted his pockets and gazed blankly around the silent cab. Cosgrove waited for it with the teeth on the blind side of his face gritted and the lips on the taxi-driver's side hooked back into the best he could do in the way of a smile. Then the taxi-driver turned to him and spoke with all the exasperation of someone who's just been robbed.

"I don't suppose you've got a match on you by any chance, mate?"

"I'm sorry," said Cosgrove. "I don't smoke."

"Strike," said the taxi driver. "I forgot to offer you one. Here, help yourself."

"I don't smoke," repeated Cosgrove.

"She's right," said the taxi-driver reassuringly. "I've got plenty."

"I don't smoke."

"Take one for later then," said the taxi-driver encouragingly.

"*I don't smoke.*"

"Don't smoke, eh?" said the taxi-driver. His tone suggested that he was quite prepared to believe Cosgrove didn't smoke, but he found it difficult.

"Couldn't do without me smokes meself. Not that I hold it against a joker that doesn't smoke. If they don't want to smoke that's their business. I don't believe in inteferin' in anyone's private affairs . . ."

He broke off to reach over and rummage in the glovebox in front of Cosgrove. "Did you see where I put me matches?" he asked.

"No, as a matter of fact I didn't," said Cosgrove, leaning back into the seat out of the way of the taxi-driver's rummaging.

"I bet that bloody Bert's got them, that's what'll have happened. Bert's lifted 'em. He's a beaut at that caper."

Cosgrove could see a box of matches between some papers in the glovebox and was about to say so when the taxi-driver found another box, all on his own.

"There y'are!" he said triumphantly. I knew I had a box of matches in there somewhere." He lit his cigarette. "Sure you won't have one?" he enquired.

"Quite sure, thank you," said Cosgrove firmly.

"Well, I'll just leave 'em on the seat 'ere so you can bog into 'em if you change your mind later on."

As far as Cosgrove could see there was now no reason why they couldn't set off. He waited to see what would happen.

The taxi-driver must have had similar thoughts. "Well, we could get away now," he said. "Don't want to hold you up if you're in a hurry."

He fumbled at himself for a few moments.

"Looks like I'm goin' t' have to get out again," he said resignedly. "I've gone and forgotten to get me keys out of me pants pocket again. Don't seem to 'ave been doin' anything but get in and out of the bloody car all day. It's tough on a man with a crook ticker, y'know." He held up the found keys.

"Knew they were there somewhere," he grinned, getting back into the car and slamming the door.

He put the key in the ignition switch, turned it on and pressed the starter. Incredibly, the car started. And then, even more incredibly, they moved off along the road with a series of gentle jerks.

Cosgrove felt an absurd desire to apologise to the taxi driver for his lack of faith in him. Instead he asked: "Is it very far to Mrs Mobberley's place?"

"No distance at all, mate. No distance at all. Just out this way a bit."

The vehicle accelerated violently and Cosgrove thought with a slash of panic of the taxi-driver's Coronary Thrombosis. He flung a look at the speedometer. They were travelling at fifteen miles an hour in second gear and had covered just under one hundred yards.

A hundred and thirty yards from the last of Ongapuni's shops (Cosgrove idly paced out these distances on a walk later) the taxi rolled gently around a left-hand turn at an elegant five miles an hour, off the town's bitumen strip and on to a long straight metalled road.

"Don't like goin' too fast just yet," explained the taxi-driver. "Pays to take it easy at first."

"Do you mean you're only learning to drive a car?" demanded Cosgrove, his voice harsh with alarm.

"Been at it close on three weeks now," said the taxi-driver proudly. "Speed's the thing causes all the accidents, y'know. I'm not goin' to do any speedin' till I get used to it."

"You mean you don't even hold a taxi licence?"

“Nar, the traffic bloke only comes out ’ere every four months or so,” explained the taxi-driver. “If I can catch ’im next time he comes I’ll hit ’im up for a licence.”

“I certainly hope you do,” said Cosgrove, and he couldn’t help adding: “But you’ll probably have to *hold* him up for it, by the look of things.”

The taxi-driver let the car drift to a stop in the centre of the road. Cosgrove mistook the grim look of concentration on his face for anger at his sarcastic remark. He hadn’t realised the man was so sensitive.

“Look, I’m terribly sorry,” he blurted. “I had no intention of offending you. I had no idea . . .” He saw by the way the taxi-driver was looking at him that something was wrong.

“What’s wrong?” he asked, clearing his throat to cover up the quavering in his voice.

“There’s nothing wrong with me mate,” said the taxi-driver.

“Then why have we stopped here like this?”

“This is where you wanted to go, isn’t it? Mrs Mobberley’s place?”

“Yes, Mrs Mobberley’s place. I want to interview her.”

“Well, you’re there, mate. That’s her house in behind them trees there.”

Cosgrove got woodenly out of the car and looked back up the road. There was the main road they’d turned off a few moments ago, still there. (Two hundred and ten yards). And there was the town. Ongapuni, less than a quarter of a mile across the paddocks, two or three hundred yards, a few minutes’ walk. And there was the letterbox, MOBBERLEY painted on it. And there in the taxi was the taxi-driver, happily puffing on that same cigarette, with all the satisfaction of having tackled a difficult job, and done it well. To him it was perfectly logical for someone to hire a taxi for a journey so short that the vehicle didn't have time to get into top gear. Cosgrove felt suddenly fond of the fumbling taxi-driver; they'd been through so much together. Incredible that it was only an hour and a half since he'd left the hotel in search of Mrs Mobberley. It seemed like weeks. It was crazy.

He walked round to the taxi-driver's open window.

"How much do I owe you?" he asked.

"Ar, cut it out mate. I wouldn't charge a man for a bit of a trip like that. Forget it — here, have a smoke."

He passed the opened packet out and Cosgrove took the cigarette his taxi-driver knew he needed all the time. Then Cosgrove moved towards the side of the road as the taxi-driver jerked away with a nod and a "See y' later," and drove away at a sedate few miles an hour, not back towards the town, but straight away along the middle of the road in the direction he was facing. It was a long time before he passed out of sight. To Cosgrove there was only one possible explanation. The taxi-driver had obviously decided to drive straight on, right around the world and back into Ongapuni from the other way, rather than go to all the bother of turning his taxi round. Perhaps he didn't know about the reverse gear.

Cosgrove walked up and down along the road outside the Mobberley place until he'd recovered a little from the strain of getting there. Then, almost completely restored, he walked up the path and pressed the front doorbell with all the confidence you get free with every lifetime of experience.

Nothing, after all, could be worse than what had already happened to him that morning.

JUST DESERTS

(Mrs Mobberley's story as told to Jeremy Cosgrove)

Years ago, during The Depression, when I was only six years old, my father got a job as a coalminer and we went to live in a remote mining settlement on the West Coast.

The owner of the mine was a great bully of a man called Big Nudd. He was huge and powerful and had the whole district in a state of confusion and fear. He rode up and down the muddy bush roads on a big flat-decked dray which was drawn by two nervous, ill-treated horses. We soon learned that Big Nudd would give a man a job and a house to live in, and then visit his wife and family while he was down in the mine. I don't think he actually got up to any real physical mischief, but he seemed to enjoy terrorising the defenceless women and children. The approach of the big dray, rumbling along the road on its iron wheels, would send everyone scuttling apprehensively for cover inside their houses.

Many of the women were too afraid for their husbands, themselves, or just the jobs, to tell their husbands what was going on while they were underground. But such conditions cannot be kept secret for long. Husbands became suspicious. Homes broke up. Occasionally a desperate husband or father would try to fight Big Nudd, but they always ended up injured and jobless for their pains, while their wives and families would have to find somewhere to live and something to eat for themselves until they'd recovered.

For some reason Big Nudd never bothered my mother or

me, and I remember Mother saying once that Father must have had some kind of arrangement with him. But my father would refuse to discuss it whenever she introduced the subject.

This was the situation in the settlement for several months after we arrived there. Father seemed content enough to simply have sufficient money coming in to keep us all going until The Depression ended. None of us could afford to move on to another place, and Big Nudd, in his brutish way, took advantage of the situation at every opportunity. I think he must have enjoyed the hold he had over the people who were forced by circumstances to work for him.

Life went on in the little settlement with a strange atmosphere of waiting; waiting for some relief from the financial rigours of The Depression, from the constant striving to keep enough food in the houses to feed the people, and from the persecutions of Big Nudd. Then relief from one of these things came in a most unexpected way.

The people of the settlement had organised a dance to celebrate the wedding of a popular young man who was bringing his bride back from one of the large towns on the Coast. Straight after the service he was to put his bride on the bus and return with her to the settlement, where he had a job and a house to live in. About five miles from the village was a hall, where they were to stop off for the usual celebration. The bus would then go into the settlement to collect all those who didn't have cars and return with them to the hall. The bus would collect them from the hall at midnight and take them back to the village.

All these arrangements were made as discreetly as possible, for fear that Big Nudd would come to hear of the function, which he would have taken great delight in crashing in on and breaking up, either by getting drunk and smashing things or by simply being there.

We drove to the hall in our car and arrived early to help with the supper and the organising of things. By the time the bus with the rest of the people arrived and had greeted and toasted the newly-weds, it was getting dark. At eight o'clock I was put to bed on the back seat of our car, wrapped warmly in blankets, as I usually was on these occasions.

I used to enjoy sleeping in the car at parties and things. I could either sit up peeping at the people and lights, or lie there listening to the singing and voices until I went to sleep. It was very exciting and my parents were always close by so I was never afraid.

On this night I knelt up in my blankets with my chin on the ledge of the car door, watching the funny shadows of the people as they passed through the band of light coming from the hall doorway, which cut across the stony area in front of the building, slicing cars and trees right in half.

It must have been about half past nine in the evening and the people were all inside the hall, dancing and laughing and drinking toasts, when Big Nudd's dray came trundling up out of the darkness, its big iron-shod wheels crackling on the stones as it passed through my patch of light, making a huge shadow across the ground and parked cars, with Big Nudd hunched like a great motionless bear with the reins slack in the lumpy silhouette of his hands. The strange contraption passed through the light and stopped with a growl on the far side. I could just see the end of the dray and one big spoked wheel at the edge of the light. I remember wondering if the horses could see me from out there in the dark if they looked.

Big Nudd scraped and creaked off the dray and clumped in his big boots into the light towards the hall doorway, almost shutting off the light completely for a moment as he passed through the door and disappeared inside. The noisy laughter stopped suddenly, and then slowly picked up again with a lower, slower sound to it.

Then I heard a voice, raised indignantly, shout, "Private function!" A roar from Big Nudd and then a bump and a shriek of screams from the women that faded quickly to indignant murmuring.

After a while the music started up again in a half-hearted kind of way, and there was nothing much to see for a long time. Once my mother came out to see if I was all right, and, as usual, I ducked into my sleeping position and pretended to be asleep. When she had gone I lay there listening. I heard some men walk out past the car towards the grass and didn't look because I was a young lady. I heard one of them say,

". . . just walked in and blew his nose on her veil."

And another said:

"There'll be trouble here tonight, you mark my words. I'm going to round up my wife and kids and get off home before he gets any more of that wine and beer under his belt."

"What about the rest of us?" asked another. "Most of us have to wait for the bus."

"Someone'll kill him one of these days," said another man.

The men then went back into the hall, taking their voices with them.

I slept a little after that and only half-woke every now and again when an uproar started in the hall, or when my mother or father came out to see if I was all right. Then I heard something I didn't recognise, but it woke me instantly. I rose up to peek carefully over the car door.

The hunched figure of Big Nudd wavered drunkenly along the wall to one side of the hall doorway, his monstrous black shadow sliding back and forth in and out of the darkness. As I watched he took a jerky step forward and put one arm out to lean on the wall. Then he turned towards me and raised one hand to wipe his mouth as though he was going to eat it like a big toffee-apple. He began to stumble and grope his way towards the car, grunting and spitting.

I was terrified, but I kept watching as he came up to the car. Just as he was about to crash the whole car, with me in it, to pieces, he veered past. I heard the faint rasp of his hand on the bodywork and felt the car sway ever so slightly as he leaned on it in passing. The sound of his boots scuffling erratically on the gravel, stopped, and then scuffled on into the darkness.

Suddenly I heard the raised voice of my mother and saw the people crowded silently in the doorway of the hall. This silence was what had awakened me. There was a slight commotion as my mother was bustled protesting into the hall, attended by several comforting women.

Big Nudd appeared, stumbling weakly along at the edge of the light towards the dray. He found it and crawled on to the tray, for all the world like a big pup trying to climb steps. He crawled along the dray until only his legs and one arm could be seen in the light. Then he lay still and in a few seconds he began to snore huge snores. Somebody at the hall doorway said in a loud voice:

"It's all right now, he's out cold. I've seen him like this before. He won't wake up for hours."

"Not surprising, with all he's drunk. It's a wonder he doesn't kill himself," said someone else.

"It's a *pity* he doesn't kill himself," said a woman.

"Okay now, back to the party everybody," called somebody importantly.

And people began to drift back into the hall. My mother and father both hurried out towards the car and I ducked quickly under my blankets and went to sleep while my mother tucked me in and shushed my father not to make a noise and wake me. When they went back into the hall I sat up and kneeled, looking at Big Nudd's half-lit shape lying out there on the cold hard dray.

It seemed like hours that I sat there, staring at him, watching the light ebb and flow across a square bulge in his hip pocket as he breathed his great beery snores. The noise inside the hall rose up in laughter and shouts and the thumping rhythm of accordion and piano. There was a lot of drinking, I could tell by the bursts of laughter that poured from the hall every now and then. Big Nudd could hear none of this.

Suddenly there was a figure standing in the dark beside Big Nudd's dray. In the shadows just beyond the light a shoulder, half-lit. I thought Big Nudd was going to be robbed, but the shadowy figure began to struggle with his shoulders, as though he was going to wake him and invite him into the warm hall before he caught cold. The strange tussle went on for some time, and then there was a slight thump and a halting snort in Big Nudd's snoring, and suddenly his face appeared upside down, framed in the light between two of the big wheel-spokes. I was first surprised and then frightened as the figure in the darkness bent forward momentarily into the light. It was my father.

I must admit that I was only frightened to see one of my own parents so close to someone like Big Nudd, whom everybody was so afraid of. My father withdrew into the darkness and even the glow of his white shirt was no longer visible. Only Big Nudd's huge face, illuminated between the spokes.

I remember wondering why my father had bothered to touch him in that strange way, and how he could be lying with his face upside down like that with his jaw hanging open upwards. In fact I lay back across the car seat to try it for myself.

When I looked back towards the dray where these strange things had taken place, I heard the shuffle and the creak of Big Nudd's horses beyond the light in the darkness. Suddenly a horse snickered and shuddered in its harness, then several quick nervous stamps of hooves, and Big Nudd's face was suddenly snatched out of sight and carried away on a plunging rattle of sound that receded into the cold blackness of the night, along a rough mill-road that joined the main road at the hall and had fallen into disuse since The Depression had closed the mill.

Although my memory of all this is very clear, I did not then realise the implications of what I had witnessed. The sounds of Big Nudd's dray had scarcely rumbled away into silence when I saw a figure, my father, move mothlike through the light from a window down the side of the hall towards the rear door.

After what seemed a long time, a man came out of the hall, looked around, and then began to move back inside.

"I thought I heard a noise out here," he said to someone just inside the door.

"I'm sure I did," said the other man, pushing past him.

Suddenly there were people everywhere, milling in the light and demanding to know what was going on.

"It sounded like horses," said a lady.

"Hey! Big Nudd's wagon has gone," called a man from over where it had been.

"His horses must have bolted with him. He was in no condition to drive them away."

"Is that kid all right?" asked my father, pushing his way through the crowd towards the car.

I got quickly into my sleeping position and lay listening, and wondering.

"She's okay," said a voice near the car. But my father and mother both came to make sure.

"Better make certain that Big Nudd's not hanging around somewhere," warned a voice. "He'll be in an ugly mood by now if he is."

"He might have woken up and just gone off home," suggested my mother, moving away from the car.

"What about all that noise we heard? It sounded as though his wagon was out of control."

"We'd better have a look," said one of the main men. "He was pretty drunk, and those horses of his are skittery enough to have bolted with him."

Nobody was very concerned about Big Nudd really, and nobody could blame them, but they brought lights and some of the men moved off to look for him, reluctant to bother but brave in a group. I sat up as my mother opened the door of the car and told me we were leaving. My father said goodbyes to some friends who had to wait for the bus at midnight, and we drove away, leaving people standing in little groups outside the hall, with glowing cigarettes and getting ready to leave.

We weren't even there when they brought Big Nudd's almost headless body in and laid it in a corner of the hall under a blanket. And nobody ever asked me if I'd heard or seen anything. Never a whisper of suspicion about the way Big Nudd died. It was put down to a simple accident and forgotten about as quickly as possible in the relief everybody felt at his passing. As far as most of them were concerned it was a matter of him having received his just deserts.

THAT WAY

Young Davey Hill was as keen on dogs as a starving tapeworm. He often had two or three hidden in the scrub along the big swamp and up the gully behind his father's homestead. Mongrels of all sizes and description that were surreptitiously fed from Davy's plate and late-night milkings of the house cow when he couldn't get scraps for them anywhere else. On an average of about once a month his father would hear Davey's dogs barking at night or catch him sneaking down to feed them, and another batch of stray mongrels would be released with a boot in the ribs and shouted and stoned off the place — on to somebody else's. Even Davey couldn't say where all these dogs came from. They just turned up and, in time, were turned out again.

Outbreaks of sheep-worrying were so prevalent that the farmers in the district took their rifles from porch corners almost as often as they put their old felt hats on. Old man Hill waited in apprehension for the phone to ring every time he heard a shot fired on a neighbouring property. Mr Hill was a very tolerant man, but when Davey turned fifteen and expressed a desire to leave school and home, he found it impossible to discourage the boy beyond pointing out the usual things about education and learning a trade. The Ringatu Rabbit Board won easily.

So two weeks and two phone calls after leaving high school Davey Hill left home with five dogs his father had never seen before and a shotgun that his father was never going to see again. He also had a lot of embarrassing last-minute advice and a bacon-and-egg pie from his wistful mother. His father drove him to the railway station in silence and there was more embarrassment while they waited for the train. Even the dogs were embarrassed.

The Ringatu Rabbit Board Inspector met Davey at the station and helped him load his dogs and gear into a muddy ute. He was a big easygoing bloke with a grin and a pipe. It was the first time Davey had ever been treated like a man; had someone bowl up to him, stick out his paw and say "Pleased to meet you, Dave, I'm Joe Scott. How did your dogs take the trip?"

As they drove madly along a road down the side of a gorge, talking about grown-up things like rainfall and erosion, Dave felt better about having left home.

"It's all dog and gun work out here," explained Joe. "We gave up the poison a couple of years ago. It's only a matter of keeping the old bunny down to where we've got him, now. We'll never get the last one or two, but we can't afford to let them breed up on us again. There'll be a Maori bloke in the hut up there with you. He's a bit rough on his dogs, old Kingi, but he's a bloody good rabbiter for all that. One of the best I've had yet. You'll find him okay to get along with."

The road left the bushed gorge and wound around into a valley that had been brought into pasture and divided into farms by the Government. You could still see patches of rank grass among the manuka and fern. The road from here on was strictly for four-wheel drive.

"There's a couple of dairy farms at the head of the valley," said Joe. "They take all their stuff in and out the other way. This is only a short cut. All this country's going back. Bushsick as hell."

Dave didn't give a flax basket of kumaras whether the place was bushsick, lovesick, homesick or seasick. It looked pretty good to him.

Night and rain fell together as they arrived at the end of the clay track that led to Kingi Cooper's hut. He opened the door and stood like a lumpy statue against the light from a Tilley lamp on the ceiling behind him. Joe and Dave climbed out of the ute, slammed the doors and went up onto the verandah of the hut.

"How's things, Kingi?" said Joe, following him inside.

"Been raining on and off all day. I worked some of the flats this morning and knocked off."

"That's the idea. There's no need to work in the rain — this is Dave Hill, he'll be giving you a hand up here for a while. Kingi — Dave."

Dave shook Kingi's big engulfing hand and said hello.

Kingi was casually friendly. He was also the fairest-skinned Maori Dave had ever seen. In fact, he looked more like a slightly-curried European than a fair Maori. He gave Dave a hand to tie up his dogs while Joe unloaded the ute.

"Where's your dogs, Kingi?" asked Dave as they walked back toward the hut in the rain.

"Got 'em tied up all over the place," replied Kingi. "You'll see enough of 'em in the morning."

Something about the place puzzled Dave. Something that wasn't quite right. It was only when he was lying in his bunk that night and Kingi and Joe were asleep that he realised what the something was. Dogs always kick up a hell of a racket when someone arrives, especially at night. There hadn't been a sound from Kingi's pack. And he was supposed to have fourteen of them.

Joe left them in the morning, which was fine, telling Kingi to ring him from a neighbouring farmer's place if they needed anything before he came again to pay them, about two weeks' time.

Kingi and Dave set out to work a strip of country along a river beyond the hut. Dave's dogs were all over the place as soon as he let them off the chain, but not one of Kingi's left his heels before he told them to. He had everything from big scarred lurchers — all chest and legs — to pocket-sized burrow dogs. Terriers, spaniels and even a sheepdog. And not a pure-bred among them. Dave's dogs looked pretty much the same, but there the similarity ended. Kingi's pack was as highly trained as rabbit dogs can get. When he put them into a patch of cover the fast dogs spread out around it at places they instinctively knew were strategic, while the small hunting dogs dived into the fern or scrub and worked methodically through it. When a rabbit was driven out into the open it had little chance of getting far. The odd one or two that escaped into a burrow were guarded by the dogs until Kingi got there and threw a handful of granulated Cyanogas into the hole and dug in the entrance to seal the gas in. Dave shot a rabbit that doubled back past him and didn't let on how surprised he was to have hit it. He could see by this time why Kingi didn't bother carrying a shotgun. With his dogs he didn't need to.

Dave was a bit ashamed of his dogs, which were getting in the way all the time, but Kingi didn't say anything, so Dave decided he didn't mind.

Dave didn't want to knock off when it was time for them to work their way back towards the hut. They got eight rabbits for the day, which Kingi said was fairly average.

They fed the dogs from the carcase of a ram that was hanging in Kingi's dog-tucker tree with a piece of fencing wire round its neck. That was how Kingi killed his dog-tucker rams.

The following afternoon when the dogs were chasing a rabbit round the side of a hill one of them started barking on the trail and Kingi seemed to be more interested in the dog than the rabbit.

"Poor old Wally. Never thought he'd go that way," he said, shaking his head sadly.

"Lots of dogs do that," said Dave.

"Not mine," said Kingi, and Dave remembered Joe's remark about Kingi being a bit rough on his dogs.

The dogs caught the rabbit and came straggling over to where the two men were leaning on a fence, one of them bringing the dead rabbit in its mouth. Kingi turned casually away from the fence and called Wally in.

"Here, Wally. Here, boy. There's a good dog now."

He began to pat the dog roughly on the muzzle with one hand and took out his sheath-knife with the other.

"Never thought you'd go that way," he said to the cringing dog as he doubled its head back, cut its throat and swung it into a clump of fern, almost in one movement. He wiped the knife on the thigh of his denims and stuck it back into its sheath.

Dave had turned away, his face as white as a cigarette paper and his ears roaring like surf. A silent circle of dogs stood twenty yards out from the fence. Dave led the way towards the next gully so Kingi wouldn't see his face. Kingi behaved as though nothing out of the ordinary had happened, which it hadn't; but Dave wasn't to know that. Kingi told a joke about a bullock-driver, but he had to do all the laughing himself. Dave had just noticed that the band of blood on Kingi's trousers where he'd wiped the knife wasn't the only one.

A few days later they drove to a farm in Kingi's old truck to get a dog-tucker cow the farmer had left a note in their hut about. The cocky was in the middle of his milking when they arrived at the cowshed.

"I've got the old girl in the yard here," he said, leading the way past cud-chewing, muddy-legged cows to the back of the yard, where the sick cow drooped near the rails.

"The vet says she's a gonner. Been going down in condition for a couple of weeks. Not much left on her, but she might be worth a feed or two for your dogs. We'll put her out into the paddock so you can shoot her and. . ."

"This'll do,' interrupted Kingi, running one hand along the cow's bony spine. Then he had his knife out and her throat cut before the farmer or Dave realised what he was doing. While they watched in silence Kingi held the cow against the rail until she sank to her knees and rolled over, kicking feebly. Then he stooped to wipe his knife on the quivering rump.

The other cows began to stir around the yard, bellowing

and snorting at the scent of blood. Cows stirred and stamped in the bails. A set of cups fell off and lay sucking noisily on the wet concrete. One by one the other three sets of cups fell and were trampled by restless feet. Dave and the farmer looked a little wild-eyed at each other and then at Kingi, who was steeling his knife to begin skinning.

"I think you've lost a set of cups mate," he said glancing at the cocky. "Give us a hand to roll her over, Dave."

Dave went over and pulled weakly at a hind leg. The cocky shut off the vacuum in the pipes and began to let the rest of his cows out through the shed. He had as much show of getting milk from bulls, the state his cows were in. He went up to the house without another word to the two rabbiters.

As they drove away with the quarters of meat glowing on the back of the truck, Kingi said: "I think he's a bit annoyed with us for upsetting his cows. How the hell were we to know they'd go that way?"

In the two weeks that followed, Dave managed to get away on his own most of the time and work blocks of country that were too small and patchy for it to be worth two men doing. His dogs were getting good at the work and he didn't miss many rabbits. Though not having any fast dogs, he had to rely on his shotgun a fair bit. Occasionally Kingi would come back to camp with one less dog than he left with and sadly explain that Biddy or Whisky or Nigger had "gone that way". Dave was so uncomfortable in his presence that it was a relief to get out on the job in the mornings, where he could forget about Kingi in the enjoyment of the work and watching his dogs improving.

Joe came, paid them and went.

Then there was the horse. An old station packhorse that they were to shoot for the dogs with a .303 rifle Joe had left with them for the job. They pulled up at the gate of the paddock with all the dog-tucker gear on the back of Kingi's truck. Sacks, rope, shovel, steel hooks, gambels and axes. The horse had seen them coming and came and hung its tired old head over the fence to see if there was anything to do or to eat or only to watch. Dave sat in the truck and said to Kingi: "You can shoot him. I'm not much good with a three-O."

"She's right," said Kingi. "I think I'll be able to catch him."

"No," said Dave, getting quickly out and grabbing for the rifle. "I'll shoot it."

But Kingi was already walking towards the horse. Dave watched as he stroked the nuzzling head and ran a hand down the horse's neck. Then he climbed up the fence and over onto its back, speaking quietly to it. The horse turned and began to walk along the fence to the gate, with Kingi sitting on its back steeling his knife. From where he was sitting, it took him four slashes to get its throat properly cut. Dave could hear the blood pouring into the ground as the horse wandered in an aimless little circle. When it went down, Kingi stepped off and deftly wiped his knife on the hide as the horse rolled over to kick out the last of its life in the mud it had made walking up and down the fence, waiting in case it was needed.

It was then that Dave began to really hate Kingi.

The next day one of Dave's dogs barked on the trail when Kingi was there.

"That Ruff of yours barking on the trail, eh?"

"Yeah."

"Never thought he'd go that way."

"No."

"Got your knife on you?"

"No, I haven't."

"I'll fix him for you. Here, Ruff. Here boy. There's a good dog . . ."

Dave just watched.

Joe came, paid them and left.

Three more dogs, a horse, two rams and a cow.

Joe came, paid them and left. They caught the Rabbit Board's old packhorse that had been turned out for the winter in a cocky's back paddock and loaded him up for a trip to a hut in the hills beyond the river. It was an area that had to be given a rake-over every three months or so. They crossed the river and let the creaking horse lead the way up a side valley to a slab hut in the tussock, four hours from the base hut.

They worked all their country in eight days. Every morning Dave shifted the packhorse to a new stake-out and occasionally cut a bit of extra grass for him. Kingi cut another dog's throat for coming into the hut after it had been chased out. Dave was getting so good with the shotgun that Kingi, who was against their use, admitted that it was handy to have sometimes. He had only seven dogs left and Dave had four.

They were loading their stuff into pack-boxes for the trip back to the base hut when two of the dogs started fighting outside. One of Dave's and one of Kingi's. Dave ran out and grabbed a hind leg but Kingi didn't need his help. He stuck his boot on one dog's neck and grabbed the other by the muzzle. While the two dogs struggled and squirmed he took out his knife with his free hand and tested the edge with his thumb. Then he doubled back the head of the dog in his hand . . .

Blood sprayed up his sleeve and across the back of his coat. Then he bent to wipe his knife, on the ribs of Dave's dog under his foot, before giving it a few casual rubs on the steel. Then he took the dog by the muzzle. Dave turned away.

They headed for the base and it was getting late by the time they reached the river. Kingi caught up the packhorse and climbed on top of it to save getting his feet wet on the river crossing. Dave stood on the bank and watched the horse stagger to its overloaded knees among the boulders in the river. One of Kingi's feet, which he'd tucked into the pack straps, went right through as he came off. The horse plunged through the water and on to the rocks across the river and stood snorting at the scent of blood on Kingi's coat. His foot was still wedged between the pack-strap and the load. He reached up to free himself, talking quietly to the horse. Dave couldn't hear what he was saying, but he knew well enough.

Never thought you'd go that way . . .

Dave raised his shotgun and quietly cocked the hammer behind the choke barrel. He knew exactly where to aim. At that range it was easy. The number four shot-pattern burnt the horse neatly across the rump. It only took the terrified animal a few seconds to reach a bend in the river and stumble and plunge around the corner out of sight. Kingi looked like a rag man, bouncing along among the boulders and hooves.

It was too late to go for help that night. First thing in the morning he'd do all the things you're supposed to do when there's an accident in the back country.

At ten o'clock that night Dave threw the dregs of his tea into the sizzling fireplace and went out to have a yarn with the dogs; to tell them everything was okay now. When the cold had drawn all the heat from the fire out of his clothes he gave the dogs a last pat each and went inside for another mug of tea.

Kingi was standing there. With all his weight on one leg and his back to the fire. He seemed somehow to be all out of shape. Something had happened to his nose and forehead. He opened his mouth to grin but it didn't look very funny.

"Didn't think you'd go that way, boy."

Cave

Bushed and beat and too far back,
Raining hard and off the track,
Where's the road now — hard to tell
Take a guess and go like hell.

Over the side of a dirty bluff,
Stuck on a ledge and no way off,
Round this shoulder — real close shave,
And here in the cliff is a hidden cave.

Dry sticks lying on the floor
And looking round there's plenty more,
And further back among the stones
A row of moulding human bones.

Bones and hair, things of the grave,
I've stumbled on a burial cave.
Outside the thunder rips the air
And I'm not going anywhere.

I light a fire, forget the storm,
And pretty soon I'm dry and warm.
But though he's weary from the chase
My dog just doesn't like this place.

I call him in, he sniffs around
But just can't seem to settle down.
His hackles rise, he growls again
And disappears out in the rain.

I must have slept an hour or so
When sounds of voices, soft and low,
Awake me from my stony bed —
And leave me staring at the dead.

People from beyond the grave,
Vague and smoky, fill the cave,
Crouched and mumbling, hairy-thighed,
Man and woman, squat and wide.

They speak in wary undertones,
A language that I've never known,
As though they might be overheard
If one should say a noisy word.

I see one as the flames leap higher,
Drag something smoking from the fire,
The carcase of some slaughtered beast —
And now they all fall on the feast.

They tear the steaming ribs apart,
One gets the liver, one the heart,
And soon the whole voracious band
Is dripping blood from chin and hand.

A hairy shoulder moves aside,
I catch a glimpse of what has died,
And with a chill that grips my spine
I see the dog they eat is mine.

Aghast and overcome with shock
I try to burrow in the rock.
The best thing I can do is crawl
To deeper dark along the wall.

And as I cringe in mortal fear
A savage bellow rends the air.
A hairy bull-man fills the door
Behind him there are many more.

They fall amongst the feasting clan
And club them senseless to a man.
Hacking, snarling, wood and bone,
Until their grisly work is done.

The floor is puddled flowing red
All the feasters lie there dead.
The victors, as they make to go,
Lay all the bodies in a row.

And as they leave one hairy brute
Looks round and sees me crouching mute.
He lifts his club with angry eye
I have to make a move or die.

I leap up with a desperate groan
And strike my head on jutting stone.
A flash of stars and nothing more —
I fall down on the cavern floor.

I wake, the dawn light fills the air
And here's the bones, still lying there,
And every skull, the daylight shows,
Is cracked and split by heavy blows.

I leave that place, I find the track,
For sure I won't be going back.
A dream's a dream, but that was weird,
And now my dog has disappeared.

If someone asks I'll have to say
He sprouted wings and flew away,
Cause who'd believe that poor old Ben
Was et by prehistoric men?

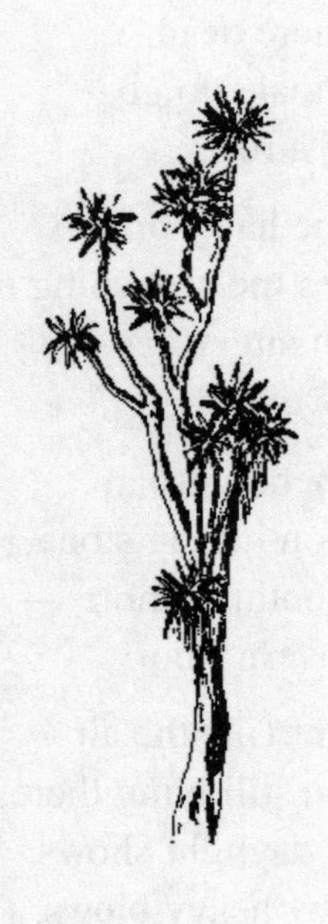

Double Scotch

I dropped the pick the moment I hit the bay and rowed ashore like a man possessed. I hadn't had a drink for days and I was sure going to enjoy this one.

It wasn't unusual for the pub to be open this early in the morning, but it looked as though I was the first customer.

Old Harvey the publican was leaning over the bar beside a drink that looked black in the dimness of the bar-room. Elbows on the bar and his right forefinger pointing straight into the middle of his heavy-rimmed spectacle-lens. The right-hand one.

I stopped and watched. Harvey had flipped his lid at last! He took his finger away from his eye and peered closely at it, turning it round and tipping it this way and that. Then he pointed it back into his eye again and held it there.

Poor sod. It had to happen. No one can drink the amount of grog old Harvey had been soaking up for years without it catching up on him in the finish. We'd all been expecting something like this — we'd had enough warning, goodness knows. But I had no idea it'd start this way.

He removed his finger and began inspecting it again with great concentration. I'd have to go and get someone. The cop? — no, better get the cook to come down from upstairs first.

She could handle Harvey better than anyone. I could leave her to keep an eye on him while I phoned the cop — and the hospital to get ready for him.

I didn't feel at all like the reviver I'd called in for. The sight of what the grog had at last done to old Harvey put me off completely.

He'd put his end-on finger back in the centre of his eye glass and was staring cross-eyed and open mouthed at it.

I thought maybe I'd better not leave the cook alone with him after all. There was no telling what he might do in this state. He might do his block completely at any moment. He might even get violent.

He muttered a broken string of curses. From where I was I couldn't hear what he was saying, except that he was cursing. I looked around the bar-room from where I stood in the doorway. The broom in the corner — he'd have to come out from behind the bar to get at that and I could run for it and raise the alarm. The bar stools — only aluminium frames, but in the hands of a berserk man one of them could be dangerous enough. What about the stuff behind the bar? All that glass! And the piece of wood for donging corks into bottles? If he started swinging that thing around! The scissors on the shelf beside the radio? Suddenly the place was filled with potentially lethal weapons.

He obviously didn't know I was there. I decided to stay and keep an eye on him until somebody came. I began to feel the need for a drink, but I didn't dare move in case he saw me and his deranged mind switched from its present harmless occupation to something more unpleasant.

Then he spoke, peering intently again at his finger.

"Well, come on in, Jack. What'll y'have?"

I stood there not knowing what to do. It sounded as though he knew I'd been standing there all the time. What if he

thought I'd been spying on him?

He went on: "I've got one of them on me blasted glasses. It'd drive you mad. It just goes round and round. He won't climb off the glass over the rim and if I take me glasses off I can't see him. If I just squash the damn thing it'll make a hell of a mess!

"Ha! There the little sod is."

He flicked something off his finger with his thumb. It landed on the bar and we watched it hurry across the bar top and disappear over the edge — an ordinary ant.

"I knew he'd climb on to me finger if I held it there long enough," chuckled Harvey. "Now what'll you have, Jack? Double scotch? Right. Sorry to keep you waiting. You'd better have this one with me; I see you've got a touch of the shakes this morning."

A Bit of a Break

Andy Rogers had never heard of the *Gazette*, nor that his name was quoted in the pages of the latest issue in terms which caused grave misgivings in the hearts of a large number of his business acquaintances. He thought it was just a coincidence that everyone suddenly insisted on his paying what he owed them within an impossibly short time. Letters which had hitherto been merely threatening became positively menacing; creditors who had previously only been firmly insistent were now delivering ultimatums.

The only thing that could possibly be called a coincidence was the fact that the gearbox in Andy's thirty-five-foot fishing boat, *South-Easter*, was down to its last few tortured revolutions. The trouble had started four unprofitable trips ago with a faint whine, and was now screaming for attention, along with his unpaid bills. The only thing he could do was to go out and try to fill his freezer with fish to pay a bit off each account and get parts for the gearbox. And hope for the best.

Andy's deckhand, Manny, who'd been with him for two years, refused to put to sea with the gearbox in that condition, and asked bluntly for what Andy owed him in wages. In defiance of the bank manager's definite instructions Andy wrote out a cheque for Manny's pay, and fuelled and provisioned the boat for a quick getaway, just in case. He was an honest enough man but things were getting a bit overwhelming. There had been some unthinkable mention of seizing his boat to pay off a few thousand lousy dollars, when all he needed was a bit of a break on the fishing. He knew the Barrier Reef as well as anyone in the game, but he'd been having a rough spin with the fishing and the weather and the boat and the store and the bank and the fuel agent and everything and everyone else a fisherman comes into contact with.

All he needed was a bit of a break.

He left the jetty and climbed the path up the cliff to home (rent eight hundred dollars in arrears), his wife, and tea. After the two kids were in bed he told her as little as possible about the strife they were in. She added a few more items to the list of debts which he hadn't remembered, including the fact that they had been refused any more leniency from the storekeeper. This didn't greatly worry Andy because by this time he was beyond the worrying stage.

Marion was a good woman, take it all round, he reflected. Never complained much and hell of a good with the kids. She didn't care for the sea much, but in a way that was a good thing. She didn't interfere with his boat or his work. Andy was specially thankful for her at this time. The one reliable one when everything was going against him. He glanced at her as she leaned across the table to take his empty plate. Nothing much to look at — in fact she was so nondescript she'd stand out in a crowd — but she was dependable and loyal, and to Andy that was worth more than anything just now.

"I'll have to get out to the reef and load up with fish, love," he said. "If I get a decent haul we can pay a few dollars off each account and keep them quiet till we get on our feet again."

"Isn't there something wrong with the boat?" she asked. "Manny said . . ."

"Oh, that's nothing. Bit of a whine in the gearbox. It'll hold out for another trip or two — it'll have to," he added soberly. "Anyway Manny's quit — did he tell you?"

"Yes," she said tiredly. "When do you want to leave?"

"I'll get away tonight and anchor on the reef. Should pick up a few mackerel and trout on the trail in the morning. I'll stay out this time till I fill the freezer if it takes me a month."

"I'll get your things ready," she said.

Good old Marion, he thought as she went off into the kitchen to fill his tucker-box. Not a single complaint. Most women would have been wailing and complaining about him never being at home, but not Marion. Good scout.

It took him half an hour to say goodbye to her and another half-hour to carry his things down the steep cliff-track to the jetty. He didn't want to use the road because it meant passing the butcher's place and the butcher might see him and get the wrong idea about him sneaking out of harbour in the night.

Three hours later he dropped anchor behind a rocky islet halfway between the harbour and the outer reef and went below to sleep till dawn. It was a relief to get away from the worry of his creditors. He could almost forget about them out here, and he slept soundly till it was time for him to start work.

He ate in near-darkness to save his batteries, started the motor, dragged in the anchor and tried to ignore the rattle of the gearbox as he motored out of the shelter of the anchorage into a fifteen-knot south-easter with plenty of sting in it. He cut her back to about three knots to nurse the gearbox and looped a rope round one of the wheel-spokes while he went forward to let down the outriggers. It was still a bit early for trailing but he let out both lines and fussed about with the gloves and gear so he wouldn't notice the rumbling beneath his feet so much.

He whistled, checked the freezer, made up a couple of spare traces, adjusted his course slightly, went forward to check the lashings on the anchor, went aft to roll a smoke, sluiced down the deck and whistled louder, but still the gearbox whined and rattled. He knew exactly what was wrong with it — it was completely shot.

It was fully daylight and he could see the scattered brown of the reef and the eye-blue of shallow water round a sand cay ahead when he got his first strike. The wire cable snapped taut and the outrigger danced against the rigging. It was a good one. He pulled on the gloves and skull-dragged an eighteen-pound spanish mackerel into the killing-pen. A good start. A few more of these would be handy. He clouted the fish with the wooden donger, cut a strip from its silver belly to tie along the hooks on the trace for a lure, and let the line out again.

A mile short of the reef he detoured to circle a low flat islet covered with birds and low scrub which leaned away from the wind in close layers like combed hair. He picked up another good mackerel there, and two more on his way across to the reef.

He trailed close in along the inside of the reef, heading north, and picked up five coral-trout, four more mackerel, two bonito and a turrum by midday. He stopped then to clean the fish and put them in the freezer.

Close to a hundred and fifty pounds of saleable fish in a morning was pretty good going. His luck must have changed. If he could keep this up he'd have a full load in a few days. He ate two bonito fillets for lunch because they wouldn't take bonito at the Fish Board lately.

Andy's change of luck didn't last very long though. When he went to take off again for an afternoon's trailing he'd only gone a hundred yards when the gearbox gave an extra loud rumble, a graunch, and then a bang that shook the whole boat. He cut the motor, threw out the anchor and went below to see what had happened.

Thick, dirty oil was running out of the cracked casing. Something had finally come adrift in there and jammed against the side of the box, breaking it beyond any hope of repair.

Andy sat in the wheelhouse for a long time wondering what to do. He was still wondering when it got dark that night, so he had a feed of coral-trout, sat on his bunk, and wondered some more.

He had four gallons of fuel for the outboard, just about enough to get him into the harbour in the leaky old dory that was lashed to the top of the wheelhouse — providing the weather was okay. Towing the *South-Easter* he wouldn't get halfway. That meant he would have to leave her anchored out there while he went for help, or wait with her and try to signal another boat if one came close enough. But the chances of another boat being in this particular area were slight.

He slept, and during the night the wind dropped so that in the morning there wasn't even a white line of water breaking on the far side of the reef as there had been the day before.

He manhandled the dory into the water, checked and fitted the old outboard, loaded water, food, a bailer and spare fuel, let out more anchor-rope on the *South-Easter* and set off for the mainland, which was represented by a faint smudge of hills in the western distance.

For a while, until it tightened up with the soaking water, the dory leaked alarmingly and he had to bail constantly to keep it from wallowing and taking water over the sides. Then he had trouble with the outboard. Dirty fuel. The trip took him all day and it was well after dark when he tied up at the jetty and stumbled wearily up the cliff towards home and bed. He was too tired to even think about his troubles. Marion would be there.

She was. He heard it before he reached the top of the cliff. Loud music, thumping, singing and shouting and laughter. Someone was having a party.

It was at his place. As he approached he could see people milling in the hall through the open front door. He stopped by the front gate, puzzled. This was impossible. Marion never had parties.

Then he heard her voice. "I can't leave the kids, you know that. Come back after everyone's gone. And for God's sake don't make it so obvious in front of everybody in there. We don't want it getting all over the district. Now let's get back inside before they notice we're gone. And don't drink too much," she giggled in a way Andy had never heard before as they went off towards the house. "I want you sober for later . . ."

Andy stumbled down the cliff to the jetty, and stood there bewildered and unbelieving for a long time.

Some time during the night he filled two cans and the outboard motor tank from a twelve-gallon drum of fuel in his little shed and set off out to the reef.

He reached the *South-Easter* in the late morning, tied the dory at the stern, went below and fell asleep on his bunk.

It was dark when he suddenly woke and remembered. He lay there listening to the familiar comfortable boat noises. The chuckle of water along the hull of the boat near his head and a faint slopping in the bilges — or was it the diesel-tank, or maybe it was in the water-tank. The faint whistle of the wind in the rigging and the *tack — tack — tack* of a loose something or other up on deck.

He woke again in dull dawn daylight and knew at once what he was going to do. It took him some time to find the stub of a pencil among the junk in the cabin.

The wind had blown up strongly and the sea was a heavy, swelling mass of green chop that pitched the dory in all directions as he headed for the coast again.

The *Harbinger*, heading south with a load of fish, passed the *South-Easter* anchored out at the reef and hailed her. They circled her a couple of times while the skipper examined her through his binoculars.

"Looks a bit queer," he said to his mate. "Doesn't seem to be anyone on board. We'd better investigate."

He nosed the *Harbinger* up to the *South-Easter's* stern and his mate jumped aboard with a mooring-line and made it fast to a stanchion. There was a choking stink of rotten fish from the freezer and a foot of oily water slopped heavily in he bilges and across the floorboards in the cabin.

Everything else seemed to be in order, except for the broken gearbox lying on an oily sack in the wheelhouse.

"Looks like they're in a bit of strife with their gearbox," observed the skipper. "They've probably been picked up and gone in for a new box. We'll pump out the bilge for them and get on our way."

"Funny they should leave the fish to go rotten," said the mate.

"Must have been held up somewhere," said the skipper. "Hang on — there might be a message here."

He moved a tin of treacle from an ordinary writing pad on the cabin table and flicked it open. "Hello, they've kept a bit of a log, by the look of it."

He turned the pages to the last entry. "Looks as though they've been gone over a week. This is dated — hell!"

He glanced quickly through the scrawly writing on the page and then turned back to the beginning.

"Get an earful of this," he said to his mate. They read:

Thursday 18th:

Left harbour late and anchored at Little Island. Gearbox holding out and doesn't seem to be getting any worse. No fishing.

Friday 19th:

Trailed out to reef and fished about eight miles north. Got a few fish but the gearbox broke up in the afternoon. Will have to wait for help.

Saturday 20th:

No sign of any boats. Took out gearbox to have a look at it. Planetary gears chewed out and gone through casing. No hope of fixing it. Feeling a bit off-colour.

Sunday 21st:

Couldn't sleep for pains in the guts but feeling a bit better in the morning. No boats.

Monday 22nd:

Bad pains in the stomach all night and doubled up with cramp or something. (Later.) Think I've got appendicitis. Stomach very sore and swollen. (Later.) Have to go for help. Try and make it in the dory. Can only walk on hands and feet. Weather blowing up from S. E. but can't hold out here.

The skipper closed the pad and looked at his mate.

"That's the lot," he said.

"Poor bastard, seems to have been on his own. Wonder who he is?"

"Who he *was*, most likely," said the skipper grimly. "Come on, let's get going. We'll have to report this. I'll put a call out on the radio and we'll scout round towards the coast. But if he's not in by this time I don't give him much of a chance."

They found the dory washed up among some rocks, thirty miles up the coast from where he'd landed.

And Andy Rogers had the break he'd needed. He's doing pretty well for himself too, in the logging business. Calls himself Harvey Wilson these days.

SEWING-MACHINE

It was okay before they got there, but once they were standing around looking into it things were a bit different. Tony's first thought was that the thick tow-rope he'd carried up through the bush wasn't too ridiculously long and thick after all. Tom was feeling embarrassed for his brother, John, who'd committed himself to going down first. John was feeling a bit embarrassed for himself too but not letting on.

"It's pretty dark in there."

"Should have brought a torch or something."

"Anyone got any matches?"

"Yes. I've got some. Here."

"You might have trouble lighting them."

"Wonder how deep it is."

"Let's throw something in."

They dropped a big lump of rotten timber down the old mineshaft. After a long time the sound of it plunging into water came up out of the black hole — — *cheow cheowcheow*.

"It's pretty deep."

"It's full of water."

"Let's find another one," said Tom suddenly. "A smaller one."

"No," said John sharply. "I'm going down this one. Give me the rope."

"What about the water?"

"Who's scared of a bit of water? I'll go down as far as the

water and have a look around and then come up again. Give me the matches."

They made a loop in one end of the rope for John to stand in and tied the other end to a small tree near the shaft. Then he took off his gumboots and they lowered him slowly down into the hole. It was a long time before he was out of sight. They shouted quickly back and forth, in and out of the darkness.

"Are you all right?"

"I can see the moon up in the sky."

"Is there enough rope?"

"How the hell do I know?"

"There's not much left up here."

"Hold me there. I'll light a match."

Tony stopped feeding the loop of rope round the tree and held it there. Looking down they saw the faint flare as John lit a match. It only lasted for a second. Then another.

"Matches won't burn. Must be something in the air down here."

"Come up again," yelled Tom. "There might be poisonous gas down there."

"Let me down a bit further," called John, "then I'll come up."

There was only a few feet of the rope left and Tom and Tony let it all out quickly so they could pull John up again, out of this stupid hole.

"That's all the rope," Tom yelled into the hole.

John's voice sounded small and strange coming in faint echoes up the shaft. "I'll try the matches again."

This time they could see no flare at all.

"No good. I've dropped the matches now anyway."

"Come up," yelled Tom. "Come on, Tony. We'll start pulling him up. He's been down there long enough."

"Wait on," said Tony. "He's saying something."

"What's that?" called Tom down the shaft.

John's voice floated raggedly up to them with a faint trace of panic in it. "You'd better pull me up. The rope's cutting my feet."

"Quick, pull him up," said Tom. "Pull him up!"

They grabbed the rope and pulled.

"Hell, he's heavy," said Tony.

"Keep pulling."

"Listen. He's saying something."

"Keep pulling," said Tom. "Harder!"

"I can't. Let's have a spell."

"No. Keep pulling."

"It's no good. I can't hold it. Let's have a spell."

"Keep pulling or I'll bash you."

"I can't."

They'd gained only a few feet and it was obvious that they weren't going to be able to hold him.

"Tie the rope round the tree. Tie the rope round the tree. *Tie the rope round the tree!*"

John was shouting something down in the mineshaft but they couldn't hear. When Tony let go the rope to make a hitch round the tree Tom couldn't take the weight. He was dragged to the edge of the hole and the rope slipped faster and faster through his burning hands until it stopped with a jerk. Tom leaned gasping over the edge. John's voice came weakly up to him. Tony stood white by the tree.

"Tom. Tom. Get me out. I can't hold on."

"Wait on. We'll pull you up in a minute."

"No, now. I can't hold on. The rope keeps turning round all the time. My feet are hurting."

Tom could scarcely hear what he was saying. It sounded as if he was coughing or sobbing. Tom jumped to his feet and grabbed the rope again, shouting to Tony to pull. But it was no use. They got a few feet of rope in the first frantic burst of energy and then it just slipped away from them again.

"You'll have to go and get someone," said Tom to Tony. "Hurry up. Run!"

"Who shall I get?"

"Anyone," said Tom savagely. "Stop a car down on the road. Go on."

Tony ran off down the bush track. There were noises down in the mine. Tom crawled over to the edge and looked down the rope to where it disappeared.

"What's happening? What are you doing?" called John in a funny voice.

"Tony's gone for help. Just hang on for a little while. They'll be here in a minute."

"I can't. I can't hold on any longer. My feet are hurting. My hands — do something."

"Hold on. Save your breath and hold on!"

There was a silence, worse than John's unfamiliar distorted voice from the black throat of the mine. Then he called again, strangely calm now. He wasn't shouting but Tom could hear what he was saying more distinctly.

"Tom. Are you there, Tom?"

"Yes, I'm here. It won't be long now."

"Tom?"

"What?"

"Tom, I'm sorry about the bike. It wasn't your fault."

"That's nothing. Don't worry about it."

Tom felt annoyed with himself for being annoyed with John for talking such rubbish. It scared him.

"Tom, tell Mum it was me who broke the sewing-machine. Tell her, Tom."

"Ar, don't be silly." Tom was really frightened now. "Hold on. They're coming."

"Tom!"

"What?"

"Promise to tell Mum it was me who broke the sewing-machine. Tell her, Tom. Tell her it was . . ."

"Yes, yes. Hold on."

"No. I can't. My feet are hurting. My hands . . ."

"Hold on. Hold on!" shouted Tom desperately.

There was a horrible sound down in the hole. Like a broken scream that had already fallen into the rocks and slime down there. It struck Tom numb and cold.

"No. No." He grabbed the rope and shook it savagely. It hung loose and slack. John had fallen into the echoing depths of the black watery earth. Tom began to be sick into the grass in great gulping sobs. Voices sounded in the bush behind him but it didn't matter any more. John was dead.

When the rope dragged itself out of his cramped hands

John heard himself shout or scream something. And then there was a thudding splash and he was suddenly sitting in six inches of rotten leaves and water.

He began to laugh and then it turned into crying and then back to laughter. Twenty feet above him four heads against the sky began to shout questions and instructions. The loop of the rope dangled in his face.

He was going to be in for it if he couldn't bribe young Tommy not to tell on him about breaking Mum's sewing-machine!

Mrs Windyflax and the Pungapeople

On a wild and windy coastline
At a place called Rockyshore,
A strange event was taking place
In nineteen eighty-four.

A funny little lady,
Dressed in possum-skins and sacks.
Went and saw the local policeman;
Gave her name as Windyflax.

She said a bunch of people
From beyond the waterfall
Had shifted onto her place,
Pungapeople, they were called.

"I've tried to build a letterbox
To keep my letters dry,
But these people just won't let me
And I've had enough," she cried.

"Can't you make them go away, sir,
Bother someone else instead?
They bend my nails, they hide my tools,
They make me mad!" she said.

The policeman was a nice man
And he took down all the facts,
And so began his strange report
On Mrs Windyflax.

He accompanied the complainant
To see what he could do,
"I'll give these pungapeople folk
A proper talking-to!"

She led him to a murky place,
An ancient river bed,
A mighty cliff-face loomed above,
"They live round here," she said.

"Well, where are they?" said the policeman,
Looking round and up and back.
"You can just see their reflection, sir,'
Said Mrs Windyflax.

"You can see them in a mirror
Or reflected in a pool,
Otherwise a pungaperson
Is, to us, invisible."

"They stand about up to your knee,
Or just a little less,
With wrinkly skin and hairy legs
And green as watercress."

"You're kidding," said the policeman,
"Who'd believe a thing like that?
Seeing leprechauns in mirrors
On a Westland river-flat!"

It was then that Mrs Windyflax,
As ladies sometimes do,
Flew into tears and stamped her foot,
"You think it isn't true!"

"Okay then," sighed the policeman,
"Get a mirror, I'll wait here."
"There's none around," she told him,
"They all simply disappear."

Now it only goes to show you
Just how nice that policeman is —
He went all the way to their place
And came back with one of his.

"Now let's see," he said, "Where are they?"
And he turned his mirror round
In the search for pungapeople
From the cliff-top to the ground.

"By George, I thought I saw one,
Something moved just over there!
There's another — gracious heavens,
I can see them everywhere!"

"They don't like being stared at,"
Mrs Windyflax advised,
"And it makes them very angry
If you look them in the eyes."

"I can see one!" cried the policeman,
"I can see him plain as day,
He's sitting on that rock up there,
And now he's gone away.

"By Jove, they're quick and lively,
Strangest thing I ever saw!
One was standing by that tree just there
And now there's three or four!

"Help me catch one, we'll be famous!
We can put it in a sack."
"It isn't quite that simple, sir,"
Said Mrs Windyflax.

"I'll bring one in for questioning;
Establish all the facts.
I'll have to take a statement . . ."
"Just take care," warned Windyflax.

Then he saw one, saw it plainly,
Saw exactly where it went,
And he crept up on a flaxbush
To detain the miscreant.

Then he sprang, "Aha, I've got you!"
Where he knew he'd seen it go.
Then he held aloft a muddy stone,
Then he dropped it on his toe.

Now although that nice policeman
Isn't anybody's fool,
He became exasperated
And began to lose his cool.

He blundered through the bushes
Where he'd seen one just before,
Calling on it to surrender
In the handle of the law.

Expostulating angrily,
He sought to bring restraint
To suspicious individuals
In respect of a complaint.

Implementing regulation twelve,
A thorough search was made,
But somehow during all of this
His mirror got mislaid.

"Now where's my hat?" the policeman said.
"I had it on — that's queer,
And the buttons off my braces . . .
Hey, what's going on round here?"

"There's nothing in my pockets,
I've been robbed, I'll make arrests!
They've got the laces off my boots
Come back, you little pests!

"I know I had a shirt on,
My coat's gone missing too
I'll get a great big mirror
And arrest the lot of you!"

"It's no use getting angry, sir"
He thought he heard her say,
"It only makes them do it worse,
Let's leave it for today."

But the policeman was indignant
At these unprovoked attacks,
And he wasn't listening properly
To Mrs Windyflax.

"It's theft of Government property,
Obstruction of a cop.
I'll call in reinforcements
If this thieving doesn't stop!"

But he found it rather difficult
(Apart from keeping warm)
To arrest a pungaperson
When you're out of uniform.

In just his long red underpants,
Enquiries incomplete,
The policeman had to implement
An orderly retreat.

"Don't approach them in the meantime,
There'll be charges to be brought.
There'll be legal implications
When I've filled out my report!

"I've had some trouble in my time
From felons on my patch,
But those would be the slipperiest
I've ever tried to catch."

* * * * * * * * * *

Any day now that policeman
Will have finished his report
(The writing of it must be
Taking longer than he thought!)

Irregardless of the rumour
That he's given up the chase,
He intends to get a mirror
And return to close the case.

He'll lay an information
And it won't be long before
Those pesky pungapeople
Feel the vengeance of the law.

So as soon as information
Comes to hand about the case
We'll let you know what's going on
At Windyflax's place.

Meanwhile, Mrs Windyflax,
To everyone's regret,
Puts up with pungapeople
And her letters gettin' wet.

Lawful Excuse

H.M. Prison, Stortford. October, nineteen sixty-seven. They'd handed me down eighteen months this time. Breaking and entering with intent, unlawfully on premises, theft, idle and disorderly, and insufficient visible lawful means of support — funny how they can make a simple job like knocking off a factory sound like a major crime wave. Anyway, there I was, and due for the big one. Preventative Detention, the next time they lumbered me, but it was eighteen months too soon to worry about that at this stage.

For the first three weeks they put me in a four-man association-cell with two other blokes because they were rearranging the system or something. I was a bit anxious to find out what kind of blokes they'd put me in with. It makes a big difference when you're locked up with them eighteen hours a day.

Now anyone who's got a bit behind him'll tell you that there's three kinds of lag. There's the bloke who got himself mixed up with the firm's money, or tickled the peter to get himself out of a jam and got lumbered. He's usually a firstie and takes it pretty hard. He's not likely to come back for another dose.

Then there's the bloke who's been plucked on a job, tried and convicted. He takes it all pretty philosophically and just waits till he gets out so he can pull the same stunt again, without making the same mistakes next time. He usually makes a different one, or a variation on the old one.

And then there's the moaner. He's been framed. A victim of circumstance. He should never have been put in here. It's the bloody cops. His mates put it across him. His wife squealed on him and then ran away with another joker . . .

There was a young bloke and an old bloke in this cell with me, and within ten minutes I knew that this young bloke was going to be a prize example of hurt, outraged and bewildered injustice. I was a bit cheesed-off about him because I always like to lie around and think things out when I first get inside. Kind of work out where I went wrong and how to watch out for it in the future. And with this bloke pouring out his troubles it was impossible to do anything but not listen as politely as possible. The old bloke had obviously heard it all before and after we'd given ourselves a knock-down to each other he didn't show any interest in anything but a book he was reading.

Young Johnny was an Irishman. He'd been in the country three years and in jail for nearly two of them. Second time inside. Car conversion both times. And both times he'd been framed. They usually start off with something like: "What have the bastards pinned on you, mate?" They think that because they're innocent, everybody is.

"What have the bastards pinned on you, mate?" Johnny asked me as soon as I'd got settled on my bunk.

"Plucked me on a job with a load of hot stuff on me," I told him. "This is my seventh stretch," I added, just to make sure he got the message.

Well, I got the works. He'd been an apprentice jockey — one of the best in the country at the time — and one night he was walking back to the stables where he worked when one of his mates pulled up in a flash car with his girlfriend, hopped out and asked Johnny to watch the car for a minute. They'd be right back and give him a lift home. Johnny sat in the car to wait and next thing round the corner comes a prowl-car. His mate had nicked off and jacked up an alibi and Johnny got a year in boob for pinching the car.

He was done in his career as a jockey and when he came out he was going around looking for a job. He was walking along the street when his overcoat he'd got off the Discharged Prisoner's Aid people blew out and caught in the rear-vision mirror on the front of a car that was parked there. He tilted the mirror back into place and left a perfect thumbprint on it. The cops picked him up a couple of hours later. The car had been stolen and abandoned. He'd got two years this time.

Johnny rambled on about crooked lawyers and the cops beating up blokes in the cells and things like that, till old Charlie on the bottom bunk told him to put a sock in it.

Charlie was a different proposition altogether. I suppose that if it wasn't for him and me teaming up about Johnny's consistent bitching about the food, the officers and everything in general, we'd never have got to be mates. We managed to freeze him into silence whenever we'd had enough of it and it wasn't long before we got to playing cards and swapping books. Charlie wasn't exactly what you'd call a talkative bloke and it was a couple of weeks before I even found out what he was in for.

Murder. He'd done eight years and still had plenty to do. Killed a bloke with a hammer. Made quite a botch of it, according to what rumours were still floating around. The bloke had taken four days to die. There hadn't been much motive except that Charlie had it in for this bloke and worked in the same building. They'd got on to him straight away. He pleaded guilty and got life. And here he was. A good prisoner — probably get full remission.

It's hard to say exactly when two blokes become mates. Things just drift along and then, without you really noticing it, you're mates. Just like that. It just kind of happens. It's the same when two mates drift away from each other. Charlie was ten or twelve years older than me and a different kind of joker altogether. I suppose it was only the mushrooms that we really had in common.

After they gave Charlie and me a peter of our own each, we still used to manage to see a fair bit of each other. And we were sitting against the wall down in the exercise-yard one day, talking about nothing in particular when Charlie found out by accident how I'd always had a secret ambition to grow mushrooms. And it turned out that the only thing that Charlie had ever really wanted to do was grow mushrooms, just like me. But his people had had hopes for him and made him go into law instead, and he'd given the mushrooms up for lost.

Now mushrooms are a thing you either understand or you don't. I don't mean eating them — I wouldn't eat one if you paid me — but growing them is a real art. Everything has to be just right. You have to get the right spawn and set it in the right manure in the right soil in the right way at the right temperature for the right length of time. The light has to be right and the moisture has to be right. Then, if you've got all these things right and you can tell a bacterial spot of a mummy virus or a truffle before it can be seen by the naked eye, they'll grow for you, provided you've got a special feeling for mushrooms. It's a very dicey business, and here beside me was a genuine mushroom man. As rare as hen's teeth, they are. Charlie was the only one I'd run into in over nine years, ever since they deported an old Danish bloke I'd been planning to go into the mushroom business with.

So Charlie and I spent all our time discussing and arguing about the best kinds of outfit and conditions for mushroom growing. And after about a year we had nothing left to argue about. We'd thrashed out every possible angle and condition of mushrooms and finally come to more or less complete agreement. Or at least as complete as we were ever likely to get.

It was only a dream really, the best way we could think of to pass the time, but we worked out how we were going into business together, just for a kind of joke or something. And then, a month before I was due to go out, Charlie told me he was coming with me so we could get started on our mushroom factory. I thought he was joking and told him not to get too carried away with false hopes, and it was then that my partner Charlie told me the most amazing "not guilty" yarn I've ever heard.

He'd been twenty-nine at the time and working in the Law Draughting Office as a clerk. The bloke he was working under planted some petty-cash discrepancies on Charlie and, to top it off, fought tooth and nail to get another chance for Charlie to keep his job. Naturally Charlie was a bit hot on him. Charlie knew it was this bloke who stung the peter but he couldn't prove it. He let the bloke know he knew about it and the bloke said that if Charlie didn't watch himself he'd arrange to plant another lot on him, and it'd be jail for sure this time.

Losing the job didn't worry Charlie all that much, he still wanted to go into mushrooms, in spite of his family. But there was a girl working in the same building who Charlie had a crush on. He wasn't the kind of joker who gets girls very easy and this was the big one as far as he was concerned. She was quite keen on Charlie too, and they were practically engaged, but the trouble was that she cooled off him when the trouble about the petty cash cropped up.

Charlie took her along to see the bloke who done it and begged him to at least tell *her* it wasn't him who tickled the peter. But the bloke raised such a stink that Charlie got a month's notice. So Charlie had it in for this bloke good and proper.

About that time the Government was turfing out the capital punishment caper and Charlie had quite a bit to do with drawing up the new Act. And he discovered that because of someone not watching what they were doing, they repealed the old law before the new one was actually fitted into place.

For about three hours one afternoon there was absolutely no law against murder or manslaughter, and Charlie was the only one in the whole outfit who knew about it.

So he bowled into the bloke who shelfed him's office and clobbered him with a dirty big plumber's hammer he'd got from the basement. As soon as he'd done it he saw how stupid he'd been. He beat it home and waited there till the coppers came and plucked him the same day. When the bloke pegged out they tried him for murder and handed him down a ten-to-twenty. Charlie never even bothered to use his big defence — that there wasn't any law against clobbering blokes with plumber's hammers when he clobbered this bloke with a plumber's hammer. He must have been pretty upset at the time. And he'd stayed in jail ever since. Reckoned it didn't make any difference about the law. He'd murdered a bloke and deserved to pay the penalty for it. But now that he had someone to grow mushrooms with it was a different matter. He'd just about paid his penalty now anyway.

I didn't quite know whether to believe my old mate at first, but he seemed sure enough. As soon as I got out I dug up a lawyer and told him about Charlie and there not being any law against clobbering blokes with plumber's hammers at the time when my mate clobbered this bloke with a plumber's hammer. It took the lawyer a few days to check up on it. It was the dinkum oil.

They took it all very quietly and sprung Charlie without too much trouble. They didn't want it getting around about the mess they'd made of getting the laws about murder changed. Imagine what would have happened if word had leaked out at the time! I met Charlie as soon as he got out and took him back to the room in a boardinghouse I'd fixed up for us. It was a great day for Charlie.

He was a bit lost at first. Everything had changed while he was doing his ten years. He could hardly recognise the cars and the women and the shops, the roads — just about everything. It was going to take him a few months to get used to things. The only thing that hadn't changed was mushrooms. Once you're a mushroom man, you're a mushroom man for life.

Charlie had a hundred and forty dollars and I did just one small job and got another thirty-five. It wasn't much to start out on, but with a bit of careful handling it might just be made to work. We already had all our plans made, all we had to do was carry them out.

Now blokes like us can't very well bowl up to a bank manager and ask for an overdraft to get started in the mushroom-growing business. We had to be a little more subtle about it.

I found the cellar. It was just right. All concrete, about five hundred square feet of it. The basement of a place where they made ladies' dresses and hats and things. They weren't likely to need the basement. They had plenty of space to work in and for storage, and the door to the basement was boarded up with boxes and crates. I had a terrific struggle with myself for and against helping myself to about ninety bucks in a safe in the office upstairs, but eventually I left it there. We couldn't risk it.

We cleaned up one end of the basement and set up our racks. Charlie had a bit of trouble getting in and out through the transom, so I rigged up an easier and safer way through a storm-drain grating from a street that ran along the back of our premises. I got most of the materials we needed from different places around the city, but I had to be especially careful pulling jobs, now that we were going straight. I wired the basement from leads in the factory upstairs and set up heater-blowers so we could keep the temperature right for our mushrooms. Charlie bought the best white-mushroom spoors he could get and we paid for all our manure and stuff. I got the right kind of soil from one of the compost heaps at the city council nursery. We didn't need much and they never missed it.

We worked at night with torches at first, and then I rigged up a subdued lighting system from the power upstairs. There wasn't much chance of us being disturbed, no one came near the place at night, but we'd often be so absorbed in our work that before we could get out of our factory people would start arriving at the one upstairs. And we'd have to wait and work very quietly all day in the sweltering temperature we'd built up for the mushrooms.

We took to keeping food and coffee in our factory and then I ran into a couple of camp stretchers and installed them so we could sleep there. We gave up the room in the boardinghouse altogether as our mushrooms started coming up. We wanted to be right on the job in case anything went wrong.

One night I had to stop a couple of clumsy kids from knocking off the place upstairs. Scared hell out of them. We didn't want anything to upset things at this stage.

I knew a fair bit about mushrooms, but Charlie was a real master at it. He could tell you the temperature in that basement to within a couple of degrees and check a drop or rise almost before it happened. He knew how many pounds to the tray we were going to get and the day they would be cropped, before they even came up. No mushroom-virus would have wasted its time trying to get into our place with Charlie there.

And it was a terrific crop. Those mushrooms grew for Charlie as though they'd been waiting ten years for him to get out of jail. They grew so quick I was flat out trying to get them sold. And that was a bit of a problem. We could only deliver at night. I fixed us up with a few dozen cardboard boxes, but they had to be all painted over because we didn't want our name getting confused with the one which was printed on the boxes. And all this took valuable time we hadn't allowed for. Then we had hell's own job getting our boxes of mushrooms out through the storm-drain grating. I had to open up the factory upstairs in the finish and get them all out that way. You have to be very careful how you handle mushrooms.

But eventually we delivered our first crop of mushrooms, in perfect condition. We're still supplying the same clients today, and a lot more besides. We cleared four hundred and eight dollars on that first crop. It had taken us just nine weeks from the time we sprung Charlie out of Stortford prison.

We've rented the basement now and put in our own entrance. They've cleared the entrance from the factory above for when we want to get anything big in, but we don't have to use it very often. There's our own sign on the door, very small in case we get too much notice taken of us. It's hard to get out of old habits. There's more to going straight than meets the eye. We've got one corner of the factory set up for experimental purposes and Charlie thinks he's onto a way to cross white and brown spawn. If we can swing that one we'll be famous. And we've got standing orders for all the mushrooms we can supply. We could expand of course, but Charlie reckons it's better to put our time and work into quality, and that's what we're doing.

And when we've had another few months at it, we'll be properly established as solid, respectable businessmen.

Anyway, I've made the place burglar-proof.

TRAP

The telephone rang. Paul and his wife looked across at it and then at each other. She turned back to her magazine. Paul got up, put his newspaper on the chair, and went over to the phone on the sideboard.

"Hello."

"Is Mister Paul Cross there?" It was a woman's voice. Quite young by the sound of it. Blurred and indistinct as though she was speaking from a long way off. He had to concentrate to catch what she was saying.

"Speaking!" he said loudly.

"Do you know Harry Newton?" asked the faint voice.

"Should do. He works for me."

"It might pay you to ask him what he's been up to with your wife over the last few months."

"What? What did you say? Who's speaking?"

The voice laughed. "Do you want me to spell it out for you, you fool? He's been skiting all over the place about it."

"What do you mean? — Who's speaking? — Are you there? Hello . . ."

But she'd hung up.

Paul stood there stunned for a few minutes, listening to the humming in the empty telephone. Then he slammed the receiver back on to the phone as though trying to extinguish what he had heard through it. His wife was looking across at him, frowning.

"Who was that, dear?" she asked.

Still without turning, Paul got a bottle of whisky out of the sideboard cupboard and poured himself a drink. He needed time. Time to think.

"Bring me one if you're having a drink, dear," said his wife. "Plenty of ginger ale, please, and a little ice."

He made the drink and took it across to her.

"Thanks," she said. "You didn't say who that was on the telephone."

"Uh — nobody," he said. "At least, I couldn't make out who it was. They must have been drunk."

She took the drink with a slight shrug and turned back to her magazine. Paul marvelled at the way she'd carried it off all this time. Of course it was all as plain as day, now that he thought about it. A lot of things she'd said and done lately suddenly made sense. The headaches — the Housie evenings — too tired whenever he wanted to go out, and always wanting to go out when he was too tired . . .

He needed time. He couldn't think. What do you do when someone rings up and tells you your wife has been cheating on you for the last few months? Harry, eh! Wonder who that girl was? One of the popsies he's always bragging about — just like he's bragging about my wife . . .

He went to bed and lay there in the dark, the words of the anonymous caller barking around in his head . . . *Harry Newton — Ask him what he's been up to with your wife — you dumb fool . . .*

Paul pretended to be asleep when his wife came in about an hour after him and undressed very quietly, in case he woke up and wanted what she preferred to give that slouching young hypocrite who was always so anxious to please him. Already a kind of plan was beginning to take shape. They were going to pay for what they'd done to him. Nobody was going to get away with anything like that on Paul Cross. He didn't sleep at all that night.

Paul had been at work well over an hour when Harry sauntered into the workshop next morning. They got to work welding up the steel frames for a prefabricated building they were contracting for. At lunchtime Harry told him about the girl he was after. Paul was surprised at how easy he found it to laugh with him.

Harry did exactly what Paul expected him to. As soon as he started drilling the hole in the wall of the workshop Harry came over to see what he was doing.

"What's the hole for, Paul?"

"I want to put a bench in along this wall," said Paul casually. "We'll stick a water-pipe through here and let a sink into the bench to wash up in."

"Good idea," said Harry. "Do you want a hand?"

"Aw, don't think so."

Paul put the electric drill on the floor. "We'll have to cut a piece of pipe to go from the one along the side of the building and put a T-joint in. I'll just nip out and measure how far above the ground this hole is."

He took a rule and went outside. Round the side of the building he picked up one of the steel rabbit-traps they'd welded pins on to for a trapper and quickly set it.

"Poke your finger through that hole, Harry," he called. "I can't see where it is from out here."

Inside, Harry unhesitatingly poked his finger through the hole. And Paul sprung the trap on it, the serrated jaws cracking shut behind the second knuckle.

"Ow! Hell!" shouted Harry. "My bloody finger's jammed! Quick! What's going on? Quick, Paul!"

Paul went inside to where Harry was dancing delicately from one foot to the other with his finger caught through the hole in the wall. He turned his head as Paul came in.

"Paul, quick," he gasped. "My finger's jammed in something outside. Quick! Hell it's hurting."

"You don't say," said Paul, lighting a cigarette.

"What's going on? What have you done? This is no joke, Paul!"

"It sure isn't," said Paul. "It's a bit of a shame really. — It's no use trying to pull your finger out," he went on conversationally, "because somebody's ground the teeth on the trap that's on your finger down at an angle. The harder you pull the deeper they'll cut. You'll tear your finger off before you get it free."

"What are you up to?" shouted Harry. "You're mad! Let me out of here!"

Paul stalked slowly towards him, holding out a sheath-knife that shone with a newly-ground edge. Harry watched him come closer, his face white and his lips trembling. Paul went slowly closer. Harry was trying to say something but no sound came from his fluttering lips. Suddenly Paul stabbed the knife into the wall near Harry. Harry let out a hoarse groan as he flinched against the agony of the metal jaws biting into his finger on the other side of the wall.

"See that knife?"

Harry didn't answer.

Paul went on: "If you want to get free, Harry boy, you'll have to cut your finger off. That's what you're going to pay for interfering with other people's property."

"You're mad," croaked Harry. "You're mad!" His voice rose to a shriek. "Let me out of here. Let me go!"

"I'm mad all right,' said Paul. "I'm mad about you and my wife, Harry boy. That's what I'm mad about."

"You're crazy. I've never touched her in my life. You hear me? I never touched her. You're mad. Let me out of here. Let me go."

Paul began to laugh.

"You're crazy," yelled Harry. "Crazy — Help! Help! Somebody help!"

"You can shout your head off," said Paul pleasantly. "No one'll hear you in here. Now I'm going to leave your welding torch going against the end of the wall there. The place'll go up pretty quickly once it gets started, so you'd better be quick with that knife if you want to get out of it alive."

"No, Paul. No — you wouldn't burn down your own workshop. There'll be trouble. You'll get into trouble. You're making a big mistake, I tell you. Give me a chance to prove it. Paul please!"

"There'll be trouble all right," said Paul. "But more trouble for you than me. The workshop's insured. And nobody's ever going to believe your cock and bull story about me making you cut your finger off, just so you can get the compensation."

"No, Paul. No . . ."

Harry slumped against the wall. Paul lit the welding-torch and threw it into a heap of cotton waste near the opposite wall to the one Harry was against. Then he left the workshop without another word, closing the door behind him.

Harry heard his car drive away.

It was unusual for Paul to come home this early in the day. As he drove into the street he saw the car parked outside his house. It looked like that flash Ford the land-agent bloke he'd bought the house through brought back from America a few months back. Bit of a slimy bastard, Paul thought. Wife about twenty years younger than he was, and a different bit of skirt in his car every time you saw him. A proper bloody ram.

As he pulled up behind the flash Ford, Paul decided that while he was on the job of dealing with things he was going to enjoy telling this greasy Newton bastard — *Newton*!

Harry Newton . . .

Paul spun the car round and drove frantically back down the road towards the workshop, shouting incoherently as he went.

The workshop was burned to the ground, but Harry Newton escaped. After Paul left him he had managed to hook his foot through the lead on the electric drill Paul had left lying on the floor and lift it to his free hand. Then he drilled a circle of holes in the wall around his trapped hand and pulled out a hole big enough to get the trap through. He sprung his finger free and got the doors open enough to slip through before the smoke got him. Then he stood back from the blazing building among the people who were starting to gather, holding his throbbing hand in his armpit.

The workshop was beginning to collapse when Paul drove wildly back down the drive — and straight into the blazing doors of the building. The workshop fell around him in a great roaring cloud of sparks and flame. There was a brief extra burst of flame when the petrol in the tank of the car exploded.

"He was mad all right" said Harry to Paul's wife in bed a couple of nights later. "We could hear him shouting as he drove past us, just before he crashed into the workshop."

Harry's Piece of Pain

Harry Roper found a bench and rested in the sun,
Studying his fellow man at shuffle, walk and run.
And as he watched with lidded gaze the bustle and the din
All the voices died away but one that said, "Come in"

"Come in" it said. And then again, "Come in," he heard it say,
And though he waited patiently it wouldn't go away.
And then he saw the passing crowd move out across a plain
Unable to resist the voice, "Come in," it said again.

He saw a shining mountain there, a door was open wide,
He saw the people shed their cares and start to move inside.
And very soon a multitude was flowing in and past
And Harry knew that humankind was coming home at last.

Everyone who ever lived, from everywhere on earth
Was heading for that mighty door, regardless of their worth.
From every long and latitude, from every tribe they came,
And everyone who entered there was greeted by their name.

And as they passed within the door the lame were made to walk,
The blind were made to see again, the dumb were made to talk.
The guilty left their fear outside like rows of muddy boots,
And very soon the plain was strewn with faulty attributes.

The rich were made to shed the load they'd carried all their lives,
The parted were united with their husbands and their wives.
The poor were lifted from the road they'd trodden all their days;
The heedless lifted up their eyes in gratitude and praise.

Humble, worn and sick at heart, and weary of the fight,
They heard the voice that said, "Come in," and hurried to the light.
And when at last they'd all gone in and left him on the plain,
He gazed around the empty world and hung his head in shame.

He saw across an oily sea great smears of greed and gain,
And over on the other side was loss and want and pain.
All the ignorance of man was there to see, and yet
The only thing that Harry felt was sadness and regret.

And now he hadn't any choice, no time to lose or win,
He had to turn and face the voice that said once more, "Come in"
And as he moved toward the door he wept, because he'd seen
A better life he could have lived; the way it should have been.

They found old Harry sitting there, a dribble on his chin,
They put him in a wooden box and said a prayer for him.
They lowered him into the ground the place from whence he'd come.
They stood and thought, the score of life? When added up, what sum?

Twice Bitten

Clive didn't mind dogs in the least. In fact he quite liked them. Although he'd never actually owned a dog himself he always had a spare scrap or a pat for the odd ones that came sniffing hopefully round the door of his bach from time to time. Neighbours' dogs, mostly. He recognised all of them. They made the place seem kind of domestic somehow.

But this one was different. Nobody seemed to know where he came from or who he belonged to. Clive called him Sadly, because he was a sad kind of dog and it didn't seem right to call a dog as dignified as this just plain Sad. And he had to call him something in order to try and send him away.

But Sadly soon made it plain that he had no intention of being sent away. He moved on to the porch of Clive's bach, where Clive found him when he came home from work one afternoon, and stayed there. He wasn't the kind of dog you throw things at, or kick, or even growl at very convincingly.

Clive didn't take much notice of him at first and Sadly took over the bach, keeping all other dogs and cats away and accepting the scraps Clive gave him as though they were well earned. Then the dog took to following Clive around, ignoring with pointed dignity any attempts to send him away or back to the porch.

That was when Clive started making enquiries about who might own the dog, but even advertisements in the papers failed to bring so much as a rumour about Sadly's past or owner. He just stayed, and the longer he stayed the more possessive of Clive he became. He'd escort him to work and come back to collect him when he knocked off in the afternoon.

At first it was only tradesmen and salesmen and casual callers Sadly bailed up at the gate with hackling snarls and bared teeth, but he soon graduated to Clive's friends or anybody at all. Their calls naturally became even less regular than ever. Once Clive actually slapped Sadly with a heavy doormat, but Sadly took absolutely no notice of him whatever. He held his ground, bristling and growling, while Lucy Scroates tried desperately to crawl through a hydrangea bush in her best stockings. Her attitude towards Clive was noticeably cooler after that.

Sadly started walking in and out of the hut whenever the door was opened, and soon took up residence on the floor of the little kitchen. He'd become very indignant if he was ever shut inside, though, because he still considered his self-imposed duty of scaring hell out of each and every visitor to be an indispensable service.

On the advice of friends, Clive at last called on the SPCA. They didn't appear to appreciate his problem.

Was the animal homeless?

"Well, not exactly, but . . ."

Was it dangerous?

"Not really what you'd call dangerous. It hasn't actually bitten anybody, but . . ."

Was it sick, or injured?

"No, nothing like that, but all the same . . ."

"Sorry, sir, in that case we can't do anything about it. Have you tried the police?"

The police weren't very helpful either.

"Have you advertised for the owner?"

"Yes. For two days in two newspapers."

"Well, in that case, if nobody comes forward to claim the dog within three months of your advertisements you can claim it as your own property."

"But I don't want him."

"Well then, after the three months are up you can sell it to defray your expenses. It's simple."

"But can't I even give him away?"

"Oh no. You couldn't do that until you've established your ownership of him. You could be charged with stealing him if the real owner comes forward."

So Sadly, who'd been waiting outside for him, followed Clive home and moved his camp to the mat on the floor by the bed, and stayed.

And stayed, and stayed, and stayed.

He ate everything that was given him with a complacent off-handedness that cost Clive two or three dollars a day.

Whenever he planned a meal he had to allow for plenty of meaty scraps. Sadly's disapproving stare at a scrapless meal was more than Clive could stand. He took to eating out, until he was seen smuggling scraps out of a restaurant and they searched him, thinking it was their cutlery. Then he was caught slipping bones into his pocket by Lucy's mother, who took them and wrapped them up for him. They didn't really mind but the embarrassment was too much for him and he ate at home again. His coat pockets were getting smelly, too.

Whenever Clive drove out in the car, Sadly sat up in the passenger's seat like a garrulous old man being chauffeured around. This attitude began to annoy Clive and he organised a departure one morning in which he managed to slam the car door before Sadly could dive in. Sadly stood aloofly on the footpath and watched him drive away. Clive felt so ridiculous and guilty about leaving him behind that he turned round the block and drove back. There was Sadly, still standing on the footpath, as though he knew he was being returned for. He stepped into the car with a distant glance at Clive and sat staring out of the window with the air of one who is above communicating with such as Clive.

After a couple of months, Clive got to depend on Sadly for company. Lucy was only allowed out once a week (and twice on long weekends) and very few of his old acquaintances ever came to see him these days. He couldn't take what was by now known as a savage dog anywhere where there were children, or for that matter anybody at all. He'd tried tying the dog up at the gate on one occasion, but Sadly chewed through the rope and followed him into the Scroates' living-room. The collar and chain he'd bought after that had never been used, and never would be, if Sadly's attitude towards it was anything to go by.

Soon it was almost impossible for anyone to get near Clive without being menaced by Sadly, who growled and rumbled restlessly all the time they were talking. And Clive tended more and more to take Sadly's side in the differences of opinion between Sadly and his other friends.

Clive and Lucy were out in the car one Sunday, with Sadly,

who'd accepted being temporarily banished to the back seat with very ill grace, drooling sullenly over their shoulders.

"I can't stand this brute of a dog any longer!" Lucy suddenly burst out. "You'll have to get rid of him, Clive."

"He's actually a very nice dog, once you get to know him," said Clive. He was well aware of the scarcely veiled hostility that existed between his Lucy and Sadly.

"I don't want to get to know him," she said, impatiently. "I'm not putting up with it any more, and that's that."

"What's that?" evaded Clive uncomfortably. He had an idea there was an unpleasant scene coming up.

"The way you treat that — that thing. It's disgraceful! Everybody's talking about it. It'll end up biting somebody and then there'll be trouble."

"Sadly wouldn't bite anybody," said Clive defensively. "He only pretends to be savage. He wouldn't hurt a flea."

"Well I'm not seeing you any more until you get rid of it, and that's final. You can take me straight home. I'm not putting up with it another instant."

Sadly drooled moodily over the back of the seat rolling his yellow eyes between one and the other as they spoke. There was a longish silence.

"Okay then," said Clive, pulling up outside Lucy's place with a resigned drag on the handbrake. "I'll take Sadly down to the vet tomorrow and have him put to sleep. They say they don't feel a thing . . ."

"And have this car cleaned out, too," she said. "I can't afford to have my clothes cleaned every time I go out with you."

She kissed him impatiently through the car window and walked quickly away through her front gate.

Clive took the next morning off work and on the way to the Veterinary Centre with Sadly he turned off towards the local boarding kennels. He'd enquire how much it cost to keep a dog there. He couldn't have him destroyed in cold blood. If only the blasted dog would get himself run over by a truck or something. He reached guiltily over and put his hand on Sadly's rough old head, and got a brief distrustful stare in return. He could afford twenty dollars a week at the very outside, until some other arrangement could be made.

Thirty-six dollars seventy-five it cost him. As he drove away he felt as though he'd-betrayed poor old Sadly in a particularly underhanded way. He'd soon forget that, he told himself. And Sadly was really better off where he was now, with all the other dogs to play with. Though somehow the idea of Sadly playing wasn't a very convincing one. Still, there would be plenty of things for him to watch for and growl at.

The bach seemed empty without Sadly there. Clive surprised himself talking to the dog once or twice. He was still on the outer with Lucy, though she didn't ask and he didn't say what had happened to Sadly.

As the days went by it got worse rather than better. Whenever he went through the back door, Clive held it open for Sadly. Whenever he got in or out of the car he paused for Sadly. Once he even bought five dollars worth of dogs' meat on his way home from work. Every knock on the door reminded him that Sadly would have warned him that someone was coming. Whenever he talked to somebody he noticed that they weren't distracted by, if not actually backing away from, Sadly. And it just didn't seem right. He began to realise that the dog had given him a certain colourful status he'd never had before and didn't have now.

Relations with Lucy didn't improve significantly but this worried Clive no more than the absence of his dog. At the first opportunity on the weekend he drove out to the boarding kennels, feeling as though he'd been away for weeks, instead of five days.

Sadly was sitting on his own in a big pen when Clive arrived with the kennel-keeper. The keeper opened the gate and Clive went in and walked smiling towards Sadly. When he was five or six feet away, reaching out to pat the dear old head, the dog, who'd been disinterestedly watching his approach, suddenly sprang up with a lion-like snarl and snapped at his outstretched hand with several loud, wet skulps.

Clive got such a surprise that he nearly fell out of love with Lucy Scroates. He backed away, horrified, until he was stopped by the corner of the pen, with Sadly stalking stiffly after him, bare-toothed and savage. As soon as Clive stopped, the dog went into a half-crouch, as though preparing to spring at him.

Two men came running and they and the keeper prodded and shoved at Sadly through the netting with long sticks and took his attention off Clive long enough for him to escape from the pen. He was unhurt but badly shaken.

"I — I can't understand it," he said bewildered. "I've had

Sadly for months. He wouldn't do that to me!"

"He's been a bit queer ever since he's been here," said the kennel keeper, leading Clive away from the pen. "He's getting worse, I meant to tell you before — I'm the only one here who can get near him. We've had to take all the other dogs out of that pen."

Clive looked back. The two men were still securing the pen as though nothing had happened.

"Something must have gone wrong with him," said Clive. "He's not like that at all."

"Dogs sometimes go like that when they get old," explained the keeper kindly. "There's nothing much you can do about it except have them put away. Would you like me to arrange it for you?" he asked.

Clive nodded and walked toward his car.

Next morning Lucy Scroates visited Clive and talked to him for about half an hour. It was all off between them.

On Monday he turned in his precarious job as a grease-monkey at the garage. On Tuesday he quit his little bach, and on Wednesday he left for the mountains, to hide away till his broken heart mended.

He never got there; but that's another hard luck story.

Time of Day

At that time of day
when the world turns away from the sun
and the last traces of sunlight
are gone from the ridgetops,
I lead my old horse down a wild river valley
with two trout in the split sack
behind the saddle.

Around the bend I see great wires
strung swooping from pylon to pylon
across the sky.

And I wonder how come
it makes that moment of sadness
waft through my thoughts,
and puts that mournful note
in the cry of the putangitangi.

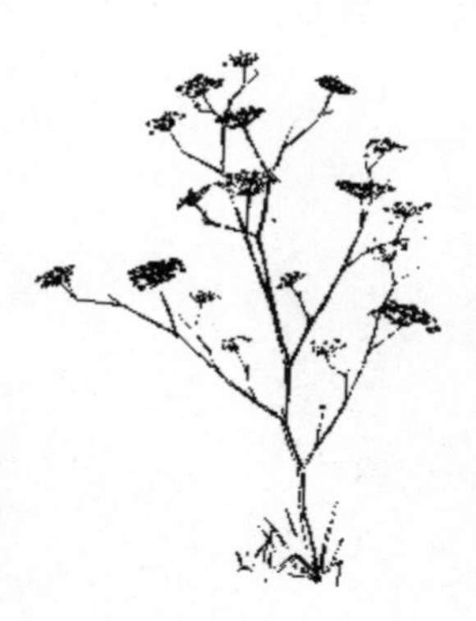

HOW DID I GET HERE?

TRAVELING THE ROAD TO RESILIENCE

My Journey and Lessons Learned From
Health Crises, Emigration and Business

ANDREW FITZGERALD

Printed in the United States of America.
Published by Fitzy's Branded Books

ISBN: 979-8-9875082-5-1 (eBook)
ISBN: 979-8-9875082-2-0 (Paperback)

Contact: fitzgerald_andrew@yahoo.com
www.AndrewFitzgeraldAuthor.com
Copy editor: Andrea Susan Glass, www.WritersWay.com
Cover design: www.100Covers.com
Formatting: www.formattedbooks.com
Images: www.Shutterstock.com

DEDICATION

My book is dedicated to

Those who have failed but gotten back up and succeeded.

Those who choose to stand tall rather than cower.

Those who have chased their dreams or have yet to.

Those who suffered a loss but stayed resilient,
confident, and trusted themselves.

To my son, Alfie; when you came into the world my
world changed for the better. You are an inspiration to
me. You are my hero, and the world is your oyster.

To my wife, Jane: you are my champion.

To my four other children who I never got to meet, hold, and
care for. You are never forgotten, and I know you are at peace.

And to myself and the resilience that allowed me to get here.

CONTENTS

PART 3: MY CORPORATE LIFE

PART 4: PREGNANCIES & MISCARRIAGES

INTRODUCTION

Hi, I'm Andrew Fitzgerald, and I died twice. Everyone dies, although not everyone truly lives. I flatlined twice and was brought back to life to follow my ambitions and embark on a journey of resilience. Yes, I died twice, yet I've lived a full life.

How Did I Get Here? Traveling the Road to Resilience follows my life from growing up in Ireland to immigrating to the United States and the trials and triumphs along the way—the failures and successes in business, the fear and excitement of a new country, the grief and loss through miscarriage, and the eventual birth of my son. I've divided this book into four parts which focus on the most significant events in my life, and as such are not necessarily in chronological order. However, as the story unfolds, you'll notice how it all fits together.

The book you're about to read recounts how I overcame fears and obstacles to realize my goals. I believe anyone who has tried, failed, and tried again and succeeded or has overcome loss and sorrow, will gain useful insights. My story shows how you can prevail over adversity using key lessons—both personal and professional—that have both helped and hindered me, yet ultimately served me well.

If you've had tough times, you'll get value out of this book. If you're in the middle of some challenge, you'll get insights. If you feel stuck or need to make a change, this book will inspire you.

I've heard that the journey is as important as the destination. I used to think the destination was all that mattered, yet it wasn't until I realized that the journey—filled with highs and lows—is often more fulfilling than the destination. So travel with me to learn how I overcame the various obstacles in my life, how I thrived, and how I traveled the road to resilience.

I've achieved so much in my corporate life and my sporting life, and yes, the journey has been more important than the destination. If you have dreams, yet have had to overcome obstacles, or you're looking for a view into the workings of the corporate world, this book will accompany you as *your* story unfolds.

My aim is for you to be inspired and encouraged, so you'll be better prepared for what life has in store for you. Ultimately, this book will help you learn to trust yourself and develop the key trait of resilience. Resilience is for everyone. ***Are you ready?***

PART I

HEALTH CRISES

"Time and health are two precious assets that we don't recognize and appreciate until they have been depleted."

—Denis Waitley, Author and Speaker

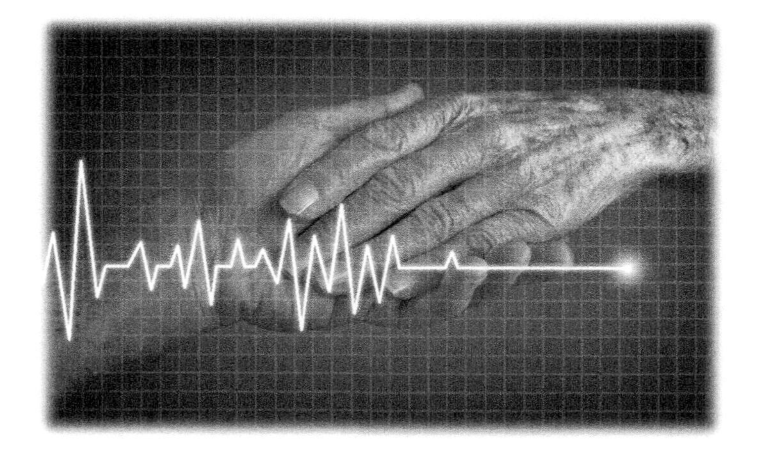

CHAPTER ONE

Last Rites

"My mission in life is not merely to survive,
but to thrive; and to do so with some passion,
some compassion, some humor and some style."

–Maya Angelou, Poet

The odors of antiseptic and disinfectant linger in the air, that omnipresent smell that can only be associated with hospitals. As I lie there on a hospital trolley staring at the ceiling, I ask myself, *"How did I get here?"*

The orderly pushing me swerves the trolley as we make our way down the corridor. The bright fluorescent lights flash in and out of my eyesight like the on/off of a light switch. A doctor and nurse are with me, and I can feel someone holding my hand but can't make out who it is. The trolley stops as we wait for the lift to open. I can't really process what's about to happen.

The hospital is eerily quiet this evening. The lift pings and the doors open. Once inside, I catch sight of the person holding my hand. I recognize the black and white clothing. It's an elderly nun with rosary beads in one hand and my hand in her other, held tightly. She flashes an approving smile at me and says, "Everything will be okay." The lift doors close and we begin to ascend. The next words she utters will forever stay with me:

"Through this holy anointing, may the Lord in his love and mercy help you with the grace of the Holy Spirit. May the Lord who frees you from sin save you and raise you up."

Wow! Am I being given last rites? I can't believe this. I'm only nineteen years old and have so much more life to live. I don't want to die, please God, don't let me die.

The trolley moves out of the lift, and now there are six or maybe seven people around me. I'm here because my heart was beating way too rapidly. The doctor explains that to bring my heartbeat down, he's going to stop my heart and start it again. He says this is the *only* course of action, the *right* course of action.

I trust the medical advice, yet I don't comprehend the severity of it. I hear what he's saying and try to hold onto positive thoughts. However, at nineteen my overriding emotions are fear, worry, and confusion. I have a difficult time processing what's about to happen.

My eyes are moving rapidly around the room, my senses amplified to the various sounds and conversations. The anesthesiologist places a mask on my face to administer gas to put me to sleep. As I close my eyes and take a deep breath, I lose consciousness. The medical team administers the defibrillation that sends an electric pulse to my heart to shock it into not beating.

I have now flatlined. I am dead. The next electric pulse is to shock my heart into restarting, which thankfully it does. I am alive again. I wake up in the intensive care unit and cry tears of happiness that I survived. *What just happened?*

CHAPTER TWO

WPW Syndrome (Wolff-Parkinson-Whyte Syndrome)

"To ensure good health: eat lightly, breathe deeply, live moderately, cultivate cheerfulness, and maintain an interest in life."

—William Londen, British Publisher

Three hours earlier, I had been playing golf with my friend Brian when it happened again: the light headiness, the labored breathing, the shortness of breath, and the unmistakable accelerated heartbeat like a pounding in my chest—similar symptoms I had experienced the previous year. Eight months before while on a soccer field, I felt a similar sensation, that rapid heartbeat. This second time though, it felt different.

I quickly left the golf course after playing only two holes and went to the locker room to change my shoes. A club member started to speak to me; however, I was so out of it, I was barely able to reply. He must have thought I'd had a few beers, starting the weekend early.

Brian had to drive me to the hospital as I knew something was wrong, so wrong. He kept asking, "Andrew, are you doing okay? Hang in there." He drove as fast as he could through the suburbs and into city traffic. I was checked into the A&E (Accident & Emergency) at the Mercy Hospital and explained that I had been there before, with the same symptoms.

Although usually a waiting game that lasts for hours, this time I was immediately taken into a room and hooked up to the heart monitor. And there it was for all to see: my heart beating at two hundred fifteen beats per minute (bpm). The normal heart range is sixty to one hundred bpm, and during exercise one hundred thirty to one hundred fifty (www.healthline.com). At two hundred fifteen it felt like my heart wanted to jump out of my chest. The doctors and nurses first wanted to make sure it wasn't a panic attack—even though this was the second occurrence and the previous time that wasn't the case.

After some time, it became clear it was not a panic attack—even though I felt pretty panicked—as my rate remained at two hundred fifteen. The doctor said they were waiting for a drug to be delivered from the Regional Hospital (now Cork University Hospital) that would assist in lowering my heart rate. However, they found out it would take too long to get there—even though it was only ten minutes away—so that was no longer an option. Therefore, another course of action had to be taken.

My parents were out doing grocery shopping as they did every Thursday night, and back in 1997, a mobile phone was like gold dust. Eventually, one of the golf club members was able to contact them and let them know where I was, which led to a frantic scramble to get out of the grocery store, into their car, and once again hope their youngest child wouldn't die.

At the time of this second occurrence of experiencing a rapid heartbeat as well as the other symptoms, I eventually received a diagnosis known as Wolff-Parkinson-Whyte (WPW) Syndrome. In WPW, an extra electrical pathway between the heart's upper and lower chambers causes a rapid heartbeat. The condition, which is present at birth, is rare and estimated to affect between one and three people per thousand. It's more common in men than women (source: bhf.og.uk). It's also one of the six contributing conditions for Sudden Arrhythmia Death Syndrome (SADS) according to the American Heart Association. But this wasn't the first time I experienced this phenomenon.

CHAPTER THREE

Flatline Take 1

"He who has health, has hope;
and he who has hope, has everything."

–Thomas Carlyle, Scottish Author

Eight months before the previous situation, I had been playing a great game of soccer having scored two goals. When I came off the field, I noticed my heart rate was elevated. I later found out it was beating at two hundred fifty bpm, and for about seven or eight hours it didn't slow down. I told my mum and dad, and they suggested we go to our family doctor. In Ireland, you have a family doctor and a family dentist who know everything about everyone in the family.

Our doctor said my rapid heartbeat was most likely from a combination of playing physically aggressive soccer and a busy weekend with of a couple of nights out. I went to bed that night but didn't feel good when I woke up. Deciding I'd better go to the emergency room, my folks took me there. After being examined, the doctor said there was no way to slow my heart down.

They'd have to stop my heart with paddles and then restart it. OMG! Really? I felt so scared, confused, and not sure what was about to happen. I really had no choice but to put my faith in the medical decision.

My parents were having a tough time with this as well. My mum was a survivor of stomach cancer, and I remember thinking what it would be like to lose her. Now suddenly, Mum was thinking the same thing about her youngest child.

As they began the procedure, I could only wonder, "Will I wake up from this?" I did my best to focus on the positive: I will be brought back to life. My heartbeat will normalize.

Thankfully I woke up, and my heartbeat was back to normal. The next course of action was to go on a medication, which I did.

CHAPTER FOUR

Flatline Take 2

"There is one consolation in being sick; and that is the possibility that you may recover to a better state than you were ever in before."

—Henry David Thoreau, Author and Philosopher

When it happened again on the golf course the following year, I didn't think the cause was strenuous exercise, as golf wasn't very strenuous at all. I was on the second hole playing with my friend, Brian. I had just hit a golf shot across my chest, and my heart started pounding. I felt lightheaded and a bit dizzy. It was hard to breathe. I told Brian I should probably go to the hospital.

Brian drove me to the hospital, to the same ER as eight months before. The doctors and nurses remembered me. They were probably thinking, "Oh, here you are again but this time in golf clothing." Again, they decided to stop my heart and start it again.

A nun with rosary beads was holding my hand and giving me the last rites. I don't think I had those the first time I was in this situation. But this time, I was even more frightened, confused, and totally on my own. My parents weren't there, although they were on their way. Of course, you can't get anywhere fast when you need to get anywhere fast. The next thing I recall was waking up the following day in the intensive care unit.

As I realized what had happened, I was incredibly thankful to wake up and to be alive. I was still here on the planet. I lay there and reflected how this was a serious moment in my life. At the time I didn't know, but it would eventually influence everything to come.

Life continued as normal, but it was all still confusing to me. Eventually, I received the diagnosis that I had an extra pathway in my heart that was there from birth and had to be ablated. Thus, I had to have a serious operation where they closed the extra heart valve.

The doctor in the Mater Hospital in Dublin explained that he'd be inserting some thin hollow tubes into a blood vessel in my groin and then threading them up to my heart to gain access to it. He'd repeat the same process down through the left side of my neck which then meant he was able to scar the tissue. This would prevent my heart from conducting the abnormal electrical signals.

Since then, I haven't had to take medication, and I never had another problem. You've probably heard of instances of kids who collapsed on the soccer field or at school activities, for no apparent reason. I'm really impressed to see that local soccer, baseball, football, and golf clubs as well as schools now have a defibrillator on site in the event of an emergency, since every second counts. And there's more awareness and education about what I had and about SADS as well.

Deaths from SADS occur primarily in young males. Families where a member has died from SADS carry a gene for cardiac disease which puts them at greater risk for sudden death. My experience with this health condition demonstrated that it's possible to overcome a condition like WPW. However, it's a silent killer and can strike at any time, so the importance of cardiology visits is important, especially for young adults playing sports.

CHAPTER FIVE

Aftereffects

"What is called genius is the abundance of life and health."

—Henry David Thoreau, Author and Philosopher

I recall now that the main aftereffect of literally dying and flatlining twice was to become inwardly focused, and I became an unrecognizable version of myself. I stopped exercising. I began overeating. I drank too much alcohol. I started going to pubs and nightclubs up to four nights a week. Looking back, I can only assume I was self-medicating, trying to ignore the enormity of what had happened.

I can't pinpoint the instant I decided to shed my excess weight and lose the twenty-eight pounds I had gained, get fit, cut back on alcohol and food, and take up swimming five days a week. I'd loved swimming as a child and found that doing twenty to thirty laps in the pool gave my heart and body a good workout. The sensation of feeling my heart beat rapidly in the water was invigorating as it meant I was pushing myself beyond my cardio comfort zone and even more assuring was that my heart regulated itself quickly after exercise which positively impacted my confidence.

Your health is your wealth, as the saying goes. We're all navigating our way through life handling whatever comes up as best we can. Hopefully you'll never experience a major medical emergency like I did. However, take confidence that anything can be overcome, and medicine is always evolving as research into various illnesses is much more improved than it was in the late 1990s.

It's only now in the year 2023 as I look back at that time, that I see how I ultimately transformed my lifestyle, which shaped my future. I started to embrace opportunities, took better care of my health, and enjoyed life more. I gained enormous wisdom, which I've been motivated to share in this book.

Later you'll learn about more of my tough times relating to starting a family after surviving numerous miscarriages before our son Alfie was born in August 2019. He was diagnosed with a small heart murmur, so now we make sure to get him checked out with the cardiologist every year. Thankfully, the murmur has gone away, but naturally we'll be mindful, especially when he's older and active, when he's playing a sport. As parents, we must be aware of these kinds of issues, especially when we don't know a child might have an abnormality like I did.

For anybody who's gone through a similar experience, perhaps you weren't as lucky as I or my parents were. If someone dies from SADS, those left behind will have a lot of questions as to what happened and why. I can't even imagine what it would've felt like for my mum and dad had I died and was not brought back to life. No parents should outlive their children and have to suffer the grief it brings.

I feel I've been given a second chance at life. It's predicted that we'll reach old age, though it's not guaranteed. If we live each day like it's the last—which it could be at any age—it sounds right in theory but isn't necessarily practical as making unwise decisions and taking risks do have consequences. It would be far better to embrace life's moments and be as present as we can with the ones we hold near and dear in our lives.

My best advice from my two near-death experiences is to do what you sincerely want to do in life. Maybe it's a dream or goal you have. Get started to put the wheels in motion, even if it may take five or ten years to obtain. And even if you never complete what you're going after, at least later in life you can look back without regret. You know you acted, even if it doesn't work out, but it wouldn't be from the lack of going for it. I want to have no regrets. I want to be able to look back on my life and know that when opportunities presented themselves, I took advantage and didn't regret not doing them. Such as writing this book which has been on my bucket list for years.

To be faced with death is a strange experience, and downright scary, but to face death twice, recover, and thrive is empowering. It only highlighted to me that there was a reason I pulled through and continued to live my life. Those two instances shaped my outlook on life and continue to shape my future. Life and death are part of an ongoing journey, sometimes at an incredible pace such as when I'm wondering how I can keep up. Other times it's a slow motion of movement and interactions.

Recently, I had a lengthy conversation with someone who said, "Man, if I told you about all the stuff I've been through you wouldn't believe it." I answered, "I would believe it." We've all had life-defining experiences. Though it might not be flatlining and being brought back to life twice. We all go through life with ups and downs, some more than others. What's a big deal to someone may not be a big deal to you.

My experiences reinforced that having empathy, consideration, and an attitude of gratitude is paramount to dealing with and overcoming almost any adversity in life. Additionally, I've learned it's important to open up to other people about your thoughts and emotions and to talk about what you're going through.

I've found solace in being brave enough to talk about whatever's going on in my life. Although be sure you pick the right forum where you'll be met with compassion and concern, and you're not just being listened to but heard. My father, who also worked in sales like me, used to say, "You have two ears and one mouth, and you should use them in that order." I've found that most people listen to respond rather than listen to hear what's being said.

During my medical emergencies and my recovery period, I did the opposite. I never once spoke about my feelings or let anyone in. In my own way, I was coping with the situation. As a somewhat naïve teenager, I thought this was just temporary and the next week I'd have moved onto something else.

I think I was compartmentalizing what had happened and not giving it air or discussing it. I felt like it would resolve itself. Well, it did resolve itself after the successful ablation of the extra pathway in my heart. However, I look back now and can see how damaging not talking about my experience was.

Hindsight is 20/20; however, I could have benefited from speaking to a therapist about my death experiences. Unfortunately, and even though I received a clean bill of health, I stopped playing soccer which I truly loved—both playing and being part of the team. It's not a regret of mine, although when I look back, I'm filled with nostalgia about my ten years of playing for the local club Avondale United in Cork. I enjoyed many friendships that built up during those days when we won and lost as a team. The soccer field represented, "where it happened" the first time, so I think I was unconsciously avoiding it to prevent pushing my heart rate to its heightened level.

I did miss the team element of sports, but being involved in teams at my local golf club in Ireland was more than a good substitute for soccer. I loved being part of the group, leading by example in my play, and winning and losing as a team. We didn't lose as much as we did at soccer since we had some seriously good young golfers in our club. One of the greatest benefits of sports is the camaraderie and the values it teaches from being part of a team.

As I write about this experience, I'm enormously grateful to be alive. Think about that for a minute: do we take life for granted? Do we only stop and think about death when we hear of a local tragedy on the news or in our community? Do we truly embrace our life each moment of each day? I sure do and I hope you do too. And I'm grateful for the resilience I've employed, that has allowed me to survive and thrive throughout my astonishing life experiences.

KEY LEARNINGS

What life has taught me, and I'd love to share with you

1. **Enjoy the life you have**. Live, laugh, learn, and hug those around you. Kiss those you love and be compassionate since everyone has something going on in their lives.

2. **Get a cardiac examination.** You owe it to yourself. Get your young kids checked regularly, especially if they play sports.

3. **Talk about your challenging experiences**. I didn't talk about my death experience until much later in life, and it would have helped me process it in the right way rather than self-medicating with alcohol and food.

4. **Exercise no matter what form it takes**. Your heart needs to get the blood pumping and flowing. Also, maintain a healthy diet but enjoy your treats.

5. **Live life.** Truly live and love your life, and chase some of those dreams you've had no matter how big or small they are.

6. **Focus on the positive rather than the negative**. You always have a choice of mindset and how you respond to adversity when the inevitable surprises come up in life.

PART II

MOVE TO AMERICA

"Only in America can someone start with nothing and achieve the American Dream. That's the greatness of this country."

—Rafael Cruz, Brazilian Athlete

CHAPTER SIX

Life in Ireland

"Change is a great and horrible thing,
and people love it or hate it at the same time.
Without change, however, you just don't move."

—Marc Jacobs, Fashion Designer

I'm standing on the balcony of the Blue Sea Lodge overlooking the beaches of Pacific Beach, San Diego, and it's like looking at a scene from the TV show *Baywatch.* As I survey my new surroundings, my attention is quickly drawn to the sights and sounds: waves crashing onto the sand, misty spray from the sea, and seagulls racing to get out of the way of beachgoers setting up their chairs and blankets. Lifeguards are putting up their stations and towers, while trainees are going through their paces. Along the boardwalk people are rollerblading, skateboarding, riding bicycles, running, and doing yoga. It's an awesome setting—something you typically see in the movies: quintessential California, not something a Cork boy would ever dream of experiencing. And I ask myself, "*How did I get here*?"

Growing up in Ireland, we had idyllic family holidays (the Irish term for vacations). We went to France, Spain, and Portugal. Because the weather isn't the best and summer sunshine isn't guaranteed, we craved the sun and the beach. Fortunately, living in Ireland we could easily fly anywhere within four hours. Our holidays included Mum, Dad, my two brothers Mark and John, and my sister Laura hanging out at the beach. These trips were real treats for us all.

My parents worked hard, so they could afford for us to go on the best holidays. They made sure to save as much money as they could, so we could go on our one or two-week holiday every year. I'm sure it wasn't cheap with four kids even back in the eighties. When I was four, we went to Edinburgh, Scotland which was a beautiful city to visit. We saw a large military exhibition and visited the castle. At age five, we traveled to France on the car ferry. Since my dad was a salesman and drove all over Ireland, it was unusual that he'd want to drive us on our holiday in France. However, it didn't bother him, as the family holiday was something we all looked forward to.

We took the car ferry from Cork in the South of Ireland to Roscoff, France. And then drove several hours to the South of France. We stayed in a local villa, played golf, went to the beach, and swam in the pool. We enjoyed the French cuisine, especially the baked goods. I liked going to France better than other destinations, because I couldn't wait to go to the local bakery (boulangère) in the mornings to get fresh French bread, croissants, and various cakes. I compared them to the pastries Mum baked at home. Even though the French might have a reputation for being a little snooty, I found them very direct. Maybe that's the type of people I like best. I wouldn't say they're the most personable, but at least you know where you stand with them.

I know Mark, John, and Laura would say our various trips were the best holidays they ever had. We had lots of fun and got on with each other, even though as siblings we were different in terms of being introverts or extroverts. Like anybody, your environment is familiar to you, so when you go somewhere else it's all new and adventurous. I enjoyed the different accents of the people we met in France, Spain, and Portugal. At some level, wanting to go on adventures stuck with me, and I think my love of travel was born then.

I was the youngest in my family, with a big gap between me and the next sibling. My sister is ten years older, and my brothers are twelve and thirteen years older, so the three of them are close. I was a pleasant "surprise" for my parents.

As a kid, I found it easy to make friends, although I was somewhat of an introvert and enjoyed my own company. Yet I was extroverted when welcoming people into whatever group I was in. Or if I saw somebody who was shy, I'd get them to come over and join in. That comes from being the captain of the soccer team.

My school days were enjoyable, and I had a good set of friends. We played in the street, hung out with each other, and called to each other's houses in the evenings to meet up. We were innocent but we got up to plenty of mischief.

I was somewhat stubborn and strong headed growing up, in that I wanted to play soccer for my local team at eight years of age, and my parents thought I wouldn't enjoy the game. Or maybe they thought I'd get injured. But I was so stubborn that I once left the house alone to go to the local soccer club, meet everyone, and start playing. It was the best move I could have made, because I made friends I still have today.

And I turned into a super soccer player and absolutely loved it. I was team captain for ten years and turned down many offers to join other teams in Cork City as I was loyal to my local community. We won and lost together, and I think the values I gained by winning and losing as a team shaped much of what's come later in life.

We'd train twice a week and then have a game on the weekend. I broke my arm, got kicked in the ankles, and pulled the muscles in my neck many times. Back in the nineties medicine wasn't as advanced as it is today. If you got injured on the soccer field, you were told to run it off rather than have your injury cared for. Most of the time we'd just throw water on it as if putting water on a bump on your arm would make it magically disappear.

As team captain I also learned how to motivate people, help them along, listen to them, and bring them up from a bad performance. No one goes out to play poorly; everyone wants to give it their best. On any day, they may not perform their best, and at times I didn't perform my best; however, those days build character and tenacity.

After primary school (elementary school), I went to secondary school (high school) which was the best six years of my life. In Ireland it extends from the first to the sixth year and then you do your final exams. I absolutely loved it as I was coming into myself and out of my shell. My personality was beginning to shine through, and I was more extroverted which sometimes meant I ended up in the principal's office.

Through sports I gained confidence and made new friends. We played a variety of sports like basketball, tennis, and Gaelic football. I enjoyed the schoolwork and put myself under pressure to do my best. Mark and John went to the same secondary school, so I had an expectation to live up to as they were model students. All the teachers knew of them, so I was often the object of comparison.

I did fine at all my classes and learned enough to pass; however, I excelled in sports so that's where I became myself. I could see the real Andrew Fitzgerald emerging in terms of passion and resilience from losing and winning to finding a better way to do something to get a fair advantage. What if we trained differently? What if we ate better? What if we were more confident as a team by adding mindfulness and a positive mental attitude? What if we discussed how we would deal with certain situations before they occurred and visualize positive outcomes? What if we could win the league this year? All these were questions I'd consider and ask of my teammates.

I did have some perfectionist traits that developed big time in sport and beyond. I had to realize there's no such thing as perfect. I could only do my very best and learn from experience; then move on. I used to give myself a hard time when I was a teenager with the high standards I set for myself. When something went wrong, I'd react with, "That always happens to me." And if I said I was going to complete a task but didn't follow through, I considered myself lazy. This might have seemed unfair, but I was still a teenager, learning and growing. Looking back, I realized I could have had more compassion for myself and accepted some things that were outside of my control.

My mum and dad liked to encourage me, so my laziness wouldn't have come from them or my environment. I wasn't as focused academically, whereas my brothers and sister were. Of course, it was since I was more into athleticism and sport where my passions were.

Growing up, you'd hear "my son the banker" or "my daughter the teacher"; that was generally everybody not just my mother and father who would say that. I placed pressure on myself to live up to others' expectations, whereas now I realize it was just parents being proud of their children. There seemed to be an expectation to do and be something bigger and better. I didn't relate to my father much when we discussed various topics or shared opinions. Like any kid or teenager, I thought I had all the answers. Though I did admire my parents for their work ethic and drive. Mum is very caring and loving, a wonderful person who survived stomach cancer in 1986 when people didn't often survive cancer treatments. John had testicular cancer and survived it. Mark had serious asthma as a kid and nearly died, so resilience runs through the family.

We can be big gossipers in Ireland, and I think everybody was self-conscious. I know I was. Certainly, the kids in my age group wondered what everybody was up to. And being liked was important. You'd hear different gossip about people, and everybody spoke about everybody's business. I found I couldn't trust anyone with any sort of openness. I was more concerned about what other people thought of me.

As a teenager, we'd go to the pub, and if you chose not to go, you'd wonder what you were missing out on. Long before this millennial FOMO (fear of missing out) was around and long before social media and cell phones, you'd feel excluded. I saw what it did to some of my friends. They would feel depressed, like they were excluded and not part of the gang, which resulted in resentment.

After completing secondary school (high school), I studied marketing in college and loved economics, accounting, and marketing of goods and services. At that time, I was playing a lot of golf which I had started playing when I was eight years old and when I was still playing soccer. I played golf as a member of the local Monkstown Golf Club, a fantastic family club. It's one of best courses in Cork, well maintained and welcoming to junior golfers who then progress through the ranks into full membership like I did. I spent many wonderful days and nights in the clubhouse celebrating with some super people like Dick, Maurice, and Dave.

My father introduced me to the game. We'd hit balls in all types of weather at the practice range which was just an open field. My dad would stand at the top, and I'd stand at the bottom and hit some shots to him, and he'd hit them back to me. Those were some beautiful moments of being together. We'd then go to the clubhouse for a glass of Coke or some ice cream. Even though it was an individual sport, and I was used to the team element of soccer, I absolutely loved golf.

I'd play regularly with a super bunch of friends, namely JP, Steve, Richie, Gary, Johnny, Roy, Brian, Ronan, and Timmy. We played on different teams together, and I won numerous tournaments. I represented my club at the highest levels, and I enjoy my All-Ireland gold medal, silver medal, and two bronze medals. In my family, Mark played golf, while John and Laura didn't. Dad and Mark were enthusiastic about the game, so they weren't too happy when the youngest in the family started to beat them.

More than merely going to the course and playing golf, I enjoyed being outdoors and appreciating the scenery. The best part of golf was playing first thing in the morning and seeing the dew and footprints on the grass as we headed off. I saw it as an adventure, imagining what the day ahead held for us. What if today is my big day? What if I have a hole in one? What if I shoot my best score ever?

These are thoughts I still think about every time I play. Since golf is played over five hours, that's a long time to be concentrating. The game will never be mastered, but that's part of the challenge, as is the enjoyment of doing your best to beat your previous score. That's all you can ever do.

At some point when soccer became problematic with injuries, and I was excelling more at golf, I decided to give up soccer. I was nineteen when I had the health scare I describe in Part I. I think that probably stuck with me, because soccer was such a physically exerting exercise that my heart would naturally race. Psychologically, I might have believed something could go wrong again. Golf was less stressful on my heart, so I gave up soccer at nineteen just before heading off to college. I knew this was the right decision as the pull and allure of golf was too great to be ignored.

After leaving college with my qualifications, I continued working in the local golf pro shop where I started working at age eighteen. I was there six days a week and played golf in the evening. Then my golf buddies and I would go out for a few pints of beer. It was a simple life, and I felt the need for some room to "breathe" after all I'd been through. Even in that early stage of recovery from my surgery, I was starting to do what I felt was right for me and not necessarily what I thought "I should be doing" hoping to fit in with the standard narrative: leave secondary school, study hard in college, and enter the work world. I felt I had plenty of time for the serious work world and that it was time for play first.

Those formative years were preparing me for something else, because even at a young age I was curious and searching. It wasn't that I was searching for or seeking material wealth; it was just a sensation wondering if this was the best life for me or was there something better.

CHAPTER SEVEN

Holidays to the States

"Every life is a journey, regardless of whether you stay in one place, live like a global nomad, or end up being something in between."

—Ranjani Rao, Author and Scientist

As time went by and I was busy building my corporate career (which you'll read about in Part III), my ambition to travel was ignited. The United States was the dream holiday for me and my wife, Jane—individually—as kids growing up. I started dating Jane back in early 2001; however, we had known each other through mutual friends for some time before that, and she grew up about thirty minutes from where I lived. Now, it might be a little stereotypical of being Irish that we'd first meet on a night out in a pub, but Ireland is famed for its welcoming and cozy pubs, and I like to say that the "pub is the hub" of the community in Ireland. We had an amazing connection from the get-go. I felt comfortable around her and fell in love early on. Jane is a strong woman who knows her own mind, is incredibly loyal, and is one of most tenacious and resilient people I've ever met and gotten to know.

We first went to the US as a couple in 2005 and spent two terrific weeks in Florida, in particular Orlando and then the stunning beach community of St. Pete's Beach. America lived up to what we imagined: bright lights, hustle and bustle, large portions of food of many cultures, and wonderful people who were engaging, open, and friendly with a "can-do" attitude. Living in another country instead of being on holiday are totally different as we'd find out later in our lives. We had rose-tinted spectacles on when we came home from our trips. Yet I loved each one so much that I wanted to go again and again, as often as we could.

Next up was a holiday to Boston in 2006. In addition to staying in the city, we spent time on Cape Cod. We absolutely loved America but specifically Boston, because it was especially Irish in terms of downtown and how many people had immigrated to the East Coast. We enjoyed Cape Cod at the end of September when the weather was changing and coming into fall. We spent time in Hyannis, a village on the Cape Cod peninsula and enjoyed the laid-back vibe and vibrant atmosphere—laid back during the day, vibrant at night. And we loved touring around my namesake's museum: John Fitzgerald Kennedy.

Jane and I were married in October 2007, and for our honeymoon we went to Cancun, Las Vegas, and New York. That was a fantastic trip. Cancun was excellent for that resort feeling we needed after getting married and going through a lot of preparation. Then Vegas was amazing; it was around Halloween, and the Strip was packed with people in every type of costume imaginable, some that were barely there. We loved the lively energy. Up next was New York which was quite different in terms of sightseeing with its history and culture.

We met Tom Cruise and Katie Holmes who were attending an event across from our hotel, and they were kind about posing for photographs with us. I don't think either Jane or I had a decent cell phone with a camera, so we used one of the old traditional cameras where you had to get the film developed before you'd see the pictures.

While the sights, sounds, and smells were so different from what we were used to, the weather was most welcoming. On most of our trips to the US, we experienced sunny weather compared to Ireland which generally has a rainy season year 'round and has been known to have four seasons in one day. I do sometimes miss the change of seasons now that I'm in California, because I think it's good mentally to have that change. However, it is nice to be able to plan a barbecue any time of year—for the most part.

We learned much about America and the people from the places we stayed or in a bar where we got to chatting with people, which was much easier in the US. In Ireland people are in groups when they go out for the night whether to a bar or restaurant and generally stick together in their own "clique". It may appear that they're not sociable or inviting others into the group. However, once Irish people get to know you, their sociability really shines. Here in America, I found the opposite. Americans are especially inviting and will tell you everything about themselves as soon as they meet you.

Anytime we were on holiday in the US, we found friendly people everywhere we went. It could have been because Americans generally like Irish people. They see us as pleasant, approachable, and sociable. Ireland and America have been intrinsically linked since so many people immigrated to the East Coast and set up lives in the likes of Boston, New York, and Philadelphia and took jobs as firefighters, builders, and policemen.

In 2010, we traveled to San Francisco and did as much sightseeing as we could fit in. We biked the Golden Gate bridge from Fisherman's Wharf and cycled down to the delightful town of Sausalito and the best lobster rolls I've ever had. We took the ferry over to Alcatraz, and as we boarded for the twenty-five-minute journey, the fog rolled in and created an eerie atmosphere which was both fitting and ominous for our final destination. I was awed by the "rock" as it's known and wondered how life must have been for the inmates.

As part of the same trip, we flew to San Diego for two weeks. We fell in love with this Southern California city straight away. It was magical with the beaches, the range of foods, the cultural diversity, the cold beer, the laid-back scene, the liveliness of the people, and most importantly, the all-year-round sunshine. Also, we were overwhelmed with all the activity in areas like downtown San Diego, the Gaslamp Quarter, and Coronado Island, as well as the attractions such as the zoo, SeaWorld, and Legoland, which even though it's mostly for kids was still quite unique and special.

And of course, I couldn't get enough of seeing all the outstanding golf courses where I could play golf year 'round—if I lived here. I'm so grateful now that I do live here, and I can do that. Believe me, I never take it for granted. When we came back from that holiday, we thought about how we could make a permanent legal move to America and change our lives by taking a leap of faith.

I had this view of America—which I still have—as a country where you can "be anything" and "do anything". I believe that's because in America people don't pigeonhole you, whereas in my experience in Ireland the culture is different. For example, if you work in a certain industry, in the Irish culture most folks stay with the one career their entire work life.

We made at least five trips to the States before we decided to move there. My mum and dad blamed themselves for our decision, because when they traveled to San Francisco in 2002, they brought back a California license plate with my name on it. It was on my bedroom door until I was thirty—foretelling the future?

CHAPTER EIGHT

The Lottery

"The American dream belongs to all of us."

—Kamala Harris, Vice President

After returning to Ireland from our San Diego trip in 2010, Jane and I started talking about the possibility of moving to America. What would we need to do? Could we make that leap? I wanted to do something different with my life and felt like I needed more space. Many times, I could have moved to Dublin, the capital of Ireland, with corporate jobs. Yet I didn't have the confidence because I had an attachment to Cork. In my mind, though, I knew it would be better for me to make some kind of move. I don't regret not going to Dublin, because it wasn't the right decision. I turned down a couple of jobs that would have gotten me to another level.

See, Ireland was different back then. It was a four-hour drive from Cork to Dublin; today it's two and a half hours with the upgraded road networks. Cork was seen as the big rival to Dublin, so I felt I was betraying my home city by moving to Dublin for work. Yet that's where the bigger opportunities were. Still, America is further than four hours and a bigger jump than going to Dublin.

But how would we get a visa to work legally in the US as the country has a strict immigration policy? The best option for us was to enter the Diversity Visa lottery program also known as the "Green Card Lottery". Each year America gives out fifty-five thousand permanent resident cards good for ten years, after which it must be renewed for another ten years. Approximately twelve million people apply from all over the world which makes it a 0.5 percent chance of being picked—a slim chance but still a chance. The only countries excluded are ones that have turned up too often in the lottery results. For example, the United Kingdom was excluded for a year, because the lottery random selection had taken fifty-five thousand residents from the United Kingdom over the previous five years. They like to have diversity, so the UK was excluded for a year.

The lottery doesn't cost any money to enter; however, there are a few fees along the way and a few requirements. Naturally you can't have a criminal history and you need to be educated with a college degree. The application process was straightforward, so we decided to go for it. We entered in 2010 for a 2012 entry, because it takes two years for the selection and application process. After two years, you log onto your account to find out if you've been picked. If you're selected you go to the next stage, which is being interviewed at the embassy and having a medical assessment to make sure you have all your inoculations and you're not carrying any diseases. Then at the end of the interview in the embassy, you'll either gain entry or not depending on how you answer the questions and how your background checks out. After all that's approved, you're given six months to get to America. If you don't go within the six months, your green card is rescinded.

In the meantime, we continued with our lives and started to save for the potential move. Each week we made a deposit into our savings account with the narrative "America" attached to it. Little did I know that action would be critical in the process when we showed our bank statements at the American Embassy, since it demonstrated how serious we were about pursuing the move.

The draw was slated to take place on March 20, 2012, and we approached the day with a significant degree of nervous tension. Will we be picked? Are we really going to do this? This could be a once-in-a-lifetime opportunity. Since we were both in the draw, if only one was picked the other could go as well. On the date of the draw, I logged into the website and entered my unique identifier number. Damn! I wasn't picked. Then Jane took the seat and entered her number. And there it was plain as day in front of us on the screen: she had also not been picked. A wave of disappointment came over us, that feeling of misery and upset. It hurt so much, and our reaction reinforced that it really did matter to us. How frustrating after building up our hopes for two years.

We went out for dinner and drinks that night at our local bar. We could barely talk. The beer and wine numbed our emotions temporarily as can often be the Irish way of dealing with feelings. The fact that we were so disappointed really hit home, because we were thinking positively about being picked and all we'd need to do to get ready for the big move.

We hadn't told any of our family or friends that we entered the lottery and were considering moving to the US. The reason was because we didn't want to worry them if we didn't get picked. If we had told them, they'd be placing too much pressure on us between our telling them and the draw, and they'd be concerned that we might be picked. They'd probably get ahead of themselves, and potentially without meaning to, could turn us off or put doubt in our minds. But they might have encouraged us and hoped we'd get picked.

A few weeks after the drawing, we were at my parents' house for lunch. My father is as predictable as sunrise and sunset and always has his lunch at 1:00 p.m. while listening to the Irish news on the radio tuned to RTE, the main news channel in Ireland. As we ate lunch, my father said something out of nowhere that had been reported on the news. At the best of times, I listen to him with only one ear, but he said something that caught my immediate and full attention. My heart raced as he said, "Terrible news about all the Irish people and the green card lottery."

My instant reaction was, "What? Say that again. What are you talking about?" Dad said that the news reported the green card lottery draw was being rescinded, because the computer spat out fifty-five thousand applicants; however, they were numbers one to fifty-five thousand in numeric order. Therefore, they'd have to have a redraw, and anyone who was picked might not be picked the next time. This was incredible news and if correct, it meant we had another chance, another shot at being picked.

Wow! Really? Sometimes my dad gets things wrong, and sometimes he gets them right. He got this one right. I drove us home as fast as I could so we could log on. Sure enough, we saw the update from the State Department that they would draw again in two weeks. We looked forward with anticipation that this time at least one of us would be picked.

For the next two weeks, we had difficulty concentrating, considering the possibility that we'd be picked. I allowed my mind to drift away to San Diego picturing us living there. Then the day came to log in once again. Holy crap! I wasn't picked but Jane was. We just stared at the screen, and for what felt like an age, we didn't say anything. Then we were screaming shouts of excitement and joy.

We decided once again not to say anything to our families as we still had a lot to do to complete the process. And we wanted to be certain we were accepted before we said anything to anyone. First, we had to track down our immunizations. My family doctor didn't have anything on a computer; it was all paper based and written down. My mum had to scramble looking for documents in the attic and was wondering why I was looking for them. I just told her I wanted to collect all my personal documents. Next, we had to see the embassy doctor in Dublin to provide our medical and vaccination records and get a full physical check-up.

Then we had to go back to Dublin to the American Embassy for our formal interview. This was the last step to becoming an American resident. We were off to the embassy in our best-looking outfits. Our interview was set for 1:00 p.m., and the level of apprehension I was feeling again reinforced how significant this process was.

Throughout my life and in my career especially, I've always been on time or ahead of time. When it comes to interviews, I like to be at least ten to fifteen minutes early, as it helps settle me. So we got to the embassy for our appointment ten minutes early, and a US Marine met us and asked what we wanted. I explained we had a visa interview at 1:00 p.m. The Marine looked at me, then looked at his watch, looked at me again and said in a booming and authoritative voice, "Well, it's ten minutes to 1:00 p.m. Go away and come back at 1:00 p.m." A slight smile raised on my face, though I quickly realized he was being serious. I guess it was my first introduction to American efficiency and directness.

We went around the corner to a coffee shop and laughed about American military efficiency. At 1:00 p.m. we passed through security and waved at the soldier. He acted as though he didn't remember us, and he wasn't going to let us know if he did. We turned off our phones and kept them off for the next several hours. Upon entering the building, I felt as though I was in an empty church. It was so quiet, and the silence was only ever punctuated by someone coughing or sneezing or the ticking of the clock on the wall. We had previously paid a fee for the medical assessment and now we paid one for the interview. Then we waited and waited until finally we were called up to a window where we were questioned about how long we knew each other, how long were we married, what we were going to do when we got to America, and how we'd support ourselves financially when we got there.

We had to supply police background checks, our educational credentials, references from work, and our bank statements. Jane worked in a bank in Ireland and kept track of the money we'd been saving each month, whether twenty or one hundred euros. We handed over our bank statements for the past two years for review. The narrative "America" we'd been attaching to each deposit reinforced to the embassy that we'd been saving for our future in America. The interviewer said, "Wow, you guys are really taking this seriously." We confirmed that we were indeed.

We spent close to four hours there that day. During some of that time everything in the embassy shut down and everybody disappeared. Looking at the clock on the wall, I remembered I had only paid for two hours of parking, so I'd need to feed the meter. I inquired if it would be okay to leave and was told to be quick. I passed the same Marine on my way out and said I'd be back as soon as I added more time to the meter. He said, "No problem, Sir." He nodded his head and watched me hurry away.

After adding enough for three more hours of parking, I walked briskly back to the embassy where once again I was asked what I wanted by the same Marine. I started to explain that I had already been inside, but quickly decided to get with the program and go through the process of saying that I was there for an interview. I cleared security once again. The Irish way of a "wink and a nod" didn't seem to apply to US Marines.

Finally, we were called back and were told, "Raise your left hand and repeat after me..." What was said was lost on me because I was in a bit of a tizzy. All I heard was, "Your visa is now approved. Welcome to America. Here's your package. Here are your documents." In addition to our diversity visa being placed in our passports, we also received a sealed immigration packet containing documents we'd have to present to US Customs and Border Protection (CBP) at our port of entry. They were in a sealed envelope which was not to be opened until we arrived on American soil. So that was it. We had our visas and now had six months to get ourselves to America.

We left the embassy absolutely thrilled but also cautious, because this was so real now, and we had so much to do before the move. We called Jane's sister, the only person who knew what was going on. She asked, "Well, are you really going to move?" And Jane said, "Yes, of course we are. Why else would we go through all this?"

We went home and started planning with lots of enthusiasm and ideas. We had to rent our house in Ireland since we didn't want to sell it. We needed packing boxes—and we needed to figure out how we were going to tell our parents and friends. We knew we weren't going off on a whim and just throwing caution to the wind. We had saved money for this and successfully obtained permanent resident cards for ten years so we could legally work.

At that time, we had good jobs, healthcare, company cars, a house—everything people think are important, and they are. It was also a time when the Celtic Tiger—a term referring to period of rapid economic growth in Ireland from around 1995 to 2007—had just burst. Therefore, the country was coming into a recession that kicked in from 2008 and lasted until 2012. Anyone would be crazy to leave a job and move away where there would be uncertainty about what we consider security.

During the boom, the country was on fire. People were drinking champagne instead of beer. I was still drinking beer because that's what I drank, but suddenly credit card companies were increasing limits without even asking. Aligned with the changes in people's social and economic lives, housing was the number one industry, and first-time mortgages were easily attained, and inflated bank loans were given out.

The company I was working for, Heineken, was amalgamating with another local company and offered some voluntary redundancies, which would give us financial breathing space and would help us with all we needed to do when we got to San Diego until we found jobs. After my conversation with HR at Heineken, I was told I'd receive a lump sum salary payment as severance pay.

America is a country where your credit rating is all important, and while we had an excellent rating from the Irish Credit Bureau, it isn't recognized in America, so we needed to use cash upfront until we could build up our rating. And now we had it.

We spent the summer getting ready, boxing up items for our storage unit, and researching America as to where to live. We searched through LinkedIn looking to see who to meet and where the jobs were. Jane had left the bank where she was working to join a mortgage broker in 2011. She'd been in the bank for fifteen years and was passed over for many promotions, so she left disappointed. She decided on the mortgage business, because it was booming even through a recession. Then everything started collapsing, and the mortgage broker laid off people including Jane.

She next went to work in sales for company called "Life's Too Good" which sells a range of hair care products. She continued to work through the summer of 2012, while I organized all we needed to do for the move. She planned to hand in her notice a couple of weeks before we were due to leave on September 24, 2012. The date is etched in my memory as it's my brother's birthday and Jane's grandmother's birthday—two significant dates.

We finally went to tell our parents during the summer, and they couldn't for the life of them figure out why we were doing it. We encountered a mix of good wishes and some head scratching. "You have good jobs and company cars. You know there's a recession and you should stay put as you both have a good set up here in Ireland." That was the Irish mentality we experienced. However, for us it was an adventure, a journey, something new to look forward to. Ireland will always be there was our thinking, and we'll meet the challenge of moving to America head on and be successful in our ambitions. We were ready to take the leap of faith and leave behind the life we knew.

After renting out our house in Cork, putting what we couldn't bring with us into storage, and saying our goodbyes, we left Cork airport on September 24, 2012, bound for San Diego in Southern California in the USA via London with much excitement, a sense of adventure, and a mix of trepidation. Armed with two suitcases, seventeen thousand dollars, and my golf clubs, of course, we set off with well wishes, prayers, and Hail Mary's from our families on our new journey.

Maybe we shouldn't have made a connecting flight, as it gave us too much time to start questioning ourselves as to whether we were doing the right thing. However, at the heart of it was that we were doing what we wanted with our lives and staying positive that it would work out. Taking a flight for a holiday or vacation had such a different feeling and experience than taking a one-way flight for a permanent move. Of course, we had some feelings of apprehension.

We landed at Lindberg Field, the main airport in San Diego, at the same time as four other international flights, which meant the immigration arrivals hall was especially busy. We spoke to a local CBP officer, and he brought us to an immigration office. We went in and he said, "These folks need processing. They won the lottery." Inside were two officers sitting on chairs watching the NFL game on TV. The Green Bay Packers were playing the Seattle Seahawks as part of Monday Night Football, and as the game was close to the end, the two officers slowly got up with one eye on us and one eye on the game.

In the final play of the tightly contested game, Seattle's rookie quarterback threw a "Hail Mary" pass into the end zone intended for his wide receiver. The wide receiver caught the ball in the air at the same time as the Packers' defender. The two game officials gave different decisions before ultimately ruling that both players had simultaneous possession resulting in a Seattle game-winning touchdown. The "inaccurate reception" pass became to be known as a "Fail Mary."

Was this a sign of things to come? Were all the prayers and Hail Mary's we'd received with our move going to turn into a Fail Mary? Was this a warning that our move wouldn't work out? We would find out.

CHAPTER NINE

The Move, Part 1

"If you're brave enough to say goodbye,
life will reward you with a new hello."

—Paulo Coehlo, Brazilian Author

After leaving the airport, we got in a taxi and headed for our hotel in an area called Pacific Beach, where we'd stay for the next two weeks as we began our adventure. We checked in and went straight to bed as it had been a long day traveling, and physically, emotionally, and mentally draining.

We didn't take long to start exploring our surroundings. San Diego County had a population of about four and a half million people at that time, and given its proximity to the Mexican border, we found Hispanic culture intertwined with American culture in terms of food, accents, and the history of the area. It was welcoming to have such a diverse culture and ethnicity, very different from Ireland.

San Diego is known for its mild year-round climate, harbor, clean beaches, parks, golf courses, and its long association with the United States Navy and Marine Corps. The San Diego/Tijuana border crossing is one of the busiest land borders in the world with more than one hundred thousand people crossing every day to go to school, work, see a doctor, or go shopping.

Later I would work with a great friend of mine Sal, who would cross the border each day to work in the beverage business and then recross back in the evening. Depending on the day in question, he could be waiting two hours or more to cross. I have a ton of respect for the commitment that Sal showed.

We had a plan and a script to follow to make that plan work: what we needed to do and how to go about it. First, we had to get our social security numbers. We made an appointment to go to the Social Security Administration office in downtown. We got strange looks from the clerks when the address where we said to mail our cards was in New York. That was the address of the only person we knew who was able to help us when we landed in America, as we'd be staying in hotels for a while. Our quick explanation, or not so quick if you're Irish, had them so confused, but they just processed the paperwork and off we went on our way. Having spent time in America, I learned to answer the question I'm asked and not volunteer any additional information.

Next up was to find somewhere to live. We stumbled on a lovely apartment complex in the coastal community of Point Loma. We toured the complex and liked the layout. A one-bedroom apartment was perfect for what we needed. The onsite swimming pool, jacuzzi, games room, gym, and BBQ area helped us make our decision. The apartment was fifteen minutes from downtown, near the beaches, and was part of a cozy village. We signed a six-month lease as our initial thinking was to give us a chance to settle in and get a feel for the city. If we decided to move somewhere else, we had flexibility. We paid the first and last month's rent in cash with a deposit upfront as well. I've often said, "America is where you have to get into debt to get credit" and this became very apparent when we moved here. While we had a top credit rating in Ireland, we had to start building our credit in the US.

Now that we had an address, the next item in our script was to visit a bank and open some accounts. As we discovered a bank down the hill from our new apartment, we decided it was as good as any to do business with. We met the bank manager who was friendly and welcomed us. She had recently moved to America from Canada so was settling into the area too. I explained that we won the lottery which allowed us to emigrate from Ireland. However, I could see she was interpreting the lottery win in money terms. She called two bank officials over to assist us. I enjoyed the fuss being made, but eventually had to explain the lottery win was a permanent resident visa. We deposited what cash we had with us and applied for a credit card. However, it would only have a five-hundred-dollar initial limit, so we'd have to start using it and paying it off to build our credit.

Next door to the bank was a large grocery store where we'd do our weekly shopping and take the hilly walk back up to the apartment loaded down with bags. Of course, I always had a bag of potatoes in my backpack which made the walk even tougher. Later I'd encounter others doing the same walk.

A bunch of Irish college students had come to San Diego on a three-month work/holiday visa called a J1, and I was aware some students were staying in the same apartment complex as us. On my way home from work one day, I noticed four guys walking up the same hill, with backpacks laden down with groceries and cases of beer. At that time, I had a rental car. I pulled up to them, rolled down my window, and asked if they wanted a ride back to the apartments. Sure enough, I heard those distinctive Irish accents as they said, "Sound out." As we drove up the hill I was asked, "Are you Andrew Fitzgerald?" I was a bit taken aback and answered I was, and once again another example of what a small world we live in. The reply was, "I'm your brothers' wife's nephew from Cork!"

Aside from renting the apartment, our next big-ticket item was furniture and everything else we required to set up the apartment. I got a brainwave that we could rent some or all of it from a rental company. I'd stumbled upon that service while doing research, as I discovered most of the rentals in America were unfurnished. For nine hundred dollars a month we could rent everything, and it would be delivered. We decided to rent a couch, dining room table, king-size bed, and bathroom and kitchen essentials, right down to a scrubbing brush. This made perfect sense as it was a quick and easy option. Although as I think back, it may have demonstrated a lack of commitment to not buy everything, make the investment, and dive right into our new lives.

As we hadn't any transport, except when we rented a car for out of the area trips, we walked everywhere. We also made use of the public transportation system which wasn't the most efficient. We discovered a great deal about renting a car as a tourist rather than a resident, and it was cheaper to use my Irish passport when making a booking for a couple of weeks. We needed a car when I entered a PGA tour pre-qualifier in October in Hollister in Northern California. If I was successful in the pre-qualifier, it would enable me to play in the tournament the following week. It was an opportunity too good to pass up now that I was stateside.

My knowledge of Hollister was based on the imaginary beach town, the trendy, cool, and vibrant clothing that bears the same name as the town but has zero connection with the place that's in California. In fact, as I continually discovered in America, everything isn't as it seems. A local business owner in the town of Hollister had tried to put her city's name on a pair of jeans, but the parent company threatened to sue, claiming they had the trademark on the word Hollister. Even the local high school had been worried about the same issue with the name on their school uniforms. Welcome to Corporate America.

In my first experience driving in America—on the "wrong" side of the road—to say I was nervous was a huge understatement. I had a trusty Garmin that wouldn't steer me wrong, unless of course, you put in the address of your destination and hit "via beach cities" which meant a six-hour trip that took eight hours. The GPS brought me off the main highway and into each beach city, back onto the highway and off again, and so on. Looking back, it was the perfect way to see so much so quickly; however, I should have known something was up when after only forty minutes into the journey I was stuck in a traffic jam in Encinitas as surfers made their way across the street to surf, the equivalent of letting sheep cross in Ireland.

On arriving in Hollister, we found a small town with plenty of charm, very much a farming and ranching community. We checked into the Best Western Hotel and went out to grab some food. When hearing our accents, the lady in the pizza shop asked us where we were from. She said she'd love to visit Ireland as she had some heritage there. Then she said in a serious voice, "You guys are from Ireland. Why would you come to Hollister?" Perhaps, we're all like that; we want to be from somewhere else or hold somewhere else on a higher pedestal than our own surroundings. It seemed that every time we said we're from Ireland, the general reaction was "Ireland is no nice, why would you want to come to America?" I guess we all think the grass is greener on the other side when in fact each country has its pros and cons.

The PGA tour pre-qualifiers are held every week preceding the actual qualifier, and for two hundred dollars you can take your chance against some of the best young and not-so-young golf talent in America. For me, it was something I'd wanted to do, and during planning the move in the summer of 2012, my game improved considerably. I finished forty out of ninety players, and while I didn't play to my potential, I classed it as an overall good experience.

Our trip back to San Diego (on the freeway) was much more enjoyable as the driving was becoming more comfortable. Once back, we continued to explore downtown San Diego full of bars and restaurants, especially in the district called the Gaslamp Quarter, which was like the Temple Bar in Dublin. The nightlife had a wonderful atmosphere with its vibrancy, and as Irish folks, we weren't short of people coming up to speak to us, to learn about Ireland, and to ask us lots of questions, which we enjoyed.

We discovered a good cohort of Irish people in San Diego, especially my best friend Mark, who's originally from County Tyrone and has been in the US for over twenty years. He continues to help me with my assimilation. In addition, we found a terrific local organization called the "Irish Outreach". It receives a grant from the Irish government and plays a significant role in welcoming Irish immigrants, helping them with local information, giving advice, and connecting fellow Irish people. They also hold cultural and social events (in a pub, where else?). Some of their advice and guidance was invaluable, and we were very grateful to them.

Outside of the nightlife, San Diego has tons of other terrific areas to explore, like Old Town which to this day is close to how it used to be and is the oldest settled area in San Diego as well as the site of the first European settlement in present-day California. In addition to the history and culture, the city boasts the most visited zoo in the US, as well as Safari Park, Sea World, and Legoland. From a sporting perspective and with the ideal year-round climate, all sports are well represented. In the winter, you could be at the beach surfing in the morning and then drive two hours up into the mountains and go skiing in the afternoon. It was a lot to take in, but we loved it.

On the last day of our car rental before we were due to drop it back to the agent, we took a trip to Shelter Island where we went for a walk. Shelter Island is like a tropical island only ten minutes from downtown with lots of palm trees, boats, and boutique hotels. We passed one called Humphreys on the Bay. Outside was a sign saying, "The Script, Live Tonight". It caught our attention because we knew of an Irish band of the same name. We walked into the hotel and found the amphitheater where chairs were being set up for the gig, while the band was doing a soundcheck.

As we stood around looking like we were meant to be there, a man named Bob approached us. We introduced ourselves and said we were from Ireland and just moved to San Diego. While doing some touring we'd spotted the sign for The Script. He confirmed it was the Irish band and asked where we were from. Of course, it's a small world and even smaller when you're Irish. Turned out he lived twenty minutes from where I lived in a town called Ballygarvan County Cork. Bob was the band's tour manager, and we had a great conversation and laughed a lot. He asked if we were going to the show that night. We hadn't planned to, and it looked like it was sold out. Naturally, I was hoping he'd say, "Come along tonight. Here are two tickets." He did better than that; he gave us two VIP tickets. We were delighted, and Jane and I said to each other, "Only in America could this happen."

We dropped off the rental car, went home, had some food, and got changed. Within a couple of hours after taking a cab, we were back sipping cool beers on the VIP balcony overlooking a crowd of fifteen hundred people. Since moving to America, I've become even more proud to be Irish. And now, on a warm seventy-seven-degree evening with the palm trees gently swaying in the background, I was about to enjoy one of Ireland's newest and talented rock bands.

During the concert, I went to the bar to get drinks, and the gentleman ahead of me mentioned he worked as a Director for TaylorMade Golf Company headquartered in Carlsbad (North San Diego County). He was chatting with the bartender about another man in the VIP area. I asked him who he was referencing, and he told me it was Scotty Cameron, the number one designer of golf putters in the world. This was a real treat for me: a VIP at The Script concert and less than twenty feet from me was Scotty Cameron.

Towards the end of the concert, I introduced myself and Jane to Scotty and told him about our move and my recent round in Hollister. Jane and his wife got on straight away, and we had a good time talking about anything and everything. I exchanged phone numbers with him, and he mentioned we'd play golf together some day.

Bob had invited us backstage to meet the band and have some drinks. We met Danny and the rest of the band members and had beers with them. What a start to living in America. Everything was going according to the "Script".

As we had completed all the paperwork in the San Diego airport, we were now officially permanent residents. We found work quickly with high-paying jobs and set about our "new life". Within six weeks after arriving, Jane found a job working with JP Morgan Chase going back into the finance world in the bank scene where she was qualified. I got a job working with a local beer distributor, the largest in San Diego. We bought a car, but since we only had the one car between us, Jane would walk down the hill from our apartment and get the bus to Old Town transit center. Then she'd get on the trolley and get off and walk about ten minutes to the bank in downtown San Diego.

That was a new experience for her, as she lost some independence by not having her own car. But we knew how costly it was to park a car downtown for a whole day. Her job was a more junior role than she was used to even though she was the most qualified person at the bank. And it wasn't like it was back home, as we were comparing everything to Ireland. There was no, "Oh hi, Mrs. Fitzgerald. Thank you for coming in today. How can we help you with your accounts?" What she had was more of a sales job, trying to sell credit cards, home insurance, or a mortgage to bank patrons.

Additionally, there was no "craic"—the word for fun in Ireland—among the staff or customers. It was very stuffy. Everybody got a different lunch break, so no one ever had lunch together, and it was never longer than thirty minutes so you couldn't go downtown, to a restaurant, or get a change of scene. I think Jane found it tough, and at times she'd cry at work. Her manager would ask her if she was doing okay. Jane would put on a brave face and say, "Just missing home," but I think it was really about how she felt starting at the bottom rung.

I suppose we tended to lean back towards Ireland at times of difficulties. My job was an outside sales job, and I didn't know where I was going most of the time, so I used the GPS. That was difficult for me, because in Ireland I could go anywhere on autopilot without even realizing I was driving. Here in 2012, the GPS was the old Garmin that you attached to the windshield. It was off you go and do your best, yet I didn't adapt to it very well. I didn't adapt well at work either, so after three months I quit the job. I didn't feel like I was learning anything new and was impatient to be doing more.

After traveling to Hollister and playing in the PGA tour qualifier where I did okay, I thought, well, I'm here in America, I'm a good golfer and maybe this won't work out and we'll end up back in Ireland. Therefore, I knew I'd regret not going to the PGA tour school. That's where they give out forty tour cards to play the Canadian PGA Tour out of three hundred and twelve people over four days. It's very competitive. You're playing against the elite golfers of America and all over the world. You must qualify to get into it, you must be a certain standing in the game, and you also have to pay six thousand dollars. That's pretty much it. Well, that's quite a lot, actually.

The tour school was in April of 2013. Jane was okay with me leaving my job and getting ready for tour school by practicing, getting fit, and running the household. Jane could concentrate on her job and take the car to work. I set about playing every day and found comfort in knowing it was the right decision for me to pursue this even though the odds were against my getting in. I knew if it didn't work out for me, I could get another sales job.

April came, and out of the blue, Jane quit her job too. She could now come to the tour school with me. When she quit, her manager asked, "What are you doing? Why don't you just take a week's vacation?" And Jane said, "No. We're going on tour." Maybe I'm too good a salesman that I'd sold the idea to Jane that it was going to work out perfectly. I really hadn't intended to do that. I was focused one hundred percent on getting fitter and better, so I'd make the tour.

Okay, let's do this tour school, we decided. It will work out. We'd be traveling throughout Canada where I'd play golf if I was qualified. And if it doesn't feel like it's working out in America, who knows? We'd talked about setting up social networks, but it hadn't happened. We thought we'd have progressed in our jobs, but we'd both quit. We thought we were comfortable within ourselves, but we felt something was missing. We expected to know our way around after seven months and could drive anywhere, but that wasn't the case.

We were impatient. We had missed being in Ireland on the first day of Christmas, which is a big deal there. We'd spent eight hours on Skype checking in with everybody. It was comforting, almost like being there, but not quite. We'd been invited to a couple of homes for Christmas Day dinner—some expats—but we said, "No, this is what we normally do." In hindsight, we realized it would have been better for us to go if only for a few hours, just to be around people and to start building those social networks.

We thought we were doing the right thing spending time by ourselves and checking in with family. Then we were back to work the next day as we were still settling into our new jobs. Ireland is generally on a go-slow mode or shuts down for about seven to ten days between Christmas and New Year's, since everything moves slowly. Everybody worked hard for the year, so people take time off as a form of respect. It's family time. It's a religious time.

Tour school was next on the agenda, so off we went in April to the school at the Morongo Golf Club in Beaumont in Riverside County in Southern California. The school was what qualified a golfer to be eligible to play full time for a year—in Canada. It's called "tour school" as it's compared to being at school where your abilities to perform are examined over four days with three days practice before, so it's intense.

We arrived on Sunday, and the tournament started on Thursday. As I rounded the corner to the clubhouse, I saw more golf bags than I'd ever seen in my life. I looked old compared to everybody else, although I was only thirty-four. I'd considered golf an older person's game. However, among those who qualified to get on the tour were many college kids who are the elite players.

We booked into the Holiday Inn, and every day I practiced and played with different people. Jane used to play golf, but she gave it up and now plays tennis. She said, "It's probably just as well we don't play golf together." However, she did caddy for me. It was a perfect experience for us, because I needed her there since I was nervous even though I'd played millions of times.

The course was a typical eighteen-hole course like the ones I was used to playing. However, I think I attached too much meaning to the outcome. In sports as in life and sales, it's better not to get too attached to outcomes; rather just go with the flow and trust yourself. Be confident that you prepared, know you may get some bad breaks, but good experiences will happen as well.

Unfortunately, I didn't play that well and finished two hundred and seventeen out of three hundred and twenty, hugely disappointing. However, I would experience PGA Tour Professional Golf in other ways when I got the chance to play with many famous golfers throughout my personal and corporate life.

I realized that week that I *liked* the game, but I didn't *love* the game. To love it, you must be totally committed, focused, and selfish. When we got back to San Diego, we returned all the furniture we rented. Our next decision was to travel for the next several months since neither of us had jobs.

We called Jane's parents, Bill and Margot, and told them we were heading off traveling, that we were taking a break from living our new life. Again, there was complete confusion on their part, but much excitement, because they thought we'd end up back in Ireland. Looking back now, I suppose they were right. They thought we were too old to be making such a big change and that it might not work out.

Yet, for us, those four months we spent traveling in America were fulfilling. As you'll learn later at our eventual success at becoming parents, we're happy we did our traveling when we were without our son, Alfie. And now we get to enjoy him when we go on mini vacations. We feel like we've done most of what we wanted and lived a full life.

Over the four months, we traveled up the West Coast into Vancouver. We stopped off in Orange County for a few days and viewed the sights, then headed up the coast on the 101, stayed in Santa Maria, went to Pismo Beach, Morro Bay, through Napa, stayed in San Francisco, and in Sausalito, where we visited years before. It reinforced what we loved about America: the different sights and people, all of whom were so welcoming.

We'd hear, "Oh my God, Irish. Where are you from? What are you doing here?" We'd say, "Just traveling, throwing caution to the wind." Many people say Californians aren't friendly, but I find the opposite. We continued on through Yosemite, Mammoth Lakes, Lee Vining, Oregon, Seattle, and drove over the border into Vancouver. We had booked a hotel on Hastings Street. The Border Patrol officer laughed at us, and we wondered why, but when we got to Hastings Street I could see why he was laughing at me as many homeless folks and people were hanging around dealing drugs. We enjoyed all Vancouver had to offer, and found Canada to be a beautiful country, much like Ireland.

After leaving Vancouver, we went back to Seattle and drove around for a day to see if we could sell our car. We had a flight booked from Seattle to Florida. We met this man in a car dealership who was a Catholic. Well, he couldn't believe that two Irish Catholics had walked in. He took the car for a "spin" as we call it in Ireland. He asked us about the country and the churches and what they were like, so we had a fun conversation. He bought the car for twenty-five hundred dollars which was perfect as we wanted to get some decent cash out of it. Then he drove us to the airport. On the way, he brought us to the bank to let us deposit the check—such a nice man. We boarded our flight to Orlando, and upon landing rented a car. We'd reserved a penthouse in Bonita Springs from an Irish guy in the middle of July. We didn't realize it was a penthouse, but since it was super hot, we were grateful for the beautiful place with two pools, a community bar, and a full gym.

Our routine was as follows: every morning I'd get up and play golf at 7:00 a.m. before it got too hot. I'd get back about 10:00 a.m. to have breakfast with Jane. Then we'd go to the gym. We got as fit as we'd ever been. We'd lie by the pool and sweat, get into the pool, come out and have lunch, have a beer, and in the evening cook dinner. We found a lovely bar across the street where we'd go to meet people and make friends. We enjoyed going to the beach for a walk most evenings and were flourishing in our surroundings.

Florida is similar to Ireland with the reeds and the dunes. And we really enjoyed the warm water which felt like I was bobbing up and down in a warm bath. I guess our families were wondering what was happening with us. My father-in-law said, "There's nothing in Florida for you."

Well...we made the decision to move back to Ireland in July. It was almost like a self-fulfilling prophecy as all along the way since we made the move our heads and hearts were back in Cork. We told everybody the news. My brother Mark said we could stay in his house because our house was still leased.

I suppose it was the culmination of a lot—no jobs, not many friends, no permanent residence. Deep down we knew we couldn't keep traveling all over America and draining our savings. Maybe we were "running away" rather than facing our homesickness, embracing our new surroundings, leaning on each other, getting advice, and giving each other a kick in the butt for support. Nevertheless, Ireland, here we come.

CHAPTER TEN

Return to Ireland

"Immigration inevitably involves error and revision.
What I imagined it would be, it's not.
For better or worse, some mistake is unavoidable."

—Siri Hustvedt, Author

We landed in Shannon airport in County Clare, and as soon as we touched down it started to rain. Of course, it had to be raining. A few Americans were on the flight cheering that they were in Ireland. I suppose we were commiserating, because we looked at each other, and Jane asked, "Is this a bad idea?" I said, "It seemed like we were acclimating to the States, but we weren't working or doing much of anything in Florida." Jane replied, "Well, we're here, so let's make the most of this."

Yet, as soon as we landed, we felt we might have made the wrong decision, because we didn't give ourselves the best chance. We weren't patient. We didn't trust ourselves. We didn't seek out support. We didn't ask enough questions. We didn't put ourselves out there. We weren't toughing it out. We were too soft on each other, because it's easy to find comfort when someone is down. We were both feeling down, so we found comfort in each other's discomfort rather than one of us being stronger and stepping up. It was easier for us to run away rather than hunker down and meet those feelings head on. We were wondering: was this an impulsive decision?

We could've gone down to the Irish pub and told people, "Hey you know we're struggling here." What could we have done when we weren't satisfied with our jobs? That's a big part of how we could have assimilated into a new country, culture, and environment. It takes time, and we needed to surround ourselves with similar minded folks and positive people. It's the same in the business world. We either flourish in our environment or flounder in it. Since we spend so much time on the job, that was where we could have started making friends and become comfortable with the customs and culture of America. However, we weren't in our jobs or San Diego long enough to get acclimated.

Family and friends were delighted to see us, even as they were shaking their heads, asking, "What happened?"

I remember one person saying sarcastically, "I never met anyone who regretted going traveling." I felt I needed to justify the decisions we made. Jane's "stock" answer to folks was, "We were trying to make a permanent move, but we just didn't enjoy it. And then we decided to go traveling." She was short, sharp, and to the point rather than when I gave long-winded answers to the questions we got.

I felt I was constantly defending myself. I saw it as criticism, although maybe it was merely observations. Yet I took them personally. I was disheartened during those summer months, still questioning our decision. Ironically Jane's company hadn't filled her job yet, so she went straight back to work with the hair product company and picked up the same company car.

We moved back into our house in September after the tenants left. And there we were on a Friday night watching the equivalent of the David Letterman show which in Ireland is *The Late Late Show,* the longest running chat show in the world. It was raining in September, the curtains were drawn, and we were back. And it was depressing.

I started work at the end of September for a local retailer called Musgraves in their head office. It was the equivalent of working at the corporate office of Ralph's or Albertson's in the alcohol trading department—back in my wheelhouse. Now the suppliers like Heineken were calling me to sell their products. Heineken invited me to the brewery for a big dinner. I was sweating buckets that day, because I felt everyone was looking at me, wondering if they were judging me. My head was spinning. I used to work for these people, and now they were falling all over me. I noticed I was overdressed, wearing a sweater, shirt, and tie.

I settled into the job, but my mind was elsewhere. I was clocking in at 9:00 a.m., then had a tea break at 9:15 where I was having a conversation with a nice bunch of people in the canteen. After thirty minutes, it was back to work. Lunch was 1:00 to 2:00 p.m. Another tea break at 3:15, and we clocked out at 5:00. Not much work got done. Then I drove my car ten minutes up the road to our house. If I left the hand brake off, it was seven minutes down the hill to work each morning.

I could see a possible career path perhaps as the trading manager for alcohol. If the current guy retired and I acquired the skills and patience, I could be in that position. However, for me it was about learning new skills while my head was elsewhere. I was booking time in a meeting room, going there to work, and sending résumés to American companies. It wasn't anything to do with my new company or the job, as the pay was good, and the people were fine. It was just that my thoughts were far away...back in America.

I went down to the local pubs where I knew many of those folks for years. But now I didn't feel I fitted in.

I imagined them thinking, "Well, who do you think you are, leaving, and now you're back?" Some people said, "I could've told you it wouldn't work out. Why did you do it in the first place?" I knew it was their own stuff, but I still took it personally. That's the Irish mentality I experienced. I'd prefer people say nothing so it wouldn't bother me. Yet, it was up to me to be resilient and not feel I had to explain myself.

Christmas came and went, and for me it was a letdown. I remembered Christmas in San Diego where all we wanted to be was back home. Yet here we were sitting at the table with family and friends clinking glasses and eating a huge meal. When you're surrounded by family, you take it for granted. Yet, when you're away from home, you miss those familiar situations. While we were in America, we should have been getting on with our new lives, as our friends and family were getting on with theirs and weren't thinking of us all the time like we were of them. Was there a happy medium?

January was dark and wet, while we knew in San Diego it was at least seventy-seven degrees and sunny. Jane and I talked about our return to Ireland. I said, "Look, I know we're both adapting, and you've got your job back and I have a job. I'd love to be as comfortable as you, settling into your old job, seeing former customers, having your sales routines. But I'm struggling. Your family is great, my family is great. But I haven't played golf since returning, and I don't love my job."

Of course, I was no longer a member of my golf club, and for some reason I decided not to rejoin. I bemoaned the fact that I couldn't play golf year 'round in Ireland. I think I was hiding away. My two good friends, JP and John, told me they were worried about me. I usually turned up on time, and if I was running late, I'd send a text. Well, I completely forgot we had arranged to meet for lunch one day. It was the first time I ever forgot an appointment.

I felt I'd benefit from talking to a therapist, or counselor as we call them in Ireland, one-on-one, just to chat through some of my feelings, like doubt, sense of loss, depression, and uncertainty. The counselor I saw was fantastic, thoughtful, empathetic, and experienced. Valerie not only listened to me but heard me and gave me some self-work to do. Her method was cognitive behavioral therapy (CBT). I did the work and got quite a lot out of it. One suggestion from her was to change my perspective, such as looking at a situation with a different viewpoint: positive instead of negative. Another directive was to discuss my feelings with Jane. I'd need to ask her, "Look, this is how I feel. How do you feel?"

I do believe to this day that it was mostly me who wanted to go back to America. But equally Jane was feeling similar longings, and to her credit she said, "Let's go for it." We sat down at our dining table with a huge sheet of paper, as we asked the hard questions. "Well, here's a blank canvas. What's going to be different this time around? What are we going to do to push ourselves? What if we're homesick? What if the jobs don't work out? What if we don't make any friends? What if God forbid something happens to someone in our families? What if a parent dies while we're in the US?" This last thought had been on my mind, though I knew we could be back in Ireland within sixteen hours.

And "What if I don't have a regular game of golf? I'd have to join a member's club and they're expensive." Having a regular game of golf is crucial for my physical exercise as well as my mental health. Early Saturday morning after a long week of work, I found I could let go of tension and enjoy the sport, and I did just that when I lived near the beautiful courses in Southern California.

We wrote down everything, designed it all, and as luck would have it, Heineken USA said we're hiring someone in San Diego directly. I decided to apply for the job. When I was in the US the first time, I had made connections with Heineken through the beer distributor I was working with. I was interviewed on Skype for the San Diego position and was offered the job straight away. This was in January when they said, "We need you here in two months." I wanted to get back into a branded company. Beer distributors are excellent people and an excellent business. However, I wanted to be with a supplier where they have more structure in place around human resources, marketing, and finance, and there's upward mobility in terms of making geographical moves and other roles. So I accepted. We'd been out of the country for a short time, so we maintained our permanent US residence status. America, here we come—again!

CHAPTER ELEVEN

Welcome to America, Part 2

"No matter who you are or what you look like,
how you started off, or how and who you love,
America is a place where you can write your own destiny."

—Barack Obama, Former US President

Our plan for the move back to America in early 2014 was that I'd go first and get set up, and then Jane would follow. However, she decided that if we were going to go, we should go together. She quit her job and we went through the same actions again. We leased our house. We spoke to our families. We packed up everything we wanted to take. And we weren't surprised that everybody was shocked. We heard, "You're too old. You tried it and it didn't work. What makes you think it will be different this time?" I don't believe anybody said, "Go for it."

It was a big decision, and I understood people's concerns and fears. Ireland was still in recession. But I had a job waiting for me, and Jane always found jobs easily. We were enthused and laser focused on what we planned to do. After landing back at Lindberg Field, we settled back into the same building in Point Loma. We realized the first time we had an adjustment problem. But this second time, everything was more familiar, so it was easier to settle in.

Interestingly enough, after a month of being back, we found out that the hair product company Jane worked for in Ireland, whose head office was in Chicago, needed someone in Southern California. What a welcome surprise that was. She rejoined the same company and covered Southern California calling on high-end hair salons and physicians such as dermatologists and plastic surgeons, many of whom recommended the products. Viviscal Professional is an all-natural, one hundred percent drug-free organic product that strengthens hair follicles and is sold at CVS, Walmart, and Walgreens.

Suddenly we were working during the week and creating a robust social life on the weekend with friends we made through work. We lived in Point Loma for three months, and then decided to take a short-term lease in Pacific Beach. We loved the area with lots of bars and restaurants and quiet areas like Kate Sessions Park. I could hardly believe it. I was walking through the grocery store doing our first full grocery shop alongside women in bikinis and guys in board shorts. You just don't see this in Ireland. I loved the liveliness, the colors, and the attitude.

This time everything was going well. Work was going well for both of us. We were making a wonderful circle of friends. I could have made a couple of geographical moves, because Heineken wanted me to work other parts of the States and take on some roles with more responsibility, as I was already a strong performer. However, here's what I was thinking: if we wound up moving back to Ireland for good, I wanted to go back with skills and experience that would get me at the right level in Ireland. So I had to make some difficult decisions, because I wanted to show enthusiasm and ambition. However, Jane and I were re-settling in the US, whereas everybody else at Heineken was in their mid-twenties and would jump at the chance. But I really didn't want to move to Miami when they offered it, because Jane would have to move, and we'd have to start all over somewhere other than San Diego.

The golden rule we both agreed to when we came back was if we had some major decisions to make, we'd talk about it. If it's not working for one of us, then we'd talk about it. No impulsive decisions anymore. And we make decisions together, as a team.

We thought it would be a good idea to check in with each other after six months and then sit down and discuss how we were feeling. We needed to be able to support each other through any feelings of uncertainty. Perhaps we went through some stages of grief when we came back, regretting the decisions we made in haste. I believe a shift occurred for us in Ireland when we realized we had to let go of blaming ourselves because of our previous choice to leave the US. And now we were committed to do whatever it took to make it work on our return to America.

I think it was essential for us to compare and contrast Ireland to America and America to Ireland to get clearer and then be able to choose what we truly wanted—both regarding jobs and lifestyle.

One activity that kept my spirits high was that I was playing golf regularly in Balboa Park with my friend Mark, and I joined the men's club near Pacific Beach. I continue to be a member of that club and play regularly with an eclectic range of members who all love the game. Then a truly remarkable golf experience landed in my lap. About a year after our return to the US, in June 2015, I found myself standing on the first tee with Padraig Harrington, a three-time major golf champion from Ireland asking myself *how did I get here?*

Some thirty-six hours earlier I had taken a red eye flight from San Diego to Connecticut—from the southwest to the northeast of the country. I landed in Bradley Airport bleary eyed, tired, yet full of excitement as I picked up my rental car and drove to the Holiday Inn in New Haven.

I remember getting the phone call as I drove back home from Los Angeles after a customer sales meeting. The person calling reminded me that six weeks earlier I had entered a sweepstakes advertised by a new golf company to win an opportunity to play golf with Padraig and two other people. I had won! Really? Could this be happening to me? I was hyper and immediately started thinking about what it would it be like. People sometimes say, "Don't meet your sporting heroes as it could be a letdown" since they're held in such high esteem. I called Jane and said, "Your favorite golfer is going to play with his favorite golfer." The rest of the ninety-minute trip back home was a bit of a blur, although I do remember playing lots of Irish music like U2 and singing "It's a beautiful day" as loud as I could.

As usual, I started to prepare by reviewing the golf course we'd be playing on. New Haven Country Club is steeped in history having been founded in 1898 along the east shore of Lake Whitney and was a demanding test of all golfers' abilities.

After much preparation and excitement like a child at Christmas, the morning arrived. I got to the course one hour before our 10 a.m. tee time, and as I like to do once I pull into the parking lot of a course I haven't played,

I soak up the atmosphere and let my senses take in the surroundings. My first impression was "Wow, this place looks amazing, and hey, there's no one here." As a general rule of thumb, country clubs in America are closed on Mondays to allow for maintenance.

It was a bright morning with blue skies, and the warm sun hit my neck as I stood around listening to the far-off hum and din of machines cutting the fairways and greens. I heard birds chirping their morning tune and smelled the scent of fresh cut grass lingering in the air which signals that the course is getting ready to be challenged. I next heard the familiar sound of "thud, thud"—new cups being hammered into the ground and holes being changed on the putting green.

I continued to the locker room where I was greeted and shown around by the attendant. I grabbed a cup of coffee which gave me a jolt and helped me get focused and warmed up on the range and putting green. I rolled some putts and noticed how fast the greens were, like putting on glass. Going through my regular routine, I kept glancing up every so often to see if "he" had arrived yet.

It was thirty minutes to our tee time, and I met the two other lucky players: Melissa from South Carolina and Samantha from New York. The owner of the golf company that ran the sweepstakes, also from New York, joined us and would be playing as well. Everyone was friendly and excited for what lay ahead. Back to the range

I went to hit a few final practice shots. Then at the top of my backswing, I heard him with his familiar Dublin accent. My swing collapsed, yet I tried to act cool as the ball sprayed way right. Just as well no one else was there other than the five of us around.

Padraig introduced himself, as if he needed to. What he first said to me was, "You're a long way from Cork!" I smiled and tried to speak, but my mouth was dry. "Come on Andrew, pull yourself together." Padraig went to the practice range and ran through an efficient warm up. I stood back, watched, and noticed how quickly he switched into his practice mode. Today was going to be a special day, I thought.

"The ladies will play from the red tees, and Andrew, Peter, and I will play from a combination of the white and back tees," the pro said. I surveyed the empty fairway ahead of me, checked the direction of the wind, the distance to carry the bunker on the right side, and took my usual two practice swings. And then it happened. The sound of the machines I'd heard earlier seemed to stop as if the composer of an orchestra had swung his baton to command them to stop. Silence enveloped the course, and I was conscious of my heart starting to beat faster. No doubt adrenaline was flowing through my veins, and I was curiously conscious of my breathing.

"You got this Andrew. Pick your target and execute." I pulled back my driver and crushed my tee shot right down the middle of the fairway. While I held my finish pose, I heard him say, “Great swing.” That did it for me for the day. That was enough; no matter what else happened, the day was incredible already. Padraig stepped up and sent his piercing drive soaring through the air. His ball probably took a cursory glance down at my ball while in the air as it landed forty yards ahead of mine. We were off! After four holes, we both abandoned the carts we’d been supplied with and walked the fairways together as much as we could.

Padraig did not live up to my expectations; he blew them away! He was so friendly, natural, and normal—not at all intimidating. He asked me questions about my life in Ireland, making the move to America, and my work life since moving. As I’m such a big golf nerd, I asked him tons of questions about his career, the resilience and perseverance he’s had to rely on, as well as his philosophy on the game. Of course, I garnered some invaluable advice from him about my game.

During our talk I told him about the book I planned to write someday. So when I was getting ready to publish I sent him a quick email saying I mentioned him in my book that was going to press. I was thrilled when he sent me this message: “Congratulations on your book and using your resilience skills to overcome all the challenges. Good luck for the future!”

The rest of our round went so fast, and while I was engaged in watching and listening to Padraig, I lost focus on my own game. As we strode up the eighteenth fairway nearing the end of an amazing experience, I reflected on how lucky I was to have had this opportunity to not only meet but play golf with my idol. So once again I asked myself, *how did I get here?*

CHAPTER TWELVE

Life in Ireland vs. America

"Some people want it to happen,
some wish it would happen, others make it happen."

—Michael Jordan, Basketball Player

My impression from being in America is that it seems anyone can do anything, like "The world is your oyster." For me that was true. I found more opportunity—personally and professionally—sport wise and for travel due to the country's vast size and overall positive attitude and encouraging nature of its people.

I've noticed that kids are much more outgoing than those in my generation. As kids growing up in the eighties in Ireland, we were taught to address people as Mr. and Mrs., and it was "speak only when you're spoken to". We were quite cautious and mannerly. Today I don't often see kids with those same manners; however, American and Irish kids are so confident nowadays, it's refreshing. I don't expect Alfie to be like me or other American kids. I prefer to leave him alone and let him do his own thing.

Alfie is mellow, a lot like me when I was young: happy to be part of a group and making friends easily. He's got plenty of confidence for a three-year-old, and I'm glad. I work with people who have kids, and they tell me they instill confidence in their kids and a serious work ethic from an early age. I've been told that in America it's important to have good grades in school and participate in extracurricular activities. A high school graduate will want to show a prospective college they can manage homework and sport as well.

Yet, since I moved here eleven years ago, I've gotten somewhat tired of hearing everybody say college is so expensive. Of course it is, but that seems to be the primary goal for their kids. A common theme at work is the employees are working hard for their yearly bonus, and the bonus gets banked for the college fund. You know what? I think that may have shifted. A significant number of people who started working from home building their own businesses realized they didn't need four years of college to do that. So maybe the up-and-coming entrepreneurs have values of "decide and do" rather than wait four years to get a piece of paper from a university.

One common everyday occurrence I hear in America is the word "awesome" being used in many situations. It took a while, but I got out of the habit of using my old answers to questions like: How are you? How are things? "Not bad," would be my reply, which is a double negative. Now using the word "awesome" has a ring of positivity that reverberates in my heart and ears. In my experience growing up in Ireland, you wouldn't hear many say, "I'm doing great," because it's almost like they don't want anyone to think they're doing better than others. Or they don't want you to think they're doing well, because they're setting themselves up for a fall— which is an old Irish phrase.

In America everything appears to be a competition. One senior manager at Heineken and I talked about soccer, and I told him I played for ten years to a high level. He said to me, "Can you believe the coach put my son as a goalkeeper? Have you ever heard of any good goalkeepers in the world?" I named off seven of them which he had never heard of. After a game he told the coach that under no circumstances was his son to be a goalkeeper, because he's going to be the guy who gets blamed when the opposition scores goals.

My love and passion for golf was tested in the early days after moving stateside. The game is so insular and singular that it took a long time for me to adapt to a "new way of playing". While golf is just as competitive in

Ireland and the standard is high there as well, the overall feel for the game is friendlier there, even in the heat of battle. Here not so much.

I find that golf is a selfish game and played mainly individually. While people say they want each other to do well, in the US on the golf course, I quickly found that no one cared about who I was, or where I was from. I wasn't on the course to make new friends or acquaintances. I was there to play competitive golf.

I play a lot of the tournaments that have elite qualifiers to get into the big ones. For a while, it was uncomfortable for me, since I didn't know all the US golf courses as well as some of the other players. While playing, there was zero conversation in our group. Once I accepted that, I played much better.

Another comparison which is not meant to be disrespectful to Ireland, is that if you fail, people remember, but if you try and fail in America, you're given a chance to try again. It's almost like, "Well good on you for trying," whereas in Ireland my experience has been, "I could have told you that wouldn't work out." The best example is when somebody you know in America has a big house and people might say, "Wow, good for them; someday I'm going to get a big house." But in Ireland they'd say, "Who do they think they are?"

Growing up in Cork City I'd hear, "There's Andrew the golfer, there's Andrew the sales guy." When I met people, before even talking to me, they'd say, "You're playing great golf," when I might have been playing terrible golf, but no one wants to know. People I'd meet would make assumptions about how well I was doing or how good my golf game was, when in fact if I were to say, "Hey, things are not so good," they didn't really want to know. It was only small talk, but not all that truthful.

I knew it would be best to say, "Yes, I am." It was like a false positivity, because I felt pigeonholed. I was living up to other people's expectations rather than my own and it felt claustrophobic. Even though Ireland has a population of a little over five million, you run into the same people regularly. I suffered from small town syndrome, where I felt like I was a big fish in a small pond when I wanted to be a small fish in a big pond in America with less attention on me.

I related to Jane one night that when I was around ten years old and gathered at the family dinner table I said, "I'm going to do this and I'm going to do that when I'm older," showing my ambition. It was often met with, "Yeah, sure we'll see. I'm sure you will." Some of what I envisioned was outlandish; I had big dreams. I thought someday I might like to become a professional golfer, to own my own company or run a company, and to move to America.

Yet, I was perceived as being boastful or overly ambitious. The attitude is simply "that's as good as it gets and we're okay with that". It wasn't for me; I didn't want to settle. It's also not for me to say that's wrong or right either. It's a difficult environment, and you do somewhat become the environment you're surrounded by.

I believed this before I moved here, and now that I'm living in America, I believe you can pursue anything you want. I don't know if it's the culture, the country, or the ability to fail and get up and go again. Or maybe it's a combination of mindset, opportunity, and a bit of luck.

In Ireland status quo is good enough. Yes, the opportunities are there, but it's a smaller country so there's a glass ceiling if you want to have certain accomplishments. I see it as a hangover from what some would say the "downtrodden" times since the days of how England treated Ireland. Northern Ireland had a war called "the Troubles", and as in most wars, it was about religion and land. The six counties in Northern Ireland (not Cork) out of a total thirty-two in all of Ireland, are even now ruled by England so there's still some division there.

Don't get me wrong. I had a wonderful family life in Ireland. Yet, when I look at life in America now with Alfie, everything is new—being a parent and being in a new country. Now that Alfie is three, I realized I didn't know how the school system worked, so I've had to learn about that. Whereas I'd know about it if still living in Ireland as a first-time parent. What might be safe would be to run back to Ireland; however, I'm following my own advice of trusting myself, asking questions, and building my knowledge. And talking everything over with Jane, and not making impulsive decisions.

Immigration in Ireland is and always has been seen as "They had to go," and "There's nothing for them in Ireland" which wasn't what I was doing. I was choosing to change my life, to follow an ambition. I didn't feel I had to explain why I was doing it. Truly, no economic, family, or social circumstance was making me do it. We knew it would be a different, better life for us. And it's where we wanted to raise our children.

CHAPTER THIRTEEN

Visits to Ireland

"Immigration isn't about continuing an old life; it's about starting a new life."

—Anthony T. Hincks, Author

Since moving to the US, we've been committed to going back to Ireland for a two-week annual vacation. It's important for us to keep in touch with our friends and family. We enjoyed seeing everybody at family dinners and catching up at the local pub. Nobody gave us any flack. It seems unbelievable now because we're in our flow. Jane and I spend our time in Ireland asking and answering questions. Our families have been supportive. Of course, they miss us, but they get to see us when we visit. And we've had some visitors here as well. Now, every time we leave, we're happy to get back to San Diego.

As I write this book, my dad is eighty-nine and my mum is eighty-four. Unfortunately, not being the most mobile, they've never experienced our life in San Diego, which I find sad. I keep in touch as best I can through electronic means. We know it's not the same as visiting, so that's why we get back to Ireland every year. When people visit us, they get a sense of San Diego—the beaches, the golf, the weather. Pretty soon San Diego became Hotel Fitzgerald with friends and family visiting nonstop. The more the merrier.

During the two years of the Covid-19 pandemic (2020-2021), we couldn't travel to visit Ireland while complying with the stay-at-home order in California. At the beginning of the lock down, Alfie was nine months old. We stayed home and watched him take his first steps and say his first words. We coped quite well since we were both working from home and enjoyed the time we had together as a family. Before Covid we were working at outside jobs and were busy. So we were grateful to have that time at home with Alfie.

As Jane was working from home full-time and I was in and out of jobs, I had the Daddy daycare role and Alfie was loving it. It was the best eighteen months of our lives. We felt secure in our surroundings, while the world was in chaos. Although, I had days I was tearing my hair out as

I accommodated to my full-time parenting role. I barely had time to even grab a cup of coffee or take a shower. Alfie would be crying because he was hungry or cutting a tooth. Sometimes no matter what I did, I couldn't soothe him. I have a huge respect for any stay-at-home parent who takes on that role and responsibility, as you quickly learn that the best laid plans go out the window when your son or daughter has needs to be met. When they need to eat, they eat; when they need to sleep, they sleep; and when they need to play, they play.

I knew what was happening in Ireland in relation to the pandemic where it was much stricter. At one stage, people were only allowed to go within five miles of their house. All in all, the situation was terrible worldwide. People lost jobs, relationships fell apart, finances suffered, and most of the world had stay-at-home orders. I guess it was at times like those when one would miss their homeland, but we were quite comfortable. That only reinforced that our move to America and the life we were building was the correct one for us.

As a result of all this time off, we made a lot of plans. We thought about places we wanted to travel as soon as we could, such as Alaska and Hawaii, two places still on our bucket list to visit and explore. I also decided I was going to write a book. I had considered this before but didn't have the right motivation. With no full-time job and staying at home, the motivation returned. Yes, I was going to write that book. I started the writing and doing some research to understand the book writing process. Then I found the help I needed in Andrea Susan Glass, a professional book coach and bestselling author—and she lived only a mile away.

I know my life inside out, but I didn't know how to structure, write, publish, and market a book. I had to get out of my own way and out of my comfort zone. I had to stop putting up imaginary barriers so I could start to write my book. I wanted to follow my passion and my dream of being an author. I knew this could help pivot my career to be being a business coach, psychologist, or public speaker—ultimately being my own boss which I've always craved. It's taken a while to get here, and you're reading the result of my efforts now.

When Covid calmed down, Alfie went back to day-care for three days a week. Every Monday and Friday, I'd hang out with him, play soccer, go to the beach, and walk the pier in Oceanside, the city we moved to in 2017. Jane, who was still working virtually, was extremely busy on Mondays and Fridays, so she needed the house to herself. I was grateful for the time I spent with Alfie.

I got into a routine and enjoyed it. I had enough time to clear my head and be ready for when I'd get back into the alcohol business in the right space. I was making connections, but people were talking about how tough it was with many bars and restaurants being closed.

Finally, after the two years of Covid raging, people started traveling again. My most recent trip to Ireland was October 2022. We look forward to going back to visit our family and friends as often as we can and for Alfie to meet all his cousins and have fun with them. We've experimented with a variety of ways of flying from San Diego to Cork. Lately, we found going from the Los Angeles airport directly into Dublin and hiring a rental car to drive the two and a half hours to Cork was the most efficient way. It's a night flight so we can sleep and arrive refreshed and ready for the many celebrations, family dinners, nights out, meeting up with friends, and playing golf—all part and parcel of being back.

During the most recent trip back to Ireland, I enjoyed getting out on the golf course with my buddies as if I'd never been away. You know what real friendship is when you can just slip back into the routine and be comfortable with each other like nothing's changed. Yet it had changed because time moved on, and I've been in America coming up on eleven years. Although it is nice that some things don't change—like the people back in Ireland.

Seeing Alfie knock on his grandparent's door, seeing them open the door, and seeing the big smiles on their face is worth the twenty-two hours to get from San Diego to Ireland. We had lots of fun, good home cooked meals, lots of clinking of glasses and pints in the pub, and a really awesome vacation. Jane and I even got to go away for a few days to celebrate our wedding anniversary. It was nice to be a little selfish and get some downtime away from Alfie. It's something we miss in America, having the regular support we'd have in Ireland.

Here in America, we have friends. Some we made through work and some through Alfie as he's developed friendships and by osmosis we've become friends with the parents. That helps with play dates and getting a sitter from time to time so we can get out and have time to ourselves. I have to say that with all the planning we did before we came back to America, we've made it work. We built the social and business connections and have a lovely home not far from the beach. And I can play golf year 'round. What more could I ask?

KEY LEARNINGS

What life has taught me, and I'd love to share with you

1. **The environment** you grow up in will dictate your beliefs, attitudes, and views on life. Do your best to create an ideal environment for your kids, with respect and manners at the core of that environment.

2. **Follow your dreams**, no matter what they are or how wacky they seem and sound to other people. It's YOUR life and only you must answer to yourself for the decisions you make. You may find out that dreams do come true. Find a way, take your time, do your research. Then just go for it.

3. **Don't get too attached to outcomes**; rather just act, then go with the flow and trust yourself.

4. **Be confident** when you've prepared in advance; however, know you'll have some bad breaks, but good experiences too.

5. **Vacations are earned** by hard work, so enjoy them. Whether for enriching travel or visiting relatives, make them at minimum an annual event.

6. **Involve children in sports**, whichever they choose. They'll learn excellent life skills such as working with others, leadership, getting up from failure, and celebrating success.

7. **Taking risks is fine** if they're calculated. Rather than being impulsive, discuss the pros and cons with your partner or a counselor first.

8. **Give yourself time to adjust** when making big life changes rather than running back to what was comfortable. As you stretch yourself, you'll find a new level of comfort.

9. **Be open to surprises** that are even better than what you expected. Enjoy them even if they're different from what you planned.

10. **Look for places** where you can build your social network: at work, with parents of other children, at sporting clubs, and at cultural events.

11. **Don't let others** try to convince you of what's "right". It may be what's right for them, but not for you. And don't make excuses for your choices.

12. **Discuss your feelings** with your partner; don't hide them as they won't go away.

PART III

MY CORPORATE LIFE

"Hard work spotlights the character of people: some turn up their sleeves, some turn up their noses, and some don't turn up at all."

—Sam Ewing, Athlete

CHAPTER FOURTEEN

The Dark Side

"The real competitive advantage in any business is one word only...'people'."

–Kamil Toume, Business Author

I'm sitting in the airport in San Diego waiting to board yet another flight to visit yet another market to work yet another territory with yet another distributor team. While I really enjoy the sales aspect of what I do, I wonder if I really need all this in my life. I ask myself, *"How did I get here?"*

Two weeks earlier, I felt like I was literally thrown under a bus. In the industry, as well as in life, the term is used for someone metaphorically throwing you under a bus to save their own skin. I sat in a board meeting after preparing my presentation on year-to-date sales which were phenomenal based on where the company had come from and the situations it found itself in.

As always, I was prepared. I believe anything worth doing is meant to be difficult, and I spent many hours preparing my presentation. But like everything else, once you have the foundations and the data prepared, it's easy to put the presentation together. I was happy walking into the board meeting and confident that the board members would receive the good news about sales in the spirit it was meant.

After taking my place at the table, I saw that the agenda for the day involved my leaving the room for about forty-five minutes while the current CEO presented her thoughts and findings on the company. Little did I know she had shared her documents with the board members forty-eight hours earlier. As it turned out, that was good news. When she asked that I leave the board room, the board members insisted I stay. I could feel tension in the air. What was going on wasn't clear to me, but I'd soon learn. Being exposed to a board meeting at a high level was an opportunity I hadn't had before.

As the meeting began, I couldn't believe my eyes. My jaw hit the ground. Up on the screen was a number of Achievements and Challenges. Under "Achievements" was much of what I had delivered, but someone else was claiming credit for my work. That was embarrassing, disappointing, and annoying enough, but what made me angry was that under "Challenges" was me in my position.

When the chance came for me to present, I stated the importance of the values I hold dear to my heart: respect, integrity, quality, and success. I spoke to each of those values which were not present in that room just forty-five minutes earlier. At no point had anyone ever criticized my performance. In fact, in my whole career, no one has ever said anything negative about my performance internally or externally with the company or brand I was working for. At times in life you choose to sink or swim, and that day I chose to swim. I maintained my composure and professionalism but delivered the utmost rebuke to the false narrative being spewed about me.

Continuing to present my information, I talked about the team energy and environment. I believe in creating an environment where people want to do their best, not because they feel they have to. That's the way I've always worked.

The above is a glimpse of what the dark side of the corporate world can look like. I wrote to the company founder soon after the infamous meeting and rebuked all the negative assertions made about me as well as communicating my anger and disappointment at what had taken place. In addition, I also reiterated my commitment to the company even after all of the unfair criticism and requested the board confirm their trust, confidence, and patience in me to continue my good work of building the brand. Thankfully, they did this in subsequent conversations with me directly which was very welcome.

Fast forward two weeks, and here I am sitting in the airport. The CEO resigned shortly after the board meeting, and I agreed to take on more responsibility which effectively added many of the vacated CEO's responsibilities on top of my role as Vice President of sales. Looking around me, I'm observing three types of people. One is the business traveler with their computer case who is usually well-dressed and looking anxious, probably heading to another city to make another presentation. They work on their laptops with PowerPoint slides like it's the eleventh hour. The second is the group of vacationers heading off to somewhere new. You see their smiles and feel their enthusiasm as they look forward to what lies ahead. The third are just passing through, maybe moving from one city to another, visiting family, or taking a quick trip.

Observing the business travelers, I think since they're on the company dime, they order a sixteen-ounce coffee instead of a twelve like they normally drink. They order a super-sized breakfast when someone else is paying. They're working away on their laptops, and though I feel an element of soullessness in them, there's equally an element of passion.

I've always approached my jobs with passion, acting like an owner. I spend company money frugally. To achieve my goals, I prefer to use my sales and influencing skills, my relationships, and my personal nature. Yes, you must spend money, and you can get business deals done much faster the more you spend. Yet it's not necessarily the right way of working to "over invest" as there will be another brand, another company with more budget. I like to create an emotional connection between me, my customers, and my brands and only then plan budgets accordingly.

The phrase Return on Investment (ROI) is mentioned countless times in companies, and it's good business to keep that top of mind with employees; however, there's another ROI I always deliver: "Return On Influence." By that I mean the influence I have with customers, distributors, and even consumers when we do in-store tastings—and that's priceless. It's not about next week, next month, next quarter, or next year. This is a long-term partnership with customers.

After the board meeting debacle, I now have full control of strategy for the company. First, I'll improve the culture and work environment. I like giving everyone a sense of purpose, and I want to give everyone a voice; we're all equal even though we have different titles and functions. We have a shared vision and a shared goal. Along the way, we're entitled to speak up if we feel something isn't working. My one request is that everybody should have a solution.

I gained many of these attitudes and skills as a young boy in my family business. How it all began...

CHAPTER FIFTEEN

It Began in Ireland

"You want to set goals that you can hit,
so when you start hitting them, you can celebrate those wins.
People start trusting in your way of projecting the business."

—Wiley Cerilli, Founder of SinglePlatform

My first job in Ireland was at nine years old working in the family business which operated out of our kitchen. My father was a sales manager, and he traveled the country of Ireland making sales calls selling ingredients for glucose energy drinks. Traveling in Ireland was different back in the eighties and nineties, because the road network wasn't as good as it is today. He'd leave on a Monday and get home on a Friday, so it seemed like he wasn't home a lot. I didn't really notice that we didn't have many material possessions that people crave nowadays. Yet, I had a great childhood, and everything I needed was provided.

My mum, who was a homemaker, worked damn hard to provide for all we needed in terms of emotional support for Mark, John, Laura, and me. Sometimes she even provided financial support, because she was a home baker and made cakes and pastries that she sold at the local grocery stores. I suppose that's where I first started getting involved in business.

On the weekends, I'd help wrap the cakes using a machine we had in the kitchen. I'd put a stamp on them for "best use before" or "use by" date. Then my father and I would deliver them to local grocery stores and merchandise the shelves. I'd ask the store managers for better quality and quantity of space: "Hey, why don't you give us a little better space? We're here every week delivering product to you." And more often than not they would. I guess that's when I first saw the impact of how your product can sell better if it has better positioning on the shelves.

I thought it was exciting to see people picking up my Mum's products and going home and enjoying them. They'd tell me afterwards how much they liked the cakes. That was inspiring. My father and mother instilled in me a good work ethic, not necessarily hard work, but to be conscientious, customer-centric, and reliable. If you can't do something, say you can't do it. And if you say you'll do something, follow through. I still have this work ethic of integrity today and have used it throughout my career.

During my formative years in secondary school, I worked part time at my local golf club under a golf professional named Batt Murphy. He had a shop that stocked clothing, golf clubs, and everything else to do with golf. He taught me so much about business and how to respect people. I enjoyed working for Mr. Murphy as I dealt with members, helping them improve their game by showing the benefits of different equipment. I liked custom fitting people to their equipment, which involved making recommendations based on their abilities. I helped them find a solution that would help them play better and give them confidence. I was also involved in merchandising the products, pricing, and making sure we made enough margin and profit on the cost of goods. All these skills would stand me in good stead later in life.

Although I was a little introverted, the job brought me out of myself. I'm still a member of that golf club today. It holds a special place in my heart and my golf life, so much that I purchased a commemorative wall tile in Alfie's name so he can be part of the club's future and continue my association.

I kept working there while in college on Fridays, Saturdays, and Sundays. After college, and during the summer months, I worked full time in the shop before I got my first corporate job as a merchandiser for Cadbury, the chocolate company, since I enjoyed the sales aspect and wanted to pursue that. That's where I hit the ground running. I appreciated having my own territory and company car—and all the chocolate I could eat. That contributed to the weight gain I had in my twenties. My territory included forty stores to look after, so I had to manage my time, my samples, and my point-of-sale equipment.

I traveled all over Cork City making sales calls to grocery and convenience stores, talking to the managers, and merchandising the shelves as well as building impactful displays. I had to make sure every shopper could find the product, and I took pride in my work. It was the best job I ever had from the standpoint of learning the business from the ground up, literally—on my knees, merchandising shelves and starting in a large corporate environment at the entry level.

I was good at what I did and got excellent feedback from my manager. Since I showed my ambition to get into a senior sales role, the company generously invested in my education. I enrolled in college at night for a persuasive selling skills course, which included psychology, statistics, finance, and economics. After about nine months, I was promoted to sales representative, which was a more senior position, although I continued to merchandise because I thought that was important. It created demand for me to capture orders.

A few times I didn't stand up for myself, because I didn't think it was appropriate. Instead, I preferred to understand what I was seeing rather than reacting. For example, I got a call on a Friday at 6:00 p.m. and was told to drive to a location that would normally take fifteen minutes on a normal day, but in Friday rush hour traffic it would take an hour. It was to put up a small display requested by the store manager who had called the head office. I was surprised, as I've often said to store managers, "Look, here's my phone number; call me if you need anything." That was a key learning for me to stand up for myself once I gathered the facts. It was clear that customers weren't ringing head office. It was my immediate boss who was sending me to complete short notice work rather than asking me directly to do it. He'd rather hide behind the head office "line". I told him, "Customers said they never call head office." That stopped those requests coming from him.

Next, an opportunity came up to work as a sales representative for Shelton Distributers, another chocolate company and a wonderful family business that gave me even more territory to expand. I'd be calling on three different counties, capturing and merchandising orders. I enjoyed having my own area and collecting payments from customers, making sure they cleared their accounts before we'd order again. It was very fulfilling and reinforced that it was exactly the role that fit me best.

Yet, I was determined to achieve even more. Another job came up with Diageo Ireland—makers of Budweiser, Guinness, Smirnoff, and Bailey's—as a merchandising manager with a team of seven sales merchandisers for one-half of the country. It was amazing that I was able to build on my experiences of when I was captain of my local soccer team. I prefer to lead by example through coaching and mentoring. True, everybody has a different style, so I'd adjust my method of leading to the style of the person I was working with. Some folks are direct, so I'm direct. Some are analytical, so I'd be that way. Some want to talk about sports, so we'd talk about sports all day, but we'd get back to business eventually. I was able to flex and adapt my style to get the best out of people.

Sometimes I'd travel for work, at times with the sales merchandiser. We'd travel together for a couple of days together spending time meeting customers, working through the correct steps in the sales call. This involved introducing ourselves, summarizing the situation, presenting the big idea, that is, what we're there to do, how we're going to do it, and then close the sales call and handle any objections.

People responded well to me. One of the best gifts anyone has ever given me is to call me looking for advice, even if I haven't worked with them in ten years. It's humbling that I've left a mark on then. And I'm not hesitant to seek out feedback, be it constructive, negative, or positive as it's the only way I can improve.

Working for Diageo Ireland was a terrific job, and I loved working in the alcohol business. It sparked an interest in me to get into another similar company. At that time Diageo was working through a third-party contractor, and the contract I was working on was disbanded, so everyone was laid off.

However, I quickly found a position working for a drinks distributor called Galvin's Wholesalers. The best way to describe them is that they ran a franchise of about fifty-six outlets called Carryout which are liquor stores. I was a regional manager with twenty-five shops in my territory. I worked with the franchisees to help them understand their business from the inside out. It was an ideal position for me, because it helped me see the business from the inside out.

For that role, I put on my retailer hat rather than the one of sales rep. Suddenly, I was looking at consolidated margins across different categories. I had to look at how to set up stores correctly with the right products and the right amount of space. That was my job for a couple of years after which I found my way to Heineken Ireland, a company held in high stature in the country. Through a recruitment agency, I was fortunate to secure the job. My knowledge of the Carryout franchisee group would be utilized in my new role.

I spent five years working for Heineken Ireland as a sales representative, merchandising manager, and retail development manager in a high-profile territory. At the time, the company sold these brands: Heineken, Coors Light, Fosters, Murphy's Irish Stout, and a couple of other what we call specialty beers. Heineken was the number one beer in Ireland at the time, and Coors Light was the number one light larger.

My job was to call on off-premise liquor stores and grocery stores to help them sell more product and make more money. We'd do window displays and dress the window for different times of the year. We did big displays and created thematic experiences for the customers. Any time somebody would come to visit from the Netherlands, where Heineken's head office is, I'd show them how the stores should look. We called it "taking people on a milk run", which is going through the routine, showing them the best of the best.

We showed a mix of good-looking stores and those that were difficult to work with as well. I explained how we provided solutions in terms of category management and how we could progress the business forward. I had a partnership with my customers and was solution oriented. Working in that job taught me a lesson that "your word is most important". I always followed through on everything I said I'd do, even if it was having tough conversations or having to say NO to a customer.

In that company, I worked with one of the best teams including super individuals like Wille, Don, and Jim. We had lots of camaraderie and loads of fun. Many nights we went out together, and we also participated in team building days. I remember one team day when we had to complete an obstacle course which was great fun and brought everybody even closer as a team. The brewery was based in my territory, so I'd be in and out regularly meeting people. This was the first time I was part of a corporate family, and it didn't feel like work. Suddenly I was meeting people from finance, human resources, marketing, operations, and logistics.

Salaries and benefits were top notch. I even won numerous trips: the Rugby World Cup in France in 2007, Oktoberfest in Germany in 2008, and Cabo and Cancun in 2014 with the Heineken USA business. In addition, I attended rock concerts and sporting events, and won numerous sales incentives.

I absolutely loved working with them. It was one of my best work experiences. I was promoted a number of times; however, I think other employees may have seen their tenure as being longer than mine and may have felt overlooked. But that was someone else's decision, not mine.

Around that time, Heineken was buying Scottish & Newcastle, another brewery, and they inherited Beamish & Crawford, a brewery based in Cork City. Heineken and Beamish amalgamated, so to reduce the problem of too many people, Heineken asked employees to ask for voluntary redundancy. They said, "Maybe you want to travel, or retire, or write a book." It was a fair way to do it, as lots of employees had thirty to forty years of tenure and had started at the brewery when they were eighteen.

The company was offering a lump sum of salary based on tenure. I had five years and was one of the top performers. Everyone thought I was a safe, solid guy, and I'd get one of the new jobs as a manager in Dublin. Transfers to another country were rare unless you were coming in at a high level. However, I felt the payoff was better for me than getting a transfer, so I finished working for Heineken in May 2012. I didn't tell them that at that time I had gotten a permanent resident card. Jane and I wanted to travel, and we had our green cards ready to make the move to America. Heineken facilitated the redundancy which gave us financial breathing space to start in America.

CHAPTER SIXTEEN

To Be Continued... in America

"The goal is not to do business with everybody who needs what you have. The goal is to do business with people who believe what you believe."

—Simon Sinek, Author and Speaker

My first job in America was working with a local drinks distributor with the Heineken USA portfolio of drinks. It wasn't much different than what I had been doing in Ireland, and it was an ideal start to a new life in America. Although it wasn't exactly what I wanted to do or what I envisioned my first job in America to be. This time, I was working on the distributor side of the business similar to a role in Ireland. Previously I had mostly worked directly for the suppliers. While I might have been selling Heineken, I was also selling hundreds of other brands the distributor carried, but I was seen as a Heineken expert.

Around that time, Jane and I weren't settling into America very well, so we decided to do some traveling. I left my job at the drinks distributor and decided to pursue a dream I always had: to qualify for the PGA Tour. I set about getting myself ready in January 2013 to be prepared to play in April, as mentioned in Part II.

After playing in the tour school qualifier, we traveled some more throughout America, and based on our experience of America not being all that we expected, we decided to return to Ireland. On our return, Jane coincidentally returned to her old job as the role hadn't been filled. I took a job working in the trading department of alcohol with Musgrave, Ireland that own and operate a franchise grocery chain and convenience stores under the trading names of Super Value and Centra. This was a super job for me to see how a big grocery chain plans their business internally and all about category management and innovation in the alcohol industry.

The return to Ireland didn't last long, and we came back to the US. This time, I got a job working for Heineken USA directly as the off-premise channel manager, which meant I was dedicated to only the Heineken brands of Heineken, Dos Equis, Tecate, Newcastle Brown Ale, and

Strongbow Cider. I was in a higher position with more salary than I'd had in Ireland. It also gave me the structure I enjoyed as well as being part of a great team environment. Southern California was my region, and I relished it.

My job was to work hand-in-hand with the distributor and help them plan accordingly to achieve the sales numbers to which the company had agreed. How I went about that was to divide and conquer the distributorship. I got to spend time one-on-one with people before meeting everybody as a group. I took each challenge head on, met all the customers, and brought new ideas. I'd work with the district managers or the VP of sales to understand their business

My goal was to build up everyone's unique experience of Andrew Fitzgerald rather than someone else's. When we met as a team, everybody had their version of me which served me well since people gravitated to me, appreciated my personable nature, loved my stories about Ireland, and enjoyed playing golf with me.

However, it's not always a straight shot in business, and at times I had to have the difficult conversations about execution at retail, not following through, and sales numbers being off or not being hit. The best way I've found to get through these situations was to be respectful, communicative, and to tell it like it is.

One of the most valuable lessons I learned was to create buy-in with people, so they feel a sense of purpose in achieving the goals they set. I've seen the largest suppliers in America come from a place of control rather than support. I've become an expert at support rather than control to get the best results. For example, I'd ask the sales teams at what percentage on the display program could they execute at. If they agreed to achieving eighty percent of all stores executed with a display, then eighty percent is the number we'd work toward.

From there, I could manage and track the progress, and if it looked like we weren't making any, we'd have the challenging conversation reminding everybody of their commitment to get to eighty percent. I like to say that in the spirit of partnership, it's a joint responsibility, and the onus is on both parties to deliver on what we agreed.

Working for Heineken in America was very different from working for them in Ireland. I did a lot of reading and researching on people who move abroad with a company they've worked with. The major difference I found was that Heineken didn't have a central hub in the US. The brewery in Ireland had a family feel to it. The culture of respect, integrity, success, and quality were evident every day. I'm not saying Heineken USA didn't have those values; it was just that everybody was geographically spread out. Obviously, the size of this country lends itself to that.

Since I was doing such a stellar job with Heineken, a company called Mike's Hard Lemonade was asking around for anybody who was a star performer and heard about me from the distributor. The job was key account manager for California, Washington, Oregon, Arizona, and Nevada, and I was seriously interested. It would be a huge step up for me in terms of responsibility, but at its most basic level, it was still just having a business conversation with customers who happen to buy and make decisions for many hundreds of stores.

As soon as I was offered the job, I had no hesitation taking it, because I felt this could accelerate my career in the United States. I called on the corporate offices of Circle K, Albertsons, Vons, and Ralphs among others and worked with the beer buyer to understand their business, talk about the category of beer, get more products on the shelf, and sell more effectively.

The founder/owner of Mike's Hard Lemonade is a Canadian man, and the US business operates out of its head office in Chicago. He started his career as a young man selling wine by himself, for himself, making the introductions, getting rejected, but being resilient and persistent, similar to my mum and dad's family baking business. When I met him for the first time, I was in awe of him and knew of his stellar reputation. Nothing about him was intimidating, because he was so friendly and passionate. I enjoyed the five-minute conversation we had.

The company did a really good job of embedding values and being a good partner, because they came from a place of support rather than control. However, I could quickly see the gaps left from previous people who called on the retailers I was now calling on. I set about to understand their businesses by asking open questions. How do you look at your business and what gaps do you see? What kind of communication style do you prefer? What are the key times during the year for your business? What suppliers are doing good business with you and why? What have we as a company not done well? What have we as a company been doing well that we could further enhance?

More often than not, this gave buyers permission to tell me more about their business. I enjoyed working for Mike's Hard Lemonade, as we had an exceptional team environment in Southern California, and I loved being the one to present plans. We talked to buyers who bought for two hundred or more stores. Some salespeople would be intimidated by that; however, I prefer to approach it like one person having a conversation with another person. If you know your buyer, you can either mirror their style or adapt your style and present your products and your ideas to them in a manner they'll understand. Ultimately though, it's the shoppers who decide which product gets picked up to put in the fridge cooler or on the floor display.

In June 2016, the entrepreneurial and innovative owner wanted to launch his latest innovation, White Claw Hard Seltzer. He wanted it to be the first to market in Southern California as other competitors were in that space and soon to release their own version of hard seltzer. For new brands to be successful they must "win California" as that dictates how well the brand can do in the other forty-nine states.

I was asked to meet with my retailers, sell it, and get it on the shelf for the summer of 2016. The company had identified the opportunity a couple of years earlier to put alcohol into sparkling water. What he developed was gluten-free, low sugar, low carb, great tasting flavors, with just the right amount of carbonation.

White Claw Hard Seltzer is five percent alcohol by volume (ABV), one hundred calories, and has two grams of sugar. Fast forward: by 2021 it had a forty-five percent market share and sales of almost two billion dollars and was the number one hard seltzer in the US. (https://no-good.io/2022/02/17/whiteclaw-seltzer-growth-marketing-strategy)

How was I going to sell this new product at a time of year when nobody takes in new products?

To understand the enormity of that request, I need to explain how the business works. All retailers make decisions for new items in April and October each year. Once those decisions are made, that's it, no more opportunity. So straight away I was up against this, in as much as it was slim that I'd get the products in the stores in time. My two best retailers, Albertsons and Vons which are now one company, and Ralphs grocery chain agreed to meet with me so I could present the brand and my ideas. Over one day, we visited a Vons/Albertsons buyer and a Ralphs buyer to present White Claw Hard Seltzer.

First however, I did research on the sparkling water category with LaCroix and Perrier which were selling well in the market. Often, it's important to know about other categories so you can build your knowledge and become somewhat of an expert. Second, I got samples for all the district managers and those in wider parts of the business. The last to get samples were the buyers. Some would say that's counterintuitive; surely you want to get samples to the buyer first. But I was thinking: What if the buyers taste it and they don't like it? It's better to get quantitative research tasting feedback from a wide range of people first.

The day came when we had our one-on-one meeting in the corporate offices. Many people from Mike's Hard Lemonade flew in, many of them senior managers. We went into the meeting room, with the Vons/Albertsons buyer on one side of the table and the senior managers on the other side. I sat next to my customer, while getting some strange looks as if to say, "What are you doing? You work with us." The point was that there were five of us and only one buyer. It's supposed to be a partnership, not a court hearing.

During the meeting, Henry, the buyer, asked me what my recommendation was for any buyer in any job and which flavors would be the right ones to bring into his stores. To be asked for your recommendation is the highest compliment you can be paid. I recommended black cherry and mango as two six-pack options. I told him I personally didn't like the lemon and lime flavor since it was too much like some established soda brands in the market. The senior managers nearly gasped when I said that. As it turned out, black cherry is still the number one flavor, and lemon and lime doesn't exist anymore. The lemon and lime had nothing unique compared to what was already in this sparkling water category. The same scenario played out at Ralphs, and Seth the beer buyer who was very enthused at being at the cutting edge of innovation in the alcohol business, wanted to be first to market as well.

The big difference with this program and launching when we shouldn't have been able to get new products in, was the plan I'd put in place, which was to do samples in one hundred and fifty stores throughout May, June, July, and August of 2016. The first case of White Claw Hard Seltzer rolled into Southern California on June 20, 2016.

To initiate my plan, I had to work both internally and externally. For me, selling is the easy part; it's the execution of agreements that brands and new startup companies fail on. Once I have a commitment from the buyer, I speak to my distributor to sell it to them, to gain confidence from them. Then I sell to my field sales team, to educate them on how it will work, on what the timings are, and what to do if they need to take any corrective action at the stores.

Next, I hire a sampling agency and get them uniforms, point of sale (POS), and all the goodies they'll need to hold a successful demo. The best ones are where we have lots of interaction and education. They don't have to sell a lot of products on that day. However, we've planted a seed in the shopper's mind. Perhaps the next time in the store, they'll pick us up, or they'll tell three or four other people.

By October 2016, we'd done such a good job at Ralphs, Vons, and Albertsons that we got eighty percent distribution in all their stores. This key metric gets you on the weekly ad circular. What this did for me though was to build up scan data through the register. I could also build a proof source to go to all the other retailers in California and show them what was happening with White Claw Hard Seltzer. It was important that we continue the momentum. and as such we managed to secure at least one six-pack in all other chains and retail outlets in California.

During that time, I came upon an opportunity to join Boston Beer Company, Inc.; it makes Sam Adams, Angry Orchard Hard Cider, Twisted Tea Hard Iced Tea, and Truly Hard Seltzer. At the time, I felt it wasn't the right move for me. However, when the opportunity came up again some months later, and we spoke collectively, I joined Boston Beer to launch Truly Hard Seltzer with Costco and to elevate the relationship with the buyer of a drug customer called Rite Aid. Also, I was tasked to re-launch Twisted Tea Hard Iced Tea with a convenience chain like 7/11, Circle K, or AMPM. Truly Hard Seltzer is five percent ABV, one hundred calories, and one gram of sugar, and in 2021 had a 17.4 percent market share and grew 35.6 percent in sales and is the number two hard seltzer in the US. (https://nogood.io/2022/02/17/whitecla w-seltzer-growth-marketing-strategy).

Costco is a fascinating establishment. In Ireland, we didn't have anything like it. When I first moved to San Diego and walked into a Costco, I couldn't believe the vast size of it—and the amount of stuff you could buy and the sizes of the packages. You could literally buy anything from a boat to a coffin. The most challenging issue for me in launching Truly Hard Seltzer, which was a competitor of White Claw Hard Seltzer, was that it was a different proposition which was also advantageous.

Truly was sold in glass bottles back then, while White Claw Hard Seltzer was in cans. Truly Hard Seltzer had less sugar than White Claw. Truly being part of the Boston Beer Company Inc. would be able to be leveraged through their existing business in bars and restaurants. Mike's Hard Lemonade didn't see the on-premise channel as right for their business at that time. I once again had to lay the foundations for my plan with Costco.

I researched where hard seltzer was selling well and cross correlated that to where Costco had their outlets. That way I could make recommendations to Tony, the buyer, about where he should put them. We had a thirty-minute meeting to get acquainted. He was a gentleman, and we hit it off straight away. His assistant Dave was also easy to work with. We talked about life in San Diego and Ireland, of course. Tony told me he visited the southwest of Ireland, so we had stimulating conversations. Our thirty minutes turned into ninety, and we did business for about fifteen or twenty minutes of that time. When we got down to the business presentation, Tony and Dave could see I had a track record with White Claw Hard Seltzer. As Henry Ford said, "You don't build your reputation on what you are going to do; you build your reputation on what you have done."

Tony was delighted that I had spent time walking his shop floors, taking photographs, and superimposing what Truly Hard Seltzer would look like in the various aisles. I told him I had done my research on where hard seltzer would sell well at the stores. People in the industry sometimes forget that everything we do is with the shopper in mind. What shoppers see is how they interact with our products and what they pay for our products. But the gatekeeper is the retail buyer who needs to be sold, who needs to be partnered with, who needs to understand the category and what we want to achieve. The buyers need to take a chance knowing there's a partner like Andrew Fitzgerald who will always follow through, who is true to his word, and is conscientious.

After getting the purchase order (PO) for Truly Hard Seltzer, I immediately filled in all the required paperwork with product dimensions, weights, and configurations needed to set up a new product. Once that was complete, I test scanned one pack to ensure it was activated on their system which then meant I could relate back to the company the new business we had received and also to the distributors who love to see POs come in for a lot of volume. Truly Hard Seltzer became the number one hard seltzer at that time with that buying office, and I worked extremely hard every day to ensure stores were pulling through the inventory, distributors were delivering, and we were replenishing inventory with new POs. My promise to Tony was "let me handle this for you", and that's what I did as that's what a good retail partner does.

I re-launched Twisted Tea Hard Iced Tea with Circle K in California, Oregon, and Washington, since the initial launch was ineffective. That was something I found enjoyable, because the brand had been around for four years and hadn't been too successful. So we put some plans and programs in place, and working with key retailers like Circle K, West Region, and the beer buyer, Mark was superb. We managed to get into all the stores. We did some promotions around it, and now Twisted Tea is one of the best performing hard iced tea products in the United States. Some of the chains enjoying it most are Hispanic ones like Northgate, Vallarta, El Super, Superior, and

Cardenas. I really enjoyed working with the buyers of these chains who have intrinsic family values a lot like the Irish culture. They didn't speak Irish, and I didn't speak Spanish, but we worked very well together.

We also had great success with Sam Adams Boston Lager repositioning it with retailers and delivering a renewed confidence in the brand. The company placed a huge importance on continuous training, learning, and development. Our internal training program involved flying to Boston for one week every six weeks. However, I didn't enjoy the traveling and being away for a week from the market. Some of the sales skills in the training were pretty junior, but when you're part of a team, this is what you do in terms of orientation. Along the way, I learned a lot and got to meet Jim Koch, the incredible founder and leader of Sam Adams who oozes passion for his company and employees. And I met his head brewer who had a connection to my hometown of Cork.

When I moved to the US, I was focused on accelerating my career. I was in my mid-thirties, and I didn't know how long we'd stay in America. The thinking was that if we ever went back to Ireland, I'd be going back with more skills and a high responsibility level, ready to go in at a top-level job in Ireland. That's why I made some of the moves I made. Each one, of course, came with more responsibility, more salary, and more benefits. And as I've learned through the years, each move and all that was attached to it, had gains as well as losses. For example, what you gain in salary, you may lose in hours. Suddenly, you need to pay attention to your work-life balance—if that even exists. Yet, it's up to each of us to manage our workload, our time, and our travel schedules—and to set expectations for people. I often tell my teams to "under promise and over deliver" so you can delight your customers and ensure you keep your word.

My next move was to Coca-Cola working under the venturing and emerging brands of which Topo Chico sparkling water was one and is now also a hard seltzer. How this occurred was a recruiter called me about an opportunity for a regional key accounts manager role for California. I was intrigued, because I could see that Coca-Cola would eventually get into the alcohol business, which they announced in 2019 and started to sell in 2022.

When I accepted the job, I used my expertise and educated the company on how to enter the alcohol market and the route to market for Coca-Cola. Unfortunately, there was a company restructure, and when Covid-19 hit in March of 2020, everything was stalled and there was a massive layoff. I've never been laid off in a big way, and it was difficult news to get. However, I could see that this virus was a worldwide phenomenon and not just company specific. I was confident in my skills and experience and knew companies were looking for what I had to offer. I got an excellent severance agreement which gave us some serious financial breathing space, and I filed for unemployment.

Although, being let go, despite the circumstances, conjured up images of my not being wanted. One of the aftereffects of being laid off was my self-esteem took a hit as well as my confidence. However, it was now more than ever that I needed to rely on my astuteness and resilience to know that Covid was out of everyone's control. I compared and contrasted with Ireland to see what was happening there, and it was not that different in terms of job lay-offs, restaurants and bars being closed down, and similar effects being mirrored with America and my own personal situation.

The bright side of this time being shut in as I mentioned in Part II was the opportunity to spend time at home with Alfie and watch him grow. He was nine months at the time, and Jane was working from home. I enjoyed staying at home. I got to see him take his first steps and say his first words. I realized the importance of those moments knowing I'd never experience them again.

Then I got a job offer from a new hard seltzer company called Elephant Craft Hard Seltzer. They weren't affected by the economy since they were starting from scratch. They had investment capital in the bank and were going forward because they felt it was the right time. Many different hard seltzers were taking off with White Claw Hard Seltzer leading the way. At that time, Elephant Craft Hard

Seltzer would have been an early adopter, whereas now in 2022 the market is saturated with hard seltzers.

I was out of work for a short time when I got the offer. The position was for me to be the national account director at a high salary. It looked like a fantastic setup, and I accepted. But a week later, the founder told me, "Sorry Andrew, the investors are pulling out." I said, "No problem." However, I had to go off unemployment knowing I was getting a job, and then I had to go back on it again.

I did get a few other job offers but turned them all down. Some I accepted and then turned down within twenty-four to forty-eight hours. Because I wasn't working, I thought I should take the job and then find something better. However, I didn't think that was fair to those companies, as I wouldn't take something and continue to work in it unless I could give it one hundred percent. My faith and my instinct told me to get myself out of situations I put myself in before it was too late to bow out gracefully.

Ultimately, I was out of work for longer than I had expected. During that time, I did some consultancy and advisory work for a small startup company with a couple of mid-twenty-year-olds who had come up with a great idea for a hard yerba maté. Yerba maté is a South American coffee/tea with naturally occurring caffeine. The owner of the company originated the idea to put alcohol into the yerba mate. It was looking like every beverage company wanted to add alcohol to all kinds of drinks. There's even an alcoholic ice cream on the market now. I was doing some advising for him on how to structure the business and enjoyed it. I thought maybe consulting could be a career move for me.

The company was self-distributed, so they had a few sales reps who called on stores, took orders, would go out to the van, bring the product in from the van, and then get their mobile printer hooked up and print out an invoice and get a check. I changed the way of working to capture orders from customers five days a week. Since we only delivered two days a week when we had a full load, this was more efficient financially.

Unfortunately, they ran out of money. I got the phone call on a Thursday night to come down Friday. I asked, "What's up?" The owner said, "Well, we have financial problems." He hadn't understood. He thought we could just be a White Claw Hard Seltzer after a month or two. Startups need to realize it takes a lot of money and a lot of patience to launch a new brand. Every brand needs a minimum of twenty-four to thirty-six months and a good distribution partner—and you must get retail business. We gained some business with Costco, a 1200 case order. We also got a little business with Ralphs once we had a good distributor. And we made it into an open call at Walmart where they invite emerging companies to present their products. It was all there for us, but they didn't have the funding or the patience for the long haul.

I'd completed my due diligence on the company before I joined and began to question my own judgment. I was feeling disappointed that it didn't work out; however, I left the business in a far better position than it was when I joined—not that it mattered anyway.

Next was a lot of downtime and depression. I spoke to the therapist again. I felt I was blindsided and didn't see it coming. I was too trusting. I felt customers would be wondering what happened. I wanted to reach out to them and get my story out there, though I had to be careful how I phrased what I said about the company: that they couldn't afford to keep me on payroll which was true. The company went out of business not long after this. I think the owner thought that because I had connections, which I do, it would be easy to put it on the shelf straight away. Perhaps he thought, here's Andrew Fitzgerald now on board with us; this will be a home run.

Many new brands that have come out since White Claw Hard Seltzer and Truly Hard Seltzer think it's simple to launch a brand and then sell it. There's nothing crasser in the industry than a brand owner just in the business to sell their business. Yes, everybody's house is for sale. If you're offered ten million for your house, of course you're going to sell it. But retailers don't want you coming in saying, "I'm just selling this brand in twelve months, and I need you to help me sell it." The buyers want to know you're partnering with them. They understand and accept that brands might get sold or merged with a larger company, but if that's the only motivation a new brand has, it will come across as a brand just using the buyers. I've never done that, as I don't think it's respectful.

In April 2022, my next move brought me to a company named Spa Girl Cocktails. It's a ready-to-drink vodka cocktail in a can, and a female-founded, female-led company based in San Diego. Karen Haines, the founder is beautiful, tenacious, and everything you'd want in a leader. She worked as a flight attendant for many years and then came up with an idea of a sparkling vodka cocktail ready to drink in a can. She'd been in business nearly six years when she reached out to me saying she stalked me on LinkedIn. So far, I've had an enjoyable time as the Vice President of sales. We're doing well in California, Colorado, Nevada, and Florida, where we're in distribution.

At the time of writing this book, we're getting an excellent reception, with buyers supporting me. We have a board of directors to report to. During the worst of the Covid-19 lockdown, the company set up a direct-to-consumer website. It was stunning and feminine with sophisticated colors. They sold the product online and did some serious business, which kept the company sustainable during the pandemic. We still have that business, but now we want to be in retail stores, hotels, and resorts. CVS is one of our best accounts for quantity of stores. We have two salespeople, me and Karen, and Robin, who's a brand ambassador and lives the brand and acts like an owner every day.

We're selling alcohol products which is considered a drug, so one must be over twenty-one to consume it in the US, whereas in Ireland the legal drinking age is eighteen. Yet ultimately, we're selling an experience. We're selling a lifestyle with Spa Girl Cocktails: sophisticated, chic, and luxurious. People enjoy our products responsibly while celebrating a party: a birthday, a baptism, a wedding, even a funeral. So we play a part in people's lives.

We've gone through some internal upheaval. Our reputation may not have been the best externally, but I'm changing that by spending time with sales reps, sales managers, distributors, and retailers. Divide and conquer; give everybody a sense of purpose. We need people to be brand champions for us, and as we hire people, we instill the values, culture, and behaviors we want in the company to be successful. Spa Girl is well-funded, but as all startup companies experience, extra funding is an ongoing process. We have a great package and a great product; the future is bright.

And now you know how I got here. It's for Spa Girl Cocktails that I'm sitting in the airport in San Diego waiting to board yet another flight to visit yet another market to work yet another territory with yet another distributor team...

CHAPTER SEVENTEEN

Business in Ireland vs America

"No matter how brilliant your mind or strategy,
if you're playing a solo game,
you'll always lose out to a team."

—Reid Hoffman, Co-founder of LinkedIn

The single most significant difference between working in Ireland and working in America is the various time zones here. I never realized this until suddenly conference calls at 5:00 a.m. on the West Coast became commonplace as it was 8:00 a.m. on the East Coast. So straight away getting up at 4:00 a.m. became the norm, whereas in Ireland is only one time zone, and generally everybody starts work between 8:00 and 9:00 a.m.

So not as much need to be up early in the morning and available for conference calls. In addition, with America being a much larger country with many more people, the pace is a lot faster. I like that fast pace as I worked at a fast pace in Ireland. I work toward my goals with the mantra: *What can I do now to save myself time in the future?*

Inevitably, one of the differences I notice is when you're driving around the countryside in Ireland, your day goes much quicker as you're heading to various locations and seeing the lush green fields and trees. And you glimpse the old stone walls that were put there many years ago to mark people's territory. All this contributes to the history and culture of Ireland.

In America, it's pretty much seventy-five miles an hour on the freeway and everybody rushing to get to the next meeting, to get somewhere else, to clock in. From a customer standpoint what's most important to remember is that we all have twenty-four hours a day no matter what country we live in or what country we're from. And we all make choices about how we use our time. We choose whether to rest, to work, or to play. Dealing with customers is about time management and being efficient. Equally it's about structuring your day to be the most effective you can be on behalf of your company and your brands.

Because Ireland is like a small community, you're generally working within your own locality and environment. Therefore, you're probably playing soccer or golf, or you're in the pub or going to church, so you're running into people you're doing business with. It's more difficult when you need to say no to a customer or have a tough conversation. You want to be prepared that you'll likely run into them somewhere around the neighborhood, the city, or the pub. You need to be able to look each other in the eye.

What I really enjoyed in Ireland was working on a long-term plan with customers. We'd focus on key holidays such as Valentine's Day, Saint Patrick's Day, Easter, and what we call the occasions in Ireland, similar to ones observed in America. We'd build big displays, do branded point of sales, and dress windows for the holidays. Retailers in Ireland are open to working with you if you show some creativity and proactiveness. American customers are more difficult to get a hold of, to fit into their work schedules. Buyers in the corporate world are dealing with perhaps five hundred suppliers, all telling them something similar, like we have the best product, we have the best packaging, we're investing in the brand, or we're all over digital.

Sometimes I have to laugh, because I've worked with so many of these brands, and yes, each has unique attributes and benefits. At some stage though, you must put yourself in the shoes of the retailer and ask how many times they've heard this. So I ask the buyer, "What do you think our brand is like?" or "What do you think the taste profile is?" or "How do you feel about the carbonation levels?" or "Do you get bloated after drinking this beer, or hard seltzer, or vodka cocktail?" More often than not, customers will open up.

What I like best about working with customers in America is when you say no to a deal, they don't take it personally. Whereas if I said no in my Irish career, I had to let people down gently which is how you give bad news in Ireland. Americans take it on the chin, and it's not held against you. Relevant, meaningful communication is what works for me. Anybody can send or forward an e-mail, yet if you put some thought and process into it, people will respond well to you.

America has a ton of opportunity for people to accelerate their career. Here you don't get pigeonholed. I've run into college graduates working in Starbucks. Then they started an alcohol company, then they're a senior vice president. You can start at the bottom and work your way up. In Ireland in my experience, you get more pigeonholed. You're a sales representative, and that's it. Perhaps there's a glass ceiling in Ireland as it's a smaller country.

Another big difference is that in the first few weeks of January, we're on conference calls in America straight away to talk about earning your bonus. Many people I've worked with know that bonuses pay for college since it's so expensive here. Of course, I love earning extra money, but the bonus isn't what motivates me or gets me out of bed every day. It's not what makes me go into the store and look for that last case of product to make sure it's on the shelf, so the shopper has the best experience. The bonus is a byproduct of doing a proficient job. It's just not the be-all and end-all.

America is more aggressive in terms of sales and hitting the bonus. See, every New Year here, it doesn't matter how many cases you sold the previous year. Let's go again today and sell more. My Irish career experience was that it would be slow in January and get going at full tilt by February.

I like that I thrive in and can manage that environment. If I work my plan, it usually comes out well over twelve months. I rarely panic or get ahead of myself. I don't get down if everything isn't going the right way. I'm very creative and like to look for new solutions and ideas. Working with marketing and finance enables me to see if we can free up some budget to get creative with customers and be a better supplier than everyone else.

One of the best examples I could give is when retailers send out various price sheets or promotional sheets to be filled in, and they give you a three-week window to return them. I usually have them back within three days. I think this signals to the retailer that I take them seriously and I'm competitive. I want the retailer to benchmark me versus other suppliers. I've had buyers comment, "Why can't you be more like Andrew?" They use me as the standard for what a good supplier partnership should be like. One time I walked into a big sales meeting—called a roundtable meeting—with Circle K. I wore my Circle K polo shirt and bought Circle K branded water and snacks, since we were going to be there for two hours discussing business strategy for the next year.

I sat on the right side of the buyer, and when the meeting started, I could see everybody who was there to represent their own brands. I was there to represent Circle K. The buyer said, "Why can't you be more like Andrew? If you were really interested in Circle K business, you'd dress like you're a Circle K person and consume the Circle K branded products." I didn't do it intentionally; I thought it was the right thing to do. When you visit a customer, you're in their house effectively, so you should behave and act as if you were one of their employees.

One key difference is that here in corporate America, there's no problem with spending money and taking customers out to play golf, which I love. I'm a good golfer, so a lot of customers like to play with me. I've paid up to five thousand dollars for a foursome, and I've paid ten thousand dollars just to play in a golf tournament with one customer. When else can you get five hours with the customer, spend time with them, and give them advice about their golf game? Also, you can usually talk to them about the business in the first thirty minutes. Then we won't revisit it again. We'll have a wonderful experience together and hang out for the day, maybe drink some cocktails and have food after.

I absolutely love that part of the business, that the company agrees to let you play golf with their customers. In Ireland we didn't do a lot of that where it wasn't seen as relevant, and it wasn't considered the right thing to do to take a day off work to play golf. I think there's a great opportunity for the alcohol industry in Ireland to do more entertaining. It doesn't have to cost a lot of money. I think here retailers recognize the opportunity to get out of the office for half a day, especially when they're so busy on weekends with their families.

Ultimately, I see pros and cons in working in Ireland vs. America. And I've been able to embrace them all to adapt my style and persevere.

KEY LEARNINGS

What I've learned and would love to share with you

1. **Be true to your values.** Define what your values are and stick to them. One of the main potential conflicts in the corporate world is that your own value systems may be compromised. Whether you're okay or not with that will dictate how you respond.

2. **Deal with the discomfort zone.** Get comfortable with being uncomfortable. Seek out and take on new challenges and embrace them. No business is all comfortable all the time. Growth often comes when we step outside our comfort zone and expand it a little at a time.

3. **Be coachable.** Be open, adaptable, and broaden your education of your company, brand, and different departments. The US Marines have a mantra: "Improvise, Adapt, and Overcome."

4. **Don't take no.** Don't give up when you get NO for an answer. Take it as an opportunity to improve your sales presentation or to understand the customer's objections. Keep going and be patient, persistent, and show resilience in the face of adversity. Sometimes

we need to walk away and say, "Look, it's not right for this person and the company, and that's okay."

5. **Be in integrity.** Always do what you say you're going to do, and let people know if you're unable to do what you promised. Others can count on you when you demonstrate that you're a person of high integrity. It's a value that's not often apparent in business and in life, in general.

6. **Be authentic.** Be real with people. Authenticity is the number one behavior that could be accentuated more in the corporate world. Being authentic in your beliefs, views, and opinions may be difficult to navigate, but you must be you.

7. **Create buy-in.** Creating buy-in with people allows them to feel a sense of purpose in achieving the goals you've set. "You can't bake a cake without all the ingredients." Involve your team and your department.

8. **Learn people skills.** It's helpful to learn how to read people. A course in body language is very helpful in sales. When explaining something to somebody, you want to be able to tell if they're getting it or not. They may cross their arms, or look like they're under pressure, or they rub their left or right elbow. That's a

signal for you to slow down your presentation, clarify, ask a question, check in, and give your buyers permission to seek more information.

9. **Ask for help.** Seek out support when you need it. You may get knocked back which makes you look at a situation differently. Ultimately, your values and gut instinct will point you in the right direction for what you need to implement.

10. **Celebrate success.** Don't take success for granted, that you were supposed to get that huge PO or close that big deal. Celebrating embeds your positive results and attracts more of the same.

PART IV

PREGNANCIES & MISCARRIAGES

"It is not length of life, but depth of life."

—Ralph Waldo Emerson, Author and Philosopher

CHAPTER EIGHTEEN

Delivery Day

"A baby is God's opinion that life should go on."

—Carl Sandburg, Poet

I'm standing in Scripps Hospital in Encinitas, a city in San Diego County. The nurses and doctors are handing me some scrubs before I enter the operating room. It's August 10, 2019, and Jane has just been called in for a C-section to deliver our first child. We've been here for nearly three days as she was overdue, and it's time for my son or daughter to enter the world. As I stare in the mirror at my exhausted face, I ask myself, "*How did I get here*?"

This wasn't our first pregnancy. No, it was our fifth. Unfortunately, we suffered four miscarriages in the space of four years. On one hand, it was an incredible thrill each time to find out we were pregnant. We had expectations and excitement, and even some planning, wondering what he or she might be like. Naturally, we were nervous.

Yet on the other hand, we had been faced with complete devastation when Jane had miscarried at various stages between six and twelve weeks. I must admit each of the four times, I felt like it was one of the lowest points in my life.

See, I've always been a solution-oriented person. I wished the doctors could have given us any sort of a medical reason for one after the other miscarriage. I was listening for them to say you need to do X or Y. Then we'd absolutely do that. All we heard, though, was that it was just Mother Nature, no other explanation. In some ways that was the hardest news to accept.

At the time of each miscarriage, I felt completely helpless. I needed to sit with the loss and soak in the information, though it was never what I wanted to hear. We knew there was no substitute for time, waiting for when Jane would be pregnant again. However, we did hold onto hope and a strong belief that positive results would come for us.

If you're a parent who is expecting, I think you'll identify with the fact that when you're expecting a child, and you're out walking, or you're at the grocery store, or you're in the shopping mall or anywhere, and you see a baby, you smile a bit more. You may take note of the different equipment and items you need to buy. I'd often watch how parents handled toddler tantrums and other issues as I was preparing in my mind: what if our son our daughter does this or that?

I suppose that was key to maintaining a solid focus on what we wanted—which was to become parents. With the traveling we did through the years and the move to America and subsequent move back to Ireland and back to America again—and without consciously realizing it—we had put off becoming parents and starting a family. Finally, in our early thirties, we were content that we'd experienced most of what we wanted in life, so we felt we had all the time in the world to enjoy our child growing up.

Back to the waiting room... Dressed in my scrubs, ready for what lay ahead, I had to temper my nerves. I'd been nervous at big golf tournaments. I'd been nervous giving presentations in front of dozens of people. I'd been nervous at other times in my life—sometimes for what seemed like no apparent reason. This time however, the nervousness morphed into complete excitement: this was it, the moment when we welcomed our child into the world.

We chose not to find out the gender beforehand. We wanted it to be a surprise. After four miscarriages, all we were concerned with were that the baby had ten fingers, ten toes, two eyes, two ears, one mouth, one nose, two legs, and two arms. When I entered the operating room,

I saw Jane was already being operated on. I took my position at the head of the table and held her hand. The anesthesiologist was a nice man, and the nurses were super and aware of Jane's long difficult trek to motherhood.

As the operation continued, the anesthetist started talking to me about golf, which was kind of distracting though in a good way. We talked about the most recent winner of the open in Northern Ireland, Shane Lowry, and what a fantastic moment it was for the country and what an amazing player he is.

The next thing I knew our baby had arrived. He was lifted up as I shouted, "It's a boy!" That moment in time at 7:47 p.m. on the 10th of August 2019 will forever live in my life as one of the greatest moments and more than likely my greatest achievement. The sense of pride, the sense of fulfillment, the sheer relief that Jane and my son were healthy, and everyone was doing fine was almost too much for me. And it was one of the few times as an adult that I cried.

They were exhausting days, but the best few days of my life. The utter excitement of seeing Alfie Rian Fitzgerald for the first time was palpable. On the way home from the hospital, I drove at forty-five mph, even though the speed limit was sixty-five. Although the roads are usually fine, we seemed to feel every bump. Certainly, California drivers weren't happy to see this guy driving slowly. We just wanted to make sure we all got home safely.

Crossing the threshold of our house bringing Alfie through the front door, was a momentous occasion. And now it all begins, I thought to myself, all the fulfilling days ahead watching him learn and grow. All the rewarding days taking part in whatever interests, hobbies, and sports he shows an aptitude for. All the satisfying days watching his personality develop.

Will he be like me? What will he do in the future? Will he have more hair than me? Turns out he had more hair than me after two years than I have now. I'm sure these are typical thoughts of new parents.

CHAPTER NINETEEN

Pregnancy & Miscarriage #1

"A miscarriage is not a failure, because a failure implies that it's something you can control. Miscarriages are beyond our control."

–Dr. Simone Whitmore, Physician of Obstetrics and Gynecology

I remember the first time Jane was pregnant. We were so excited. It was a new adventure, and everything was going well as we settled back in America. We were up and running with our new life, with a social circle. We wanted to be parents so much that we went for our first scan after week five or six.

As we entered the lobby at the doctor's office, we saw other couples waiting to be seen. They were as excited as we were, though probably nervous as well. Some couples were coming out from their exams after finding out the sex of their baby. They'd have either a pink or blue balloon or a little gift package. And we wanted one of those as well. However, we had decided to keep the gender a surprise.

When we went in, we spoke with the doctor as she examined Jane. Then we were hit with the news, "I'm so sorry, but the pregnancy has stopped." Such devastating news, those four words. "The pregnancy has stopped" reverberated in my ears. Jane and I hugged each other and cried.

That had to be one of the most difficult times in my life. We were shown the back stairs out of the building rather than having to go through the lobby. At the time I thought that was somewhat crass; however, I realized the doctor was used to giving bad news to parents and seeing how crushed they were. So it seemed best to go out the back stairs to the parking lot and get out quickly.

We decided not to tell anyone about this. In Ireland, the general rule of thumb is you don't tell anyone you're pregnant until after twelve weeks, you've had your scans, and you've been through what's considered "the safe period". Whereas in America, I've met people who told me after four weeks they're expecting a child or after six weeks they have a name picked out since they found out whether it's a boy or girl.

Jane and I remained private about our loss. We didn't want to worry anyone. As time has gone on though, we realized it would have been helpful to seek out support and comfort from others. After this experience, I'd advise those who've been in this same situation that by leaning on each other and talking or just sitting with the feelings and even venting, you'll find your partner is probably the greatest support for you, even if you choose not to share the news with others. Jane's mental health was important to me. I was there when she needed me to hold her, to let her cry, or when we needed to cry together.

If you're each coming from a place of empathy, understanding, and listening, and if you both agree to focus on the future and have hope at the center of all you do while being realistic, you can navigate a loss like miscarriage.

The doctor said there was nothing we could do to achieve a positive outcome. It was just Mother Nature at work, no fault of either one of us. She said to go home and get busy in a different kind of way. So as time began to allow us to heal, we got busy with our jobs.

CHAPTER TWENTY

Pregnancy & Miscarriage #2

"You're never really ready to be told that there's no heartbeat. But stay strong because life goes on and it is nobody's fault."

—Elisabeth Canalis, Italian Actress

During our second pregnancy, we had visitors from Ireland. This time, Jane had been pregnant for eight weeks when she started to miscarry at home. I was at a sales meeting in Huntington Beach about ninety minutes north of San Diego. She called me to say what she believed was occurring, and I left the sales meeting worried and stressed that this was happening again. I felt helpless that she was on her own, as at the time the visitors were out exploring San Diego.

I called the police and telling them I was going to use the carpool lane, that Jane was in the middle of a miscarriage, and I needed to get home urgently. The carpool lane in America is only for two or more people, so I gave them my license plate and name.

The dispatcher on the call said, "Sir, I wouldn't advise you do that." However, I did weave in and out of the carpool lane as I believed it was the right thing to do. It was important for me to get home quickly but safely as well. On arrival at our house, I could hear Jane withering in pain. We called the doctor, and the nurse immediately sent a prescription for pain medication to the local pharmacy.

This experience was totally different than the first one. The pain was intense as Jane passed the fetus. I can only say it was devastating to see our future child in the toilet, our son or daughter, the creation of life flushed away. The very term "flushed away" means you're removing it, getting rid of it.

The following few days, weeks, and months were extremely difficult. We couldn't comprehend what we'd seen and been through…again. We kept asking ourselves, "What can we do?" One answer was: Well, you can go into a state of depression, which would be perfectly normal. Another answer was: You can turn a blind eye and try to ignore what happened. And yet another answer was: You can meet it head on and speak with each other about it. Have emotional conversations and let it all out—which is what we chose to do. And again, we didn't tell any of our close friends and relatives in Ireland, choosing to keep it to ourselves.

We were still looking for answers. Why was this happening? What did we do wrong? What else could we do? Was it our diets? Was it stress? Jane, in fact, is a very laid back of person, so it would take a lot to fluster her. I didn't think it was stress, and our diets and exercise were fine. We were both very healthy—and for the most part happy. At least as happy as we could be under the circumstances. All we could do was keep our hopes up for the next time to have a positive outcome.

CHAPTER TWENTY-ONE

Pregnancy & Miscarriage #3

"Just because we lost a life, doesn't mean we have to lose ourselves."

—Tamara Gabriel, Russian Poet

Our third pregnancy was again a joyful moment, though we were also wondering, "Here we go again." But this time we were positive it would work out. Jane's doctor, who ironically sees women every day and gives good news and bad news, was going through IVF treatments and opened up that she'd been trying for years to get pregnant. So it was reassuring that we were at least able to conceive naturally, albeit we couldn't get past the golden number of twelve weeks.

Unfortunately, we miscarried again. This time, Jane needed to go in for a procedure called a D&C. It was a surgery Jane hadn't had to have before. In fact, she'd never had any surgery at all. And here we were, the two of us, no one in our lives knowing what was happening, heading to the hospital for a procedure. Like any surgery, there can be risks, so it was a traumatic day for us. Afterwards, the doctor once again reassured us that it was just Mother Nature, and there was really nothing more we could do other than go home and get busy. "Go home and get busy" was the recurring mantra from the doctor, so that's exactly what we did. We buried ourselves in work—again.

"Go home and get busy" was a what we needed to hear as it lightened the mood, but on the drive back to our house after the surgery, Jane broke down, and it was then that it became about us rather than Mother Nature.

Why was it happening to us? Why did it keep happening? Why us? What more can we do? What's going wrong? Was it our age? Jane's pregnancy was classed as a "geriatric pregnancy" since she was over thirty-five years of age. Being called a geriatric in Ireland is a term most people don't like as it implies you're ancient. However, Jane couldn't care less what it was called; we thought this was the one, we had been so sure of it.

These and many other questions were what we were asking. And there were no apparent answers available to us. I guess the most difficult emotions to deal with were the frustration and confusion. The doctors couldn't give us any further information on why it kept happening and what we could do to prevent it from happening again.

It was difficult to see the friends we grew up with either pregnant or just becoming parents. While we are naturally happy for them and to see them happy, we felt a tinge of "feeling left out". No doubt, that was a common human emotion. When we were expecting, it seemed everywhere I went, I saw new babies or strollers or new mums and dads with smiles the size of the Atlantic Ocean. I guess they were always present as I went about my business, but of course now I started noticing them more.

Jane and I sat down together with the emotions, with the frustration, with some anger or what we perceived as anger—not angry with each other, just angry at whatever forced caused this to happen again. And we sat and sat with the choice: either wallow in self-pity or adopt an attitude of positivity and hope, we chose the latter and "got busy".

CHAPTER TWENTY-TWO

Pregnancy & Miscarriage #4

"When we lose one blessing,
another is most often unexpectedly given in its place."

—C.S. Lewis, British Author

Our fourth and final miscarriage happened right before our twelve-week scan. We were so close. The night before the big day, the special week, the golden twelve-week scan, Jane started spotting. We looked at each other, and on some level we knew. But we said, "Let's just go to the appointment tomorrow." As soon as Jane mentioned spotting to the nurse practitioner who was checking us in, I could see on Jane's face that she knew it would be sad news.

The doctor examined her and told us she had miscarried—again. The pregnancy had started and stopped, and again she needed a D&C. This last miscarriage was probably the hardest one, because we'd been through so much already and because we'd gotten so close to the twelve-week scan.

Getting past twelve weeks is a milestone. It doesn't mean everything will go smoothly, but it does give you that reassurance—especially to us in our situation, already having had three miscarriages. All miscarriages are devastating, but the hope that came out of this one was because we nearly made it to twelve weeks. We felt that for some reason we were being tested—perhaps on our journey to parenthood, although we knew the destination was to get to the hospital and give birth to a healthy child.

Who knows why we needed to go on this journey, or even enjoy the journey, accept the bumps along the way, until arriving finally at our destination on August 10, 2019.

I'll never forget how stoic and resilient Jane was during our four losses. For the male partner, I think there's a range of emotions. But straight away I felt my role was to project confidence. If I showed too many negative emotions, I thought it might have a negative effect on Jane who was already dealing with a lot. Though because we had been around each other for so long, by osmosis we just rubbed off on each other, that is, we both became resilient. We really had no other choice.

Jane works in the corporate world as I do, so we threw ourselves right back into work after each miscarriage. That worked for us, although it may not have been the healthiest of distractions. Yet, we knew at some point we had to face the loss. We had to sit with and accept it, let it seep into our souls. We realized we were working ourselves too hard and our work was masking our pain and heartbreak. One Friday night after dinner, we broke down in each other's arms and let it all out: the grief, the sadness, the endless tears. And this feeling we both had of being cold, as if we were in shock. I think sometimes you have to breakdown before you can build up again.

For anyone going through miscarriages, you know you'll have those tearful moments. However, you must be hopeful, for without hope what is there? At one time we had considered IVF or adoption. We didn't have any problem conceiving; it was just that we couldn't carry the baby to full term. We could have gone other routes, yet we remained confident we'd be successful and have our baby one day.

If Alfie hadn't been born three years ago, we feel we'd still be happy now. I can't say for sure that I would or wouldn't feel deprived of parenthood, but I know Jane would have missed out if she hadn't become a mother. And our lives are incredible now with Alfie here. Had he not arrived, we would have missed so much.

Would we have tried for a sixth time if Alfie hadn't come along? Yes, absolutely. Forty-one was still young enough to keep trying. Though some people might choose to accept that it's not going to happen. Maybe it would happen by not focusing attention on it, at tracking ovulation dates, and being conscious of it all the time. And maybe that's part of it too—when you're trying so hard for something or you're thinking about it so much, perhaps you need to just chill out, turn off, and forget about it.

Most of the doctors told us to get away, take a vacation, get relaxed, remove ourselves from our everyday surroundings, and wonderful things would happen. And they did.

CHAPTER TWENTY-THREE

The Five Stages of Grief

"There is no right way to grieve; there is only your way to grieve and that is different for everyone."

—Nathalie Himmelrich, Grief Expert and Author

Denial * Anger * Bargaining * Depression * Acceptance

Any loss, whether a miscarriage or death, is dreadful, absolutely shattering. You naturally go through a lot of emotions. You may be able to identify with some of them—not necessarily because you went through a miscarriage, but because you've had areas of your life where you felt excited and then crushed after the bad news.

In many cases of loss, people go through five stages of grief: *denial, anger, bargaining, depression,* and *acceptance.* I'm not sure in what order we proceeded, but we definitely went through all five stages.

We didn't experience any specific order to get to acceptance, that is, we didn't necessarily go through all five in any the "recommended" order. We replaced acceptance with hope that one day we'd become parents, hope that one day we'd bring a child into the world to grow up, hope that one day we'd experience what isn't a God-given right but generally the way the life cycle works. We're creative beings, and we procreate for the next generation.

The way we went through the five stages of grief was unique to each of us. Jane and I were at various stages throughout all five, and we found that it wasn't a linear step-by-step process.

For me, the *denial* phase was thinking this isn't happening, this must be a mistake. And that quickly led me to the *bargaining* phase, because I like to fix things, therefore I wanted to figure out what the biological problem was. Was there something we could be doing? Could it be: get healthier, do more exercise, eat a better diet, take some medication, check out alternative methods, anything that could contribute to being more successful in carrying a baby for a full term? If so, then we'd do that. But the doctor simply said it was Mother Nature and just one of those things.

The *anger* phase was masked by us throwing ourselves into our corporate lives. That wasn't necessarily the right thing to do, but it was a welcome distraction. We certainly were never angry with each other. We were more compassionate with each other. I guess internally we did harbor some anger and resentment that something was taken away from us that was completely out of our control. But we didn't express anger outwardly.

And we didn't spend much time in the *depression* stage, because we made a commitment to each other to be kind and to communicate, and more importantly listen to the other person. This is what probably got us through the depression phase that we might have been in at different times, only mildly.

The last stage was the most difficult to handle: *acceptance*. It was tough to accept that it was only Mother Nature four times in a row in the space of four years. That's probably one of the toughest facts to accept, that some circumstances happen for whatever reason, and it's no one's fault. It seemed we had no other choice than to accept that it was the way it was. We might not have liked it, but acceptance was the only answer. The question was: How do we find a way forward? Our way forward was to forget about the four miscarriages—or at least not dwell on them—and be hopeful and confident that one day we *would* become parents.

How you navigate the treacherous road through miscarriage to the ultimate goal of parenthood is an individual journey. The choice is yours to choose how you decide to handle it and what's best for you and your partner. Jane and I survived fairly unscathed through our journey to our joyful destination—our son Alfie.

KEY LEARNINGS

What life has taught me, and I'd love to share with you

1. **Be supportive and kind to yourself and your partner.** Offer compassion and kindness to each other. Be there for the other and offer whatever support your partner requires. Express confidence that everything will eventually work out.

2. **Know the facts and face the emotions.** About ten to twenty percent of known pregnancies end in miscarriage (MayoClinic.org, miscarriage facts). In addition, one in one hundred women experience recurrent pregnancy loss (www.tommys.org, baby loss support). Recurrent pregnancy loss is defined as two or more failed pregnancies and includes loss of pregnancies that were confirmed by a pregnancy test or ultrasound (www.yalemedicine.org/conditions/recurrent-pregnancy-loss). Our doctor told us to get busy, which we interpreted as throwing ourselves into work as a distraction. However, taking time off work would be far better, so you could face the facts. You'd benefit from taking quiet time to see what kind of emotions come up.

3. **Talk about what's going on.** Both partners need to be open, to sit with the news, and speak to people they know—whether a friend, a family member, a therapist, or a support group. When you talk about it, you'll discover more about what's going on.

4. **Take care during the pregnancy.** After the fourth miscarriage, when Jane was pregnant for the fifth time, we were very careful and conscious about doing everything we could to ensure we made it past the twelve-week mark. We got excellent medical care and regular scans every week for the first twelve weeks and then every two weeks for the remainder of the pregnancy. We went through complete physicals, and no unusual issues were found.

5. **Live your life while you're waiting.** Some people might choose to accept that it's not going to happen. However, when you have little control over the results, it's best to keep going and keep a positive focus. Do what you usually do, a combination of work and play, time with friends and family, and enjoying each other. Be happy with what you have and be open and ready for the day you'll eventually greet your child.

WHERE DO I GO FROM HERE?

"There will always be obstacles and challenges that stand in your way. Building mental strength will help you develop resilience to those potential hazards so you can continue on your journey to success."

–Amy Morin, Author

I emigrated from Ireland to America in 2012, and I've been asked countless times: "Why did you leave Ireland?" and "Why did you move to America?" and "Will you move home to Ireland?" I don't have a crystal ball to predict the future of whether we'll remain in America or return to Ireland.

I'm reminded of a Chinese proverb that states: "The future is for those who know how to wait." I think that's one of the most important lessons I've learned: you can't fast track anything you want to achieve in the future. You must be patient and enjoy the journey. You have to trust in the process and trust your instincts that what you're doing will ultimately lead to what you want to achieve.

As I write this book, I've taken on the added responsibilities vacated by the CEO of the vodka cocktail company I work for. We're ready to accelerate this brand and be significant in 2023. I'm enjoying the leadership aspect of the company as well as the strategy and the multi-state focus I have on the business.

I've always wanted to do something for myself, march to my own beat. Maybe get into my own business and carry the full responsibility for one, pivoting from corporate life and building on my life and business experience. I suppose this book reflects that desire. I'm not sure what, but something along the way was keeping me stuck.

During the pandemic of Covid-19, I had time to reflect on my life. I realized I liked writing, and English was one of my strongest subjects in school, because we had to write a lot of essays on different topics. I'd write about soccer or golf, because it was about something I knew well. I was very descriptive, and my schoolteachers commented on the imagery and creativity of my essays.

Naturally, I know about my life and feel it's important to write a book about it. My first motivation was for my son, Alfie. We have forty years between us, and at some stage in our lives, he'll want to know more about his father. I'd love to be able to hand him this book and see him get some insights out of it. I hoped he'd cherish it as much as I cherish watching him grow.

Second, I don't want to have any regrets. When I'm in my nineties and looking back, I won't have regrets that I didn't write a book. I'm not writing it to become a millionaire or be on the bestseller list, as I know those are rare for most authors. I'm not looking to be on newsstands, radio stations, or podcasts. I'm writing it for me and my son first, and second for you the reader.

My wish is that you'll see opportunities to work on resilience in your life. I want to encourage you to overcome the obstacles you may be facing, that many people face in all walks of life in the various areas of life. Somewhere along the line we can draw parallels to what happens to us and how we rebound and deal. How we sit with the pain; how we reflect; how we succeed and celebrate any success.

The third reason I'm writing this book is I feel I have the opportunity to impart skills and wisdom which I can do through public speaking and/or coaching. I'd like to speak to people in a group setting where I'm able to introduce my book and discuss various aspects of it, whether it's the health scares, pregnancy loss, corporate life, or for people thinking about making a major move. Not necessarily about immigrating, but about making a big shift in their life. I know I can help people thrive and build traits of resilience, because I did it, so I know it can be done.

For example, many men and women have gone through a traumatic time with miscarriage. And while it's much tougher undoubtedly for the female, the man also goes through emotions and must be a strong partner for his wife. Jane and I survived four miscarriages, so I feel I can offer wisdom from my experience.

Writing and speaking for me has never been about the money. Sure, we all need money to live, and we must find a balance. At my current age of forty-five, I still consider myself a young man. Yet after all that's happened in my life, I have a unique outlook. To see my book in print will be a fantastic day for me. It's been a difficult time in the last two years: I'd sit down to write and get blocked. I'd think, "I wonder who would be interested in this?" or "Will people buy this book?" or "Will they believe all of this?"

I realized that was the wrong approach to take. This book is not about people buying it and believing it. It's about my experience being shared with others so they can draw inspiration from it that it might reinforce what they've also gone through.

Life is a journey with the destination unknown. I've learned so much every day here in America. I meet so many amazing people from different cultures and ethnicities. I experience different types of food. I find so much to do and to discover. Alfie is growing up here so it will be a distinct experience for him.

Ireland will always be there; it will always be home in my heart. I do go back to get a shot of Ireland every eight or nine months for vacations and to keep in touch with friends and family. It's important to stay connected, and with technology, we're in touch regularly. I also get visitors from Ireland which allows us to hear the stories and gossip from back home. Sharing moments is what life is all about. The future is bright though unclear, which is a major contradiction in life.

Now I can finally answer the question: "*How did I get here*?" By planning, persistence, prayer—and resilience. Are you ready to travel the road to resilience—with my guidance?

ABOUT THE AUTHOR

Andrew Fitzgerald is a native of Ireland and now resides in Oceanside, California. He's the author of *How Did I Get Here?* As a global beverage brand builder, Andrew has launched, managed, and scaled some of the world's biggest alcohol brands through his unique approach with retailers, distributors, and sales teams. Additionally, he's an expert in negotiation and coaching sales teams in the corporate world.

Andrew has traveled extensively throughout the United States which ultimately resulted in his making a permanent move with his wife in 2012. His immigration resulted in many challenges, fears he faced, and the resiliency he demonstrated in facing adversity. Andrew enjoys all sports, especially golf, as well as cooking and hiking when he's not thinking about the next big brand launch.

A father, husband, and author, Andrew speaks on what it takes to be successful in the corporate world and how to overcome health crises and other losses. His experiences allow him to show others how to recover in order to survive and thrive with resilience. He's available to work as a coach/consultant with individuals, teams, and companies in all industries.

You can contact Andrew at fitzgerald_andrew@yahoo.com and visit his website at www.AndrewFitzgeraldAuthor.com.

Printed in Great Britain
by Amazon

33193752R00118